Love Potion

An Ariel Kimber Novel

To Nikki B. -

I hope you enjoy Ariel Kimber's world of boys, witches & magic.

Much Love -

Mary Martel XOXO

Mary Martel

#UnclePantyThief

1st Edition Published: November 2017
Cover Design by: Mary Martel
Stock Photo From: Shutterstock.com

ISBN-13:
978-1985267053

ISBN-10:
1985267055

Dedication

To my Aunt Chariety.
When I put Brothers of the Flame out there, I forgot to say thank you.
Thank you for coming up with a title for my first book in the series.
And thank you for helping me name my boys.
This one's for you.
Love you.
xo

Chapter One

IT HAD BEEN three weeks since my mother's death and I felt like I hadn't been able to fully catch my breath since. First the shock, then reality had set in. I really was alone in this world, a motherless girl, a fatherless girl. A girl with no family to call my own. Once that reality set in, I had become depressed. It hadn't helped when Mr. Cole came home in his own depressed state. We mourned our losses together. He thought my mother had taken off on us, abandoning her only child when really, she was as dead as dead could get. Marcus Cole would never find out the truth, not from me he wouldn't. My lips were sealed.

His brother had been in a terrible car accident and, unfortunately, he hadn't made it. I had never met the man, but I had been forced to meet his entire family when Mr. Cole had dragged me along with him to the funeral. They were nice and all, but I hadn't wanted to go in the first place so the entire ordeal had been awkward on my part.

That's not even getting into the way people had looked at me. They'd met my mother and they hadn't liked her. And it was made worse by them thinking she'd up and left Mr. Cole while his brother was dying in the hospital, leaving me behind for him to deal with. The looks I'd been given were a lot of things and nice hadn't been one of them. If I hadn't been so depressed and deep in my own sorrow, I might have been bothered by this. As it was, I didn't have it in me to give a crap.

With my mother dead, I needed to figure out what I was going to do with myself. I was seventeen, eighteen in less than nine months, I should be able to take care of myself. Mr. Cole had other ideas. Which is why we were facing off in the kitchen, discussing the future.

I stared at him, trying to not look as freaked out as I was on the inside. I'm almost positive I failed at this endeavor. I had no poker face to speak of. Thankfully, he didn't call me out on it.

Mr. Cole was an undeniably handsome man.

My mother had never had a shortage of good looking men around for her to sleep with whenever she felt like getting off. Which had been often.

None of the others had been anything like Marcus Cole. Although, good looking, they'd all been from the bottom of the barrel. The kind of men who had had no problem with their lady love being a woman who danced mostly naked on a stage to pay her way in life. There wasn't anything wrong with being a stripper. If done right, the way a dancer's body moved while on stage could be, not only highly erotic, but extremely beautiful. Mesmerizing even.

Believe me, I know what I'm talking about.

When I was younger, before my mother simply started leaving me home alone, she would drag me to work with her. I was supposed to stay backstage in one of the dressing rooms, always out of sight. Sometimes I'd sit there quietly like a good girl, doing my homework while pretending to be somewhere else in my head. Sometimes I would mess around with the dancer's makeup, making myself into a bright red lipstick-wearing, glittery-eyed beauty.

Often times, I would sneak out of the dressing room and make my way to the side of the stage. And I would watch them dance. This is how I know some dancers made it look beautiful, like its own form of art. Vivian Kimber had not been one of those women who'd made stripping and pole dancing into a beautiful, sexy, seductive form of art.

No, much like everything else in her life, my mother had made it look cheap and tawdry.

And the men she attracted and brought home with her had reflected upon this, her being trashy. No matter how good looking they were, it never diminished the fact that they'd been just as trashy as my mother. And a lot of the time, they'd been worse than my mother because they had actually taken notice of me and it had never been good. They had all been the very bottom of the barrel.

Marcus Cole wasn't at the bottom of anything. The only time he'd even ever gotten close to the bottom of the barrel had been when he was sleeping with my mother.

Harsh, but true.

What's worse is that he'd paid for it. I tried really hard not to think about this fact because I didn't want it to taint the way I looked at him. He was the only one out of the whole bunch who was different than the rest.

Starting with his looks.

Marcus Cole wasn't simply good looking. He was downright handsome. There was a difference. Handsome seemed a more refined word and totally suited to Mr. Cole.

He was in his late fifty's but looked maybe forty. Tops. He had short, what looked to be incredibly soft, light brown hair with a sprinkling of salt at his temples. That salt at his temples being the only visible mark on him to hint at his age.

His eyes were a soft, warm brown that always seemed to be filled to the brim with kindness when they were aimed in my direction. I had never seen such kindness in a man's eyes before when they looked my way.

He ran several miles every day on the treadmill and I was pretty sure he lifted weights. Only pretty sure because I had never actually seen him do it with my own eyes. But the evidence was plain to see in the well-defined muscles on his arms. He had a fit body and was in shape due to the fact he'd worked hard to earn one.

He also dressed nice, like no other man my mother had been with before. He was a wealthy business man and he *always* dressed the part. Like now, standing across from me in his kitchen. He was dressed up in his wealthy, business man attire.

Pristine, winter white long-sleeved button up shirt. He'd left off the suit jacket, but it wasn't abnormal to see him with his hips resting against the countertop in the kitchen, a coffee cup in his hand with his suit jacket on, for all the world looking like he was getting ready to head into the office for the day.

Given he worked from home, I never understood why he dressed the way he did. Silk tie, expensive looking slacks and black dress shoes that always shined. His clothes looked expensive because they simply were expensive.

He wore them well and they looked good on him.

"I want you to come with me," he told me for the second time and I shook my head in frustration. "I understand you're almost an adult, and seeing as I'm not a parent or a legal guardian, I have no real say over what you do. But I want you to seriously consider coming with me, Ariel. Your mother may never come back and, after I sell the house, there will be no place left to come back to. And where will you stay?" He shook his head and frowned at me. "No. The best place for you is with me. At least with me, you'll have a roof over your head and the chance at a real future, a bright future."

I bit my bottom lip hard and the pain chased the tears away, like it always did.

I could not believe this shit.

With his brother dead and my mother gone, Mr. Cole had decided to up stakes, sell his house and move closer to his family. And he wanted me to go with him.

Before school had started and I'd met Tyson and the guys, I might have even considered going with Mr. Cole simply to get away from my mother. Now my mother was dead and I was left devastated at the thought of leaving this place for good. I couldn't move away from the guys, not when they were my only link to magic. Not to mention, I'd been away from them for three weeks now and I missed Tyson and the twins terribly. I didn't want to never see them again, but if I didn't go with Mr. Cole I'd find myself homeless real quick. I didn't want to be homeless. Being homeless sounded horrible.

I swallowed my heart back down my throat and stared down at the fuzzy black socks covering my feet. I could really use a break from my life right about now.

"Just think about it, sweetheart. You don't have to make a decision right this second. But you should figure it out sooner rather than later because I don't think the house will be on the market for long and I plan on being all moved out by the end of the month."

I felt faint. The end of the month. I counted in my head. Sixteen. He planned on being all moved out of here in sixteen days. And he wanted to take me with him. I had sixteen days to figure out what in the heck I was supposed to do with myself.

Anger, something I hadn't felt in over three weeks, flared to life inside of me. The lights in the kitchen flickered on and off for a second, shocking me. I blinked slowly, letting the anger go as fast as it had come on.

Holy shit. I needed to get control of myself before I turned into *Carrie*.

An extremely warm hand landed softly on my shoulder, bringing me out of my thoughts and making me flinch. I really did not want him touching me, even out of kindness, and he'd been doing it a lot lately. Maybe he found it comforting to touch me, to reassure himself that he really wasn't alone, I didn't know. What

I did know was that I was lying through my teeth to him about my mother and had added to his, already tremendous, grief. I didn't like lying to him, and I didn't like feeling guilty when I'd, essentially, done nothing wrong (well, save for the whole lying bit, that part was wrong). Every time he'd gently pat my shoulder in a fatherly manner, my guilt would threaten to devour me, eating me alive.

Mr. Cole squeezed my shoulder gently. "What she did, her leaving, doesn't say anything about you, Ariel. It doesn't reflect on you, either. It does, however, say everything about your mother and what kind of a woman she is. You're not alone. You have me and we have each other. We'll get through these hard times, together."

Oh boy.

I liked the sound of that, but at the same time, it sounded terrible.

He gave my shoulder one last squeeze before letting go and stepping away from me.

"I have a business meeting and I won't be home until late," he said. "You'll be okay here by yourself?"

I nodded in answer, my throat too tight to speak the words out loud.

I thought about the last time I'd been left alone and almost cringed but managed to stop myself. I didn't want him to think I couldn't be left on my own, that would be terrible. Over the past three weeks, the only space he'd given me was allowing me to be in my room by myself. And when we'd gone to the funeral, I'd felt his eyes on me everywhere I went. I think he was afraid I would disappear on him like my mother did.

The guilt I felt threatened to swallow me whole.

He left the kitchen without another word and, as soon as I knew for sure he was in his bedroom, I bolted out of the kitchen and headed towards the stairs. I practically ran up the stairs and locked myself in the safety of my bedroom.

Once I had the door locked, I turned and pressed my back against it. I blew out a deep breath and let my feet slide out from underneath me. My ass hit the carpet and I pulled my knees up to my chest. I wrapped my arms around my legs tightly and held on for all I was worth.

My body started to shake as I felt wetness begin to slide down my cheeks. I was crying. Why was I crying? I hadn't cried once in the last two weeks and now I was crying. Why? Because I might be moving again? Because Mr. Cole wanted to take me with him? Because I was finally wanted by a parental figure for once in my life, or because my own parent was no longer living and could never ever want or love me? Not that she'd ever done either to begin with. Or, could I be crying because I thought I might have to walk away from the only people I'd ever really had a connection with?

I didn't know the answers. Maybe it was a little bit of everything.

In the quiet of the house, I was able to hear when the garage door opened and closed behind Mr. Cole's car as he left.

Alone at last. For the first time in three weeks.

I laid my head on my knees and let my tears soak into the soft fabric of my leggings.

When my tears had stopped, my knees were soaked, and I had to get up to change out of the wet pants. I dropped them into a white laundry basket in my closet. I found a pair of dark, blue jean shorts and slipped into them.

I was pulling up the zipper when the doorbell went off. I froze for a heartbeat before quickly doing up the zipper and pushing the button through the little hole created just for it.

My heart skipped a beat as I thought about who could possibly be outside ringing the doorbell. Could it be Tyson? The Salt and Pepper twins? Maybe even Quinton? I cringed at the thought of it being Quinton. Not because of Quinton himself, but because of the feelings and emotions seeing him might bring out in me. And, if I were being honest with myself, which seemed rare these days, I had to admit that the man scared me just a little bit.

The doorbell rang again, then a third time. Whoever stood out there was clearly starting to grow impatient. My money was on Quinton. He seemed like the type to get annoyed when the door didn't open up the second after he rang the bell. Who else would it be? All of Mr. Cole's friends and family called before stopping by.

Knowing it was one of seven, I left my bedroom and slowly made my way down the stairs. I wanted to see them but they'd backed off, giving me the space I had needed. The space I still thought I needed, if only I weren't now running out of time.

Before my last conversation with Mr. Cole, I would have hidden out in my bedroom, not going anywhere near the front door. Probably not for the next six months or so, I thought it would take me that long to be able to face them all again after I'd run off, taking the cowards way out.

The doorbell rang a fourth time while I unlocked the front door. I was rolling my eyes as I pulled open the door.

"Listen," I said as I looked up and past the hand raised and ready to start knocking on the door, ready to give whoever it was an earful for being obnoxious with the bell. I said no more because my mouth was too busy hanging open as I gaped at the person standing in front of me.

This…

This was unbelievable.

"Wha… What…" I sputtered.

Chucky's dimples popped out as he grinned at me.

What in the actual fuck?

Chapter Two

CHUCKY.

FREAKING CHUCKY had been ringing my doorbell like an A-hole.

The last time I'd seen him, he'd gotten weird on me. He'd knelt at my feet, wrapped his arms around my legs and told me he'd do anything for me, anything. And he'd gotten uncomfortably close to sticking his face in my crotch. I hadn't liked it much.

Tyson and the salt and pepper twins had been convinced Chucky's weirdness had been Quinton's doing. Quinton had admitted to messing with Chucky before with his magic, to them it made sense that he'd do it again. I was in agreement with them. Quint was a dick that way, and there wasn't much he wouldn't do for me. Not to mention the small fact that he was all kinds of crazy.

I hadn't seen Chucky since because I hadn't been back to school since then. And now he was here, at my house of all places. My house he'd never been to before, and he certainly hadn't been invited to now. At least not by me he hadn't. I didn't see Mr. Cole inviting him over to shoot the breeze with him either.

Chucky lowered his hand and continued to grin at me. I was not smiling. In fact, I imagined my face looked downright scary, all covered in red splotches from crying. My nose was probably bright red, and I'd bet anything my eyes were bloodshot and puffy. I'm sure the scowl on my face didn't help much either.

Chucky, on the other hand, looked his usual chipper, smug self.

His light, brown eyes twinkled at me, full of a secret I did not want to know. His short brown hair had grown a little bit longer since I'd seen him last, not enough to warrant a haircut because it had been so short to begin with.

His large, broad shoulders were incased in a tight, white short-sleeved t-shirt. The front said something about football and Devils in red, cracked and faded lettering. His dark blue jeans were faded in places and frayed at the right knee.

I never realized before how Chucky's clothing did not match the quality of clothing his friends wore. Chucky's clothes were worn and clearly had been laundered a great deal. The Pretty Princess, Ken and the minion had all been dressed in expensive clothing. Chucky's weren't expensive. What they were was absolutely normal.

I wondered how he fit in with the rest of those snobs.

Must have been his winning personality.

When he continued to grin at me while saying nothing, I mumbled, "Uh, Chuck, what are you doing here?"

Way to go, Ariel Kimber. Rather brilliant. I was surprised I'd managed to get even that out past my shock.

His dimples went away as he frowned at me. His eyes turned calculating, watchful, and I was suddenly reminded of just who it was I was dealing with here. Chucky was not my friend and likely never would be. Not because he hadn't tried, but because I did not want him as a friend. Frankly, I did not want him as anything in my life.

Apparently, I could hold a mean grudge. Something I hadn't known until just then. I'd never held on to anything like anger or resentment before. I'd always chosen to let it go in order to maintain my own sanity and version of happiness. But times had changed for me and I did not like Chucky in the least bit.

On the first day of school Chucky had tripped me in class, causing me to fall to my hands and knees before an entire classroom of people. I'd been hurt and humiliated while they'd all laughed at my expense. A few days later Chucky had called me a freak show and asked me to go out on a date with him, all in the same conversation.

Yeah, I didn't like him. Not at all. It was a wonder anyone did.

Thanks to Quint and his magic, Chucky and his not so nice friends had ended up puking up their own blood all over themselves during lunch one day. It hadn't been their finest hour and had scared the crap out of a whole lot of people, myself included.

The sickness had only lasted for a few days then it had miraculously gone away. It was after that when he'd gotten weird on me in school and I hadn't seen him since. Heck, I hadn't even thought of him since he'd walked away from me in the hallway at school.

His smile slipped a little when I called him Chuck. I remembered him telling me before how much he didn't like being called Chuck, which is why I kept on doing it. He preferred to be called Chucky because there was clearly something wrong with him. I preferred Chuck because he didn't.

"It's Chucky," he reminded me like I figured he would. "We already went over this before."

I wanted to roll my eyes but somehow managed to refrain from doing so.

I crossed my arms over my chest and frowned at him. "What… Are… You… Doing… Here?" I asked him slowly, enunciating each word so he wouldn't miss anything. He wasn't the smartest person I'd ever met and repeating myself was starting to grow tedious.

He tucked his hands in the front pocket of his jeans and shrugged his shoulders casually. "I missed you at school so I thought I'd stop on by to check on you, make sure everything's okay. So, is it?"

I stared at him, dumbfounded. Now, why did these things have to keep happening to me?

If I wasn't so ashamed of my own behavior, I would have marched across the grass and the driveway so I could smack Quinton upside the head for putting me in this position. After the whole bloody fiasco, he should have left Chuck alone. Instead, he had to go and mess with his head and I was the one who had to deal with it.

I didn't want to deal with anything.

"Listen, Chuck," I said as I took a step back so I could shut the door on him. "Thanks for stopping by, but everything is fine." It wasn't actually, but no way were we going there. "It was very kind of you to stop by and check on me. Now that you know I'm fine, you should probably be on your way. I'll see you at school. I plan on going back next week."

That last part was a complete lie. I had no intention of ever going back to that school. I'd rather take the test to get my GED and find something better to do with my time.

I stepped back into the house, intent on shutting the door but he didn't let me. Quickly, he placed his shoulder in the door and pushed his way inside. I gaped at him as he moved past me.

"Wha… what are you doing?" I stammered out past my suddenly dry lips.

I didn't want him in my house and I absolutely did not want to be alone with him.

Slowly, his lips moved up and he smirked at me. I swallowed past the sudden lump in my throat and dug my fingernails into both my palms. The sudden pain helped keep every other emotion at bay. I did not want to be afraid. Not of Chucky, not of anyone. Never again.

He glanced around the entryway nervously. "Nice place."

Something in his voice had me cocking my head to the side, examining him closer. He'd sounded resentful and a little snide. Since the first time I'd met him, I wondered about Chucky's life. What made him act like a dick? What did his home look like? Did he live with both of his parents? Were they nice? I didn't want to know but I kinda did. I made no damn sense to myself sometimes.

"It's not my place," I murmured softly. "It's Mr. Cole's."

And it wouldn't be my home for much longer, nor would it be Mr. Cole's. I pulled in a shuddering breath, that thought broke my heart. The only father figure I'd ever had and he wanted to take me away from the only people who would likely ever really understand me. And I was too big of a pussy to go over and explain the situation to them to see if they could help me get out of it.

"Heard your mom skipped town," Chucky said quietly, cutting into my thoughts.

My head lowered, and I closed my eyes, searching for strength. Yeah, I just bet he heard all about my mother supposedly skipping out on us. I was willing to bet that the whole damn town was whispering about the harlot who fucked Marcus Cole over and the bastard she'd left him with. Leaving the house at this point would be a brand-new horror simply waiting to befall me.

I could see it in my head. Me, parking my sweet Rover at the grocery store. Getting out, beeping the locks and heading towards the entrance. I wouldn't notice them until it was too late for me to do anything about it. They'd hold in their hands rocks, glass bottles, one brave sucker would probably have ahold of a brick. They'd snarl ugly names at me while lobbing their heavy objects at my body. And I'd stand there like a fool and do nothing about it. I'd be too shocked to use my magic in defense.

The image faded away before the first object could crash into my face. I blinked, slowly coming back to the room I stood in. My thoughts were heavy, slow, like I was treading water and not moving. I had to stop doing this to myself. I'd probably get another headache. Seemed I couldn't go a day without getting one of the stupid things.

"Hey," he murmured as a cold hand brushed against my warm cheek.

I jerked back, the touch of his skin against my own making me feel funny, and not in a "ha ha I'm gonna laugh my ass off" kind of way.

I slapped his clammy hand away from my face and stepped back.

He laughed at me, causing the skin on my arms and the back of my neck to prickle as my hair rose.

My back straightened as I lifted my chin. I squared my shoulders and looked him straight in the eyes. He would not intimidate or frighten me. Not in my own home, not anywhere. Not ever again. I wasn't alone or a weak little girl anymore, my magic would never let me down or abandon me. I was stronger than this A-hole. Not physically, but I could kick his ass with my magic any day of the week. I'd been practicing.

I stared him down and whispered vehemently, "Do not touch me again. Not unless you're invited to do so. And just so we're clear, *Chuck*, I wouldn't hold my breath while waiting for that particular invitation because you're never gonna get one. I can promise you that."

His nostrils flared like a wild beast and he snapped at me, "I knew it. Nobody believed me when I told them, but I knew I was right. You're fucking Tyson. What I want to know is why. What's so fucking great about Tyson Alexander? Why does everyone want to ride that? Because he's got money? It can't be because he's so damn nice. He's a dick, Ariel. I saw the way he treated you on the first day of school. What's so different with the way he treated you from the way that I did? I already said I was sorry. What more do you want from me? I already got on my knees and begged. What more do you want from me?" He finished speaking in a tortured whisper.

My eyes were as wide as they could get as I took a step back and away from him. He'd started out practically snarling at me and ended sounding as if I had done something to personally torment him.

I'd never done anything to him that would make sense for him to be speaking to me in such a way. And I'd done absolutely nothing to garner his devotion. No, crazy Uncle Quinton had gone and done that.

Quinton's name and the offenses stacked against him were quickly filling up the empty slots on my shit list. Soon, I'd be forced to retaliate in some way. I couldn't let him get away with doing this shit to me, even if it was involuntary.

"I'm not-" I started to tell him I wasn't sleeping with Tyson but snapped my mouth shut. What business was it of his who I was sleeping with? Not that I was sleeping with anybody, but…

He grabbed my chin forcefully and jerked my face towards him.

"Don't even try to lie to me," he snapped as he put pressure on my chin, likely bruising me.

I'd had enough of people trying to push me around or abuse me. More than enough.

I closed my eyes and concentrated as he kept snapping words at me. I ignored him and his brutish behavior. All the books the boys had given me had stressed the importance of concentration and control. If I let my emotions rule me, there was no telling how this would go. I needed control or I might fry him, and I didn't want to run to the neighbors and ask them to dig another hole. I shuddered at the thought of Chucky's body being buried beside my mothers.

I took a deep breath, let it out and focused on his fingers on my face, trying to crush my jaw. I could see the flame in my mind, burning bright, waiting for me to play with it. It was at my disposal. Completely and utterly mine.

I licked my lips and focused on the rough feel of his fingers on my face. I pushed my flame out and into Chucky's fingers.

He screamed, dropped his hand and backed away from me. His eyes were huge in his head as he held his injured hand cradled to his chest protectively.

"What… what did you just do to me?" He whispered in horror and, I was surprised to see, awe.

I couldn't stop my lips from curling up in a small smile. Finally, I had a means to take care of myself, to fight back.

"Babe," a deep voice rumbled from behind me. "You can't just go around doing shit like that to people."

I sighed.

Why didn't I shut the front door? I knew better.

Chapter Three

QUINTON STOOD IN the doorway with his arms crossed over his chest and his shoulder against the doorframe. He looked the same as he had the last time I'd seen him, only a whole lot more amused.

Quinton Alexander was a dangerously beautiful man. Tall, broad shouldered and slim-hipped. He wore his dark brown hair buzzed close to his scalp. His eyes were so dark brown they were almost black, and they were always, always burning with something I couldn't quite read but was almost positive it wasn't ever anything good.

Today he'd switched out the small, silver hoops in both his ear lobes for black ones.

The black, long-sleeved button up shirt he wore hid the orange and red flames he had inked into his skin. They started at his wrists and slithered up his forearms. I wanted to see the ink and wished he hadn't hidden it away.

He had on a pair of dark, blue jeans tucked into black, scuffed up cowboy boots.

The cowboy boots were a nice touch.

He looked hot.

My face smoothed out, the smile now entirely gone, and I tried my hardest to look innocent. When he smiled at me, I'm pretty sure I failed.

"Shit like what?" I asked sweetly. "I didn't do anything."

Funny thing, lying to Quinton made me feel like crap and my stomach started to hurt. I fought the urge to rub at it, and I won.

He chuckled as he shook his head. I think I amused him. I didn't like him laughing at me. Not at all.

Instead of calling me out on my lie, he turned those dark, dark eyes on Chucky, his smile fading as soon as he locked eyes on him. I was thankful not to be on the receiving end of Quinton's scary look. He could be one downright frightening man when he wanted to be.

"What the fuck are you doing here at Ariel's house, boy?" Quinton growled.

Chucky shrugged his shoulders casually, seeming to not care about Quinton's growling, and said, "That's not really any of your business. Man, it's not like it's your house or anything. And, I could ask you the same thing."

I sighed and rolled my eyes.

Boys were so stupid. Especially Chucky. One look into Quinton's dark eyes should have been enough to let him know how dangerous he was. Any smart person would have kept their mouth shut.

Quinton laughed. I jumped, not having expected it. I stared at him with big eyes. What was he playing at here?

"Uh, hey, Chuck," I said loud enough to be heard over Quint's laughter. "I think you should be leaving now. Like, right now."

That made the laughing stop.

"Ariel," Chucky whined. "I'm so sorry. You just make me so crazy that I can't help myself when I'm around you. You haven't been to school in weeks. It's been weeks since I've seen you last and I feel like I'm lost. I can't eat. I can't sleep. All I think about is you. Morning, noon, middle of the night. It doesn't matter. You're always on my mind. Please, please don't kick me out. I'll be nice, I promise. Just don't kick me out."

He sniffled and wiped at the wetness under his eyes. Good God, he was crying. The big football player was crying. Again.

I couldn't take it. Fearing it might set him off if I laughed at him, I quickly looked away, hiding my face from his view.

Quinton caught my eye and he made a rough noise in the back of his throat when he saw the look on my face.

It wasn't funny. It really, really wasn't funny. So why did I want to laugh so badly? I could tell Quinton wanted to laugh too.

"Who are you?" Chucky asked as he sniffled again.

"I'm the neighbor," Quinton told him.

"I thought Tyson was your neighbor, Ariel."

"He is," I told him.

"So am I," Quint said.

Sounding confused, Chucky asked, "You live with Tyson?"

Once again, I sighed. This was not how I envisioned my day going. I could not win for losing here.

Quinton kept the information flowing and told Chuck, "Ty's my nephew. He's lived with me for a few years now."

"Huh," Chucky said. "I knew his folks were dead, but nobody said anything about him living with an Uncle."

My lips parted in surprise as I watched the two of them interacting. I wondered what would happen if I were to tell him it was Quint's fault he threw up blood all over himself? Or, what he'd think if I told him his sudden infatuation with me was also due to the other man in the room? And, oh, hey, we're witches.

"Yeah," Quinton said. "They died a few years ago. Look, I need to ask Ariel about a few things and I'm going to need you to be gone for that. How about you go, and she'll see you in school tomorrow."

I didn't care why Quinton was here, but I was happy he was. I'd had more than enough of Chucky and having Quinton here to get rid of him worked really well for me.

Chucky gave me a hopeful look as his eyes lit up. "You're going to be at school tomorrow?" He asked.

I absolutely was not going to be at school tomorrow. If I was lucky, I'd never go back to that place.

"Sure," I lied easily. "I'll see you tomorrow. At school. Definitely not at my house."

"Ariel," Quinton said, interrupting me.

Right. I snapped my mouth shut. I'd been rambling. I did that when I lied or got nervous.

Chucky exhaled loudly. "Good," he said. "Good. I don't know what's wrong with me, but I feel like I *have* to be around you, or I'll go crazy."

Being around him was going to make *me* go crazy. I hoped Quinton would be able to reverse whatever it was he'd done to the football player.

"You promise?" Chucky pushed it.

"Sure," I told him cheerfully. At this point I'd tell him just about anything to get rid of him.

He ran his hand through the hair on the top of his head and nodded. "Alright," he said. "I'll see you tomorrow."

He grinned at me and his dimples popped out. Then he was gone.

One down, one to go.

"What are you-"

I didn't get to finish my sentence because he rushed me. He came at me fast, stalking me. I backed up and kept going until I hit the wall. He didn't stop until he hovered over me, mere inches away from my body. His body hovered over mine as he placed both his hands on the wall on either side of me.

I was caged in and had no idea why.

His intense eyes roamed over my face. "I felt you, ya know?" he whispered. "I felt you when your mother was drowning you and I felt you just now when you were afraid of that stupid fuck. I don't know how you do it but when you're feeling something extreme, you call out to us with your magic. What did he do to you?"

My breath caught in my throat and I struggled to draw in air.

"Don't talk about her," I croaked.

"Why?" He shot back. "It's true, she tried to drown you in the bathtub. She beat on you. And I felt you panic and we all felt your pain. She's dead now and you've got no reason to hide from her anymore."

He was wrong. So very, very wrong. There was still plenty to hide from. Like my feelings. And *her*. I'd never escape her. I couldn't hide from her when she was alive. She was always there, like my shadow, ready to drag me down kicking and screaming by my hair. Now that she was dead, she haunted my mind and my dreams. I thought about her every day, the guilt never left me alone for very long.

I couldn't talk about her yet. Not with Quinton. Not with anyone. I wasn't ready.

Maybe he saw it, maybe he didn't, either way he left it alone and went back to his original topic. "What did he do?" He demanded.

I sighed. Lying to him wouldn't do me any good and I knew he'd be relentless until he got what he wanted.

"He got too pushy with me and it freaked me out a little." I glared at him. "It's your fault he's like this. You need to fix whatever it is that you did to him so he will leave me alone."

A wall slammed shut over his eyes, hiding his intense emotions from me. Until that moment, I hadn't realized just how much he hadn't been holding back from me.

"I can't do that," he said quietly. He watched me wearily, like he feared my reaction.

"Why not," I demanded to know. I hoped he was kidding.

"It's the Love Potion, babe." He rubbed at the back of his neck awkwardly. "I figured it was my safest bet when it came to dealing with him. You didn't like it when I made him sick so I found a way to ensure he wouldn't hurt you anymore. I don't know how to stop it, or how to reverse it. Honestly, I didn't think you'd care so long as I didn't hurt him."

"Love…" I sputtered. "Love potion? What love potion?"

"Just something I whipped up to keep you safe. Now he'll never hurt you because he's in love with you."

This was so wrong I didn't have words for it.

Thankfully, I found some.

"Quinton, he wasn't going to hurt me. He's just some stupid bully who decided to pick on the new girl. In time, he would have gotten bored with it and moved on to the next person. You should have left him alone. Instead, you turned into a crazy person and did terrible things to him. I mean, seriously? Would you want to be in love with someone because someone else forced you to? I know I wouldn't. That's so messed up."

Everything Quinton did was messed up in some way.

"Maybe it is messed up," he admitted. "Maybe I'm messed up. But, Ariel, I can't help it. It's the only way I know how to be. And I'm not gonna change. I tried it before when I got Tyson. I tried to be different. I tried to be better and I missed something important because of it, something that almost wrecked my family."

"Annabell," I whispered, understanding him completely.

His eyes narrowed dangerously and he moved closer to me. His forehead brushed mine as he tilted his head down and growled, "How do you know that name?"

This was one of those times where honesty was my best option but I didn't want to throw my sources under the bus.

"Ariel," he demanded in a rough voice, "answer me."

"The twins told me about her," I mumbled, hating to give them up. I hoped Quinton didn't go home and give them shit for it.

"Fuck," he swore harshly. His arms fell away from the wall and he stepped back. "You should never have heard about her. I didn't want you to know about her. Fuck, Ty's gonna be so upset when he hears you know this story."

I could only imagine they wouldn't want me to know about her and what Quinton had done to her face.

The Salt and Pepper twins had told me about Annabell and they'd also told me about what Quinton had done to the beautiful girl's face. Addison had said Quinton made an example out of Annabell to let the other covens know who they were dealing with when it came to him, to them. And it was, like most things with Quinton, extreme.

Quinton had concocted some special potion and mixed it in with her facewash. I have no idea what it was he'd used but whatever it was had been potent because it had ruined half her face.

The ruined half of her face was covered in horrific burns. Even half her mouth had been burnt, frozen for the rest of her days in a melted frown. I know this because I dreamed of her and my dreams always meant something. I couldn't always figure out the meaning but I knew, I just knew, the face I'd seen in my dream had really been hers.

And she looked that way because of Quinton.

His eyes were wide and filled with fear. What was he afraid of? Not me? Maybe my reaction to him? I didn't know but I'd never seen him look afraid before. It was worrisome.

"Quinton-"

He closed his eyes tightly and whispered, "Please don't be afraid of me now. Please, please, Ariel, do not think I would ever do something like that to you. None of the guys would ever do any-"

I now understood the fear in his eyes. Quinton and I did not know each other very well even though we'd been through some serious situations together and I spent most of my time running away from him.

From what I had been told about Annabell, I knew she was a horrible person. The twins claimed that if you were a female witch you were treated differently than the males because there were so few of them. They're given whatever they want and supposedly can pick whatever coven of their choosing. And every coven wants their own girl. Their own girl to share. Yes, you heard that right, they all share their girl. That way there would be no fighting over who got the girl. Female witches were precious and, I'd been told, every coven wanted one. So much so they were supposed to have no problem with sharing her amongst them. Considering

I'm female and a witch, I had a bit of a problem with this.

Annabell, it seemed, had had no such problems. She'd wanted her own coven to rule over but she didn't want a pre-made one. She wanted to pick and choose her members, stealing them away from the covens they were already a member of.

She went from coven to coven, seducing specific members with her beauty and her magic. She liked the rich ones who were willing to give her whatever she wanted. And she wanted to be some kind of queen.

It was unfortunate for my guys that she'd showed up so soon after the death of Tyson's parents. They'd been too devastated and grief-stricken to see her for what she really was.

She got to Tyson, Julian *and* Damien. My Salt and Pepper twins hadn't liked her at all. They talked to Quinton. Quinton investigated her. And, well, Annabell ended up with half of a ruined face as a result.

I sighed and looked Quinton straight in the eyes. Apparently, he needed reassurance. Not that I blamed him, I *did* bail on him, on them, for weeks.

"Quint, I'm not Annabell and you're not my mother." He snapped his mouth shut and stared at me with wide, startled eyes. It was a cute look for him, though, I'd never call him cute. He was dark, broody, sexy even, but not cute. It looked good on him. "And for some weird reason, I'm not afraid of you either. Now, forget about Chucky and forget about The Not So Beautiful Anymore Annabell. I've got something bigger to worry about."

The corner of his lips curled up on one side of his face. "Just like that," he snapped his fingers, "we forget about Annabell and the douche bag?"

I shrugged. "For now, yeah. Mr. Cole is selling the house and moving. He wants to live closer to his family. He wants to take me with him, Quint. I don't want to lose him, but I don't want to go with him either. But I also don't want to be homeless. I have no idea what I'm supposed to be doing. What am I supposed to be doing? I don't have a mother anymore to make those decisions for me." I lifted my arms and spread my hands wide. I sounded as desperate as I felt when I begged, "Tell me what I'm supposed to be doing."

His body heat engulfed me as he surged forward and wrapped his arms around my shoulders. He pulled me into his chest and I didn't hesitate to wrap my arms around his middle.

I inhaled deeply. He smelled like incense and spice. Like Tyson, only darker. It matched his personality.

He kissed the top of my head and whispered, "Just breathe, baby. Everything will work out how it's supposed to, you'll see. You're not alone and you don't have to figure it out on your own. We're all here for you."

He sounded like he really believed his words. I wasn't so sure. It sounded like another one of their promises they were so fond of dishing out. I wasn't entirely sure I deserved his kindness since I ran from him, ran from them all and cut them out.

"I don't think you should be nice to me. Not when I haven't been very nice to you these past few weeks. I mean, I even turned my phone off so that-"

One thin, scarred finger covered my lips, silencing me. How did he get those scars? I wanted to know but wasn't brave enough to ask.

"We get it. Every one of us gets it. Take as much time as you need. We aren't going anywhere."

And wasn't that the problem? Time. I was running out of it. He said to take as much time as I needed but what if I needed more than I had?

Quinton's hand went to the side of my face and he ran the backs of his knuckles down my cheek. Soft, gentle, barely a whisper of a touch across my skin.

My lips parted in surprise as I watched his eyes darken and fill with a heat I'd never before seen.

"What-"

"Quiet, baby," he murmured as his eyes dropped down to my mouth.

Did he… did scary dude Uncle Quinton want to kiss me?

I think he did.

Did I want him to?

He didn't give me the time to think about it.

He kissed me.

My lips parted in shock when he leaned in. His soft lips brushed mine and he took advantage of my parted lips, darting his tongue inside.

I gasped. It came out as a strange noise due to the fact he had his lips fused to mine as his tongue explored my mouth.

My arms came up and I rested my hands on his hard stomach, clenching my hands in the soft fabric of his shirt. I'd never voluntarily touched him before.

As soon as I touched him he broke the kiss, stepping back. My hands fell away from his stomach and I blinked my eyes open, not remembering when I'd closed them. His tongue snaked out and he swept it across my bottom lip as his dark eyes bored into mine.

"I'm gonna take care of everything," he whispered against my lips. "I'm gonna take care of you. You'll see."

He winked at me before moving away. I had his back for a few seconds while he made his way to the open front door. Then he was gone.

It seemed the Uncle was just like the Nephew and they both wanted to take care of me.

I pressed shaking fingers to my tingling lips. Uncle Quinton had kissed me… and I could not wait for him to do it again.

Not even Chucky's sudden appearance and the fact he'd tried to manhandle me could chase away the warm goodness I was feeling.

Chapter Four

I DREAMED I was drowning. And I dreamed of the hand that pushed me down, shoving me further into the dark abyss. And I dreamed of another hand.

The only hand that reached for me while I'm sinking, while I'm drowning, while my world fades to black as the darkness surrounds me.

Long, lean, scarred fingers reached for me.

Quinton.

Quinton was here.

My light in the dark.

I sat up in bed with a start. My breath was coming too fast, too quick. I raised a shaking hand and wrapped it around my burning throat.

It wasn't real.

None of it was real.

Tears trailed down my face, leaving a trail of wetness behind.

Drowning, I dreamed of drowning, as I had been doing for weeks. This time it was different. I'd been dreaming this same awful dream over and over again and no one had ever reached for me, tried to help me, tried to save me. The dream had always ended with me being swallowed by the darkness, screaming for all I was worth and choking to death on icy water. I would wake up crying, my throat burning, and entirely alone because I had pushed everyone away.

Tonight was different.

Tonight, someone had been there to save me, to pull me out of the darkness. I knew it had been Quinton by his fingers. Those scarred fingers I had looked at on more than one occasion and wondered where the scars had come from. I wouldn't hold back my curiosity next time, I would ask, and because he was Quinton, he'd answer me.

I looked around my dark bedroom and could feel the walls closing in on me. Panic overrode my fear and the tears stopped seeping out of my eyes. I frantically searched the dark corners of my room looking for what, I had no idea, but I could feel something pressing into me, smothering me.

I couldn't breathe.

The room was too warm, the walls were closing in on me and I escaped one nightmare just to choke on my own panic in another, only this one was of my own creation.

I felt like an idiot.

I flung my pretty light blue comforter with the pretty red rose blossoms on it to the side. Without the comforter the room was still too warm.

I had to get out of here. Now.

The fact that it was the middle of the night and I didn't really have anywhere to go never occurred to me.

I crawled out of bed and practically ran to the door. I needed to get outside, to get to fresh air so I could breathe. I stumbled down the stairs, clinging to the railing and almost tripped when I made the landing.

I crossed the foyer and made it to the door. I unarmed the security alarm and unlocked the front door. If I forgot the damn alarm the thing would rage at me, loudly.

I opened the door and stepped out into the night. The cement was cool beneath my bare feet and I shivered. I should have thought to put on shoes and maybe some real clothes. The thin tank top and short-shorts, although cute (they were green and covered in cute little pink hearts) would not save me from the chill in the air.

At least it wasn't pitch black out. The moon hung from the sky like a bright glowing orb, full, or close to it.

I stood there in the moonlight and simply breathed in the crisp night air, chasing back my panic. My chest rose and fell with every deep breath I took.

I stood there until my breathing returned to normal and my throat stopped burning. Since the nightmare started, I never understood how part of it could follow me out into the real world. It bothered me because I didn't understand it and I didn't enjoy being in pain even if it only lasted a short while. It scared me, the bad things weren't supposed to be able to crawl out of your dreams and chase you back to reality. My throat burning was a physical reminder that I had drowned in a dream. That wasn't supposed to happen and that's why it was scary.

My dreams had always been weird as far back as I could remember. They'd meant something, I just wasn't always very good at figuring out what it was. I had never told anybody about my dreams before. Then again, before coming here there had never been anyone to tell except for my mother and I shuddered at that happy thought. I could tell the guys and they'd help me to understand them and wouldn't think they made me a freak.

I realized with a start that I missed them. I missed Tyson and I missed the Salt and Pepper twins. I hardly knew them but I knew them enough to miss them. Tomorrow I would go and see them, I had let it go for too long. What would I do if they didn't want to see me? What would I do if they treated me the way I had treated them? That would crush me, break something inside of me I'd somehow miraculously managed to keep safe all this time. A place inside of me where I'd hidden away all of my hopes and dreams, if they rejected me that small place would be snuffed out. I always thought that I didn't have hopes and dreams but seeing that place inside of myself for the first time, realizing it was there, I knew I had been lying to myself for the longest time.

It made me wonder, what else had I been lying to myself about?

I don't know how long I would have stood there for if I hadn't caught movement at the edge of the tree line. A dark, hooded figure moved, entering the forest. Another hooded figure followed.

Those now hidden figures were bigger than the average human being and they had moved in a way that was eerily similar. What were the Salt and Pepper twins doing out here, skulking through the shadows in the middle of the night?

Another figure disappeared into the forest, this one still tall but thinner than the first two. I was betting on Tyson.

If they were going to be traipsing through the forest they should at least do it on their own property and not on Mr. Cole's. Not that it would be his property for much longer.

I waited a heartbeat, then two more. When nothing moved I figured it was safe. I turned and shut the front door as quietly as I could, the only sound it made was a soft click when it shut. It was still too loud for me and I flinched at the sound.

I whipped around and watched the tree line, looking for any sign of movement. There wasn't any so I hopped off the front steps, landing in the soft grass. I had an urge to curl my toes into it but I didn't have the time to waste. Who knew how deep into the woods they'd already gotten. And, they likely knew where they were going, I, on the other hand, had no clue.

Mr. Cole would be so pissed if he found out I didn't lock the door or re-arm the alarm. I would have to go back inside and find my keys if I wanted to lock the door. I didn't have the time for all that.

I ran across the front lawn, towards the tree line where I'd once seen Quinton spying on me like some kind of creeper. I was thankful not to have shoes on when my feet made next to no noise as I glided across the grass.

When I made it to the edge of the tree line and stepped on something hard and sharp I mourned the lack of footwear. Suddenly, this didn't seem like such a wise idea.

A branch snapped from somewhere in front of me and I fought the urge to scream. Swallowing down my fear, I did the brave thing, the stupid kind of thing and walked close to the trees and their shadowy depths. I looked up and let out a shaky breath. The glow from the moon bled through the trees in places, lighting up the forest floor.

This isn't so bad, Ariel Kimber, you can do this.

Yeah right.

We'd see about that.

I put one foot in front of the other and forced myself to walk deeper into the woods. There were footprints in the dirt, boots, big enough to be male. At least I thought they were big enough to be strictly considered male. The thought of a woman with that size feet had me wincing. I followed them. It was a better idea than playing eenie meenie to determine the direction I wandered off in. If I played that game I'd likely get lost, fall into a smelly, weirdly damp pile of leaves and twigs, get tangled up in them and be eaten alive by rabid, foaming at the mouth, beady eyed squirrels. Death by furry little creatures? No thank you.

I was so busy paying attention to the tracks in the dirt that I wasn't paying attention to what was in front of my face. A branch came out of nowhere and slapped me across the cheek, catching the corner of my mouth.

"Son of a bitch," I swore, tasting blood on my bottom lip. My cheek stung from the impact. I'd likely have a small bruise come tomorrow.

I'd like to say it deterred me from going any further but sadly it did not. I was being braver than my usual self would and I think part of it had to do with the dream. I didn't like feeling afraid. The dream, I couldn't control. Real life, however, I could. There wasn't anything out here that really would eat me.

I argued with myself in my head about the merits of turning back as I pushed forward. I was trying to talk myself out of being brave.

Fifteen minutes later and I was about to call it quits and head back when I spotted a clearing through the trees.

The sound of masculine voices drifted to me, carried on the wind. I had been right. Tyson and Abel and Addison. What were they doing out here?

I moved off the trail I had been following and crept closer, mindful of where I stepped.

I huddled behind a tree and peeked cautiously around it. The moonlight lit the clearing in a soft glow. A fire blazed brightly in a metal barrel.

I held my breath as I watched the three cloaked figures moved around the fire. Their voices may have reached me but their words did not.

They moved around the fire, the three of them, with their arms spread wide and aimed up at the sky. They stood in a triangle and started to circle the fire. They were chanting something, low, their words mingling together.

I leaned my body against the tree and stared at them in fascination.

A wind swept through the clearing causing my hair to blow out around my face. The hooded robes billowed out, dancing on the wind and I caught the sight of naked flesh. A smooth expanse of stomach with a line of dark hair trailing down. The figure moved before my brain caught up with what my eyes had seen.

My face burned as I blushed hotly. They weren't wearing any clothes under those robes.

They continued to circle the fire as the wind picked up. The fabric swished and swirled through thick, muscular, *naked* legs.

I clung to the rough bark of the tree, not caring that it scratched against my smooth cheek as I tried to make sense of what I was seeing. I already expected a bruise on the one cheek, what was a few scratches on the other?

They stopped moving as one and when they did the wind suddenly stopped as well. All was calm in the clearing save for the rhythm of my beating heart. A heart trying to leap out of my chest so it could run far, far away from me and the things we were seeing.

I had no business being out here spying on them. Especially if they were all as naked under their robes as the one twin I'd gotten a glimpse of. I felt like a Peeping Tom and the worst kind of pervert. They deserved better than that from me. Well, Tyson did. The Salt and Pepper twins had had no problem checking me out when they'd seen me naked after my mother's death. Tyson was different and I wasn't going to ogle his naked body unless he was aware of me doing it.

As I stood up straight and stepped away from the tree, they pulled back their hoods. It had been Addison whose naked body I had seen. I'd now seen his dick. I wondered if Abel's would look exactly the same as his twins. Probably. Everything else about their physical shape was the same, why not that part too?

I shook my head to shake out all thoughts of naked twins and all three of the guys dropped their robes to the grass covered ground. I got an eye full of Tyson's firm, tight, *very naked* backside before averting my eyes.

Yes, sticking around for this show wouldn't be right. Not at all.

I turned, to flee, when I was grabbed roughly from behind. One hand covered my mouth, silencing my scream. An arm wrapped around my chest. My back met with an extremely warm, solid, male body. I was going to struggle, to fight, when I looked down and caught sight of flames slithering up the arm wrapped around my chest. I relaxed against him immediately.

It's like Quinton was stalking me or something. Thankfully, I could feel that he at least had clothes on.

Soft lips brushed against my ear. "If I move my hand, you better not scream."

I nodded as best as I could with his hand clamped over my mouth. Now that I knew who it was, I had no intention of screaming. The last thing I needed was to draw attention to myself with three of my friends standing not twenty feet away from me, naked, with their dicks hanging in the breeze for all to see.

Quinton removed his hand from my mouth and wrapped his now free hand around my waist. He pulled me in tightly against his front.

"The others are coming and I don't think you want to be here when they arrive," he whispered against my ear.

I shivered and nodded, he was correct. I had seen more than enough penises for one night, thank you very much.

"Do you know what they're doing?" he continued to whisper and this time I shook my head, no. "You can draw energy, power if you will, off of a full moon if you offer something in return. Remember, Ariel, everything comes with a price and absolutely nothing is free. Magic takes energy to use. If you burn enough energy, you'll crash. It's why Julian brought you food that one time at the house."

He was using my first name when he usually didn't. I wondered why. Maybe he wanted me to take what he was saying seriously? I did. I took everything Quinton told me seriously.

I remembered what he was talking about. It had been the first time I had ever used magic, I hadn't even known for sure that I had magic before that, but I'd been doubtful. Good things had never happened to me before and I was nothing special, or so I had thought. In a fit of rage and extreme emotions (some would have called it a slight temper tantrum, only a slight one, though.) my magic had just sort of pushed its way out of me. It had been the single most exhilarating experience I had had up until that point in my life and probably still was. But the magic had burned bright and fast. I had been left feeling giddy, happy even. For a short amount of time. When the giddiness faded I'd been left feeling empty, entirely drained and oh so very tired. I had learned since then that what Quinton had just told me was very true. Magic came at a price and when that much energy was used, it needed to be replenished. Usually food worked wonders, especially with loads of sugar in it.

"We try to come out here every month, unless it's summer and we're camping or traveling. But this is our place when we're home and we've been coming out here for years. Usually, we offer up something small, sometimes our own blood. Just a little prick, a few small droplets, nothing big."

Quinton's hand slid up my chest where he lightly trailed fingers across my shoulder then along my collarbone. Over some of my burn scars.

I wanted to cry.

Of course he would notice my scars. I was fond of wearing tank tops, which did nothing to hide my scars. He had probably noticed the scars the first time I had worn a tank top in front of him, or maybe it had been the time I had been naked in front of him. Either way, I didn't think Quinton missed much when it came to me.

"Stop," I whispered harshly, thickly.

Stop what, exactly?

Stop caressing my scars so softly, so sweetly? Stop reminding me of something I fought so very hard to forget? Stop touching me altogether?

I wasn't entirely sure what I was telling him to stop doing. Trouble was, his touch on my bare skin did not bother me. It was where he touched that caused me discomfort.

"What caused these?" he whispered so quietly I barely heard him.

I shook my head in answer as my eyes drifted towards the fire, unseeing. I would not tell Quinton those stories, not ever. He was by far the most vindictive and ruthless person I had yet to meet. And that was saying something because my mother had held those titles before I met Quinton. At least he had good reasons for most of the shit he did, if not fucked up ones. He did messed up things to protect the ones he cared about or to teach the person who hurt his loved ones a lesson. Neither were concepts I fully understood, but I knew enough to be semi-grateful towards him. Quinton and Tyson both wanted to take care of me. I had thought their care would come in separate forms. With Quinton's arms wrapped tightly around me, I wasn't so sure anymore if his idea of taking care of me would be so different from Tyson's.

My mother's way of showing me she cared always ended with me being covered in bruises or taking a trip to the emergency room. It had all depended on her mood.

Which is why it was so hard for me to trust the guys. But she was dead, she couldn't hurt me anymore. I needed to remember that. It was hard. That part remained where the damage was still done and I wondered if I would ever be able to trust another human being. If my own flesh and blood could do such horrid things to me… what else was everyone else capable of?

I didn't know and that scared me.

I turned my head to the side, ready to tell Quinton that *he* scared me, when three more hooded figures entered the clearing. I'd momentarily forgotten what was going on around us.

Julian, Damien and Dash had arrived. I did not want to see if they were naked under those robes. No, thanks. I had seen enough male bodies for a good long while.

"Time to go," Quinton whispered urgently.

Maybe he didn't want to see anymore dicks tonight either?

I didn't think that was it but I could have been wrong. I didn't really know him well enough to guess.

Chapter Five

THE ARM QUINTON had a hold of screamed in protest as he dragged me along behind him through the dense forest. He seemed to be in a hurry so I didn't complain. I didn't think he knew he was hurting me.

"They wanted to see if you would be interested in going tonight but I told them I didn't think you were ready for that yet," he said. "If I had known I would find you out there, I would have told them to at least have some damn underwear on."

That was interesting. What did it matter if I saw them naked now when he figured it was an inevitability? Sometimes I did not understand him at all.

"So, why are *you* wearing clothes when no one else is?" I blurted before I could really think better of it.

Holy shit! Why in the world would I ask him that? Stupid, stupid girl.

He shot me a dirty look over his shoulder and growled, "I was out here because someone's got to watch your crazy ass. I saw you walk out of your house in the middle of the night in your goddamn pajamas. And I followed you into the woods. You're not even wearing any goddamn shoes and you don't even have a fucking flashlight. Who does that? What's the matter with you?"

Uh oh. Seemed he was mad at me. Normally, this would freak me out, but if he was willing to let my naked comment slide then I could over look his anger issues. Right? Yeah, I didn't think so either. Dare I try to explain myself so that maybe he will calm down? Nah, I would let him get it out of his system.

He kept on ranting, which made me think he didn't really want to hear an explanation from me. Oh well.

"Seriously, what in the hell were you thinking? You could have gotten hurt out here in the dark, all by yourself." He shook his head furiously. "Not smart, babe, that's what this bullshit was. First, that shit with that idiot guy who is in love with you and is showing up at your house out of the blue because he missed you so much he couldn't help himself. Now, you're wandering the woods barefoot. Jesus, I'm going to have to find you a babysitter, someone to watch your crazy ass all the time. Just for your own safety."

He stomped through the trees and into Mr. Cole's front lawn, dragging me along behind him.

I yanked angrily on my arm, forcefully, and he let me go.

I spotted a decent size rock on the ground at the edge of the lawn by my feet. I bent at the waist, picked it up and curled my fingers around it. With it sitting in the center of my palms and my fingers curled around it, you couldn't see it. Not too big, not too small. The perfect size for what I had in store for it.

"What the hell are you doing?" Quinton barked at me.

I stood up straight and faced him. He was wearing a black, short-sleeved t-shirt tonight. I had never seen him in anything but a long-sleeved button up shirt. The dark, blue jeans were tucked into the same cowboy boots I had seen him in earlier. His hands rested on his hips and he glared daggers at me.

Whatever.

Like he had any right to look at me in such a way. I looked at the ground and shook my head while I struggled to rein in my anger.

The things he'd said about Chucky… he was not to be believed. I was in the whole ridiculous situation with Chucky to begin with because of Quinton. Now, he made the whole thing sound like not only was it my fault but he talked like the whole thing with Chucky had been entirely my idea to begin with. Like I would do anything that would saddle me with Chucky for possibly the rest of my life. Get real.

Needless to say, I failed at getting a handle on my anger.

"Hello," he said sarcastically, "anyone in there?"

That did it. He was simply too much for words and he pushed me too far.

I cocked my arm back and chucked my rock at him. I aimed for his head. His eyes widened in either shock or surprise before the rock smashed into his nose.

I stared at him in open mouthed horror as he bent forward at the waist, clutching at his nose.

"Jesus, fuck," he yelled.

I took a step back and away from him. I so totally should not have thrown that rock at his head. Not only had it been completely uncalled for but it was just a wee bit on the insane side.

"Fuck," he snarled as he pulled his hands away from his nose.

I was ashamed and horrified to see blood on his hands. A quick glance at his face showed blood streaming out of his nose.

Oh shit.

Why did I have to lose my temper and throw a rock at him? How stupid was I?

"Nice aim," a deep, rough voice spoke from behind me.

I whirled around to find Tyson standing not two feet away from me. I blinked at him, slowly, as if I were waking from a dream.

"Wha… what…" I stammered stupidly. Where in the hell had he come from? I hadn't heard anyone come up behind me.

He smiled at me and it was a good one, a show stopper, if you will. It was a smile I had come to love because it was bright and transformed his face from handsome to incredibly beautiful. Most men couldn't be described as beautiful but it was the perfect word for Ty when he flashed that smile. It was a smile that showed off his straight, even, white teeth. Teeth that looked like he got them professionally bleached and they practically glowed in the dark.

The hood on his cloak was pulled up over his head, covering his hair and leaving half his face hidden in the dark shadows of the night. The night had made his dark brown eyes look like black orbs sunk into his face. His long, shoulder length dark brown hair spilled out from his hood, curling around his face. It was slightly longer than it had been when I'd seen him last.

Tyson was tall like his Uncle, with broad shoulders and narrow hips. They were both lean, but muscular, built like swimmers. And so very attractive, even Tyson with half his face hidden in shadow was extremely attractive.

"You nailed him a good one," Tyson muttered proudly around his grin.

I was glad one of us found the fact I'd injured Quinton to be amusing.

"Tell me, sweetheart," he said, "what did he do to deserve such treatment from you? You're normally a whole lot nicer than this, and I never dreamed I would see you throwing rocks, of all things, at someone's head." At the end, his voice vibrated with laughter.

I frowned at him. "It was only the *one* rock," I bit out. "And, he had it coming." My voice came out angry and slightly sullen instead of angry and mildly confused. Good. I preferred it that way.

Tyson threw back his head and burst out laughing. His hood fell away and his thick brown hair was suddenly on display. He had lovely hair far prettier than my own. Any girl would be jealous. Or hope to one day be privileged enough to be able to run their fingers through those glorious, thick locks whenever the mood to do so struck them. I bet if I asked, he would allow me to do so whenever I felt the urge to do it.

His robe gaped open and I noticed he now wore a pair of black boxer briefs. Where had those come from?

Not that I wasn't thankful for their appearance or anything because I absolutely was.

A warm hand brushed against my hip and I jumped at the sudden contact. I tore my eyes off of Tyson and looked to the side to see Quinton had come up beside me. Thankfully, he'd transferred his angry glare to Tyson.

"It's really not that funny," Quinton snarled at Tyson.

I was glad to see the blood flow had slowed down to a small trickle. I hoped that meant nothing had been broken by my rash actions.

Tyson stopped laughing and glared back at his Uncle. I wanted to move away from Quinton, away from the both of them and the anger they were radiating.

"Why aren't you with the others?" Quinton demanded to know.

"Why aren't you?" Tyson shot back.

"Guys-" I was going to try and be the reasonable one but was very rudely cut off before I could get more than one word out.

"Don't fuck with me, Ty." Quinton said. "Why aren't you with the others in the clearing?"

Instead of answering his Uncle, Tyson looked at me and said, "I get it, why you threw that rock at him. Right now, I'm wishing you had thrown it a little harder. And maybe aimed for his eye. A black eye would look good on him, don't you think?"

I cringed at the reminder of my stupidity and Tyson turned back to his Uncle. "I saw her there," he said. I was glad to hear the anger had left his voice entirely. "I also saw you drag her away and I wanted to make sure she was okay."

"She's with me," Quinton said, "of course she's okay. You know she's perfectly safe with me."

"No," Tyson bit out, "I don't."

"What the fuck is that supposed to mean?" Quinton asked and he sounded confused.

I was with him on this one because I believed him when he said I was perfectly safe when I was with him. It was everybody else that needed to worry.

"I'm not talking about her safety," Tyson said with a straight face. "I'm talking about her virtue."

My eyes about bugged out of my head as I stared at Tyson like I had never seen him before.

"Come on, Ty, give me a little credit here. It's not like I'm gonna do her right here on Marcus's front lawn."

My mouth dropped open to accompany my bugged-out eyes and I gaped at Quinton in what I imagine looked a whole lot like horror. I did not like the way he'd said that at all.

"Nobody's doing anybody," I breathed out.

They both started laughing and I backed away from them, slowly.

I didn't find anything funny and I certainly didn't like the casual way they were discussing having sex with me. I hadn't agreed to have a relationship with any of them and no way was I ready to talk about sex with them.

Maybe I shouldn't have let Quinton stick his tongue in my mouth? Did he think just because I had allowed him to kiss me that now I would be open to other things? I surely hoped not. My life was a mess, I couldn't imagine how much messier it would get if I started knocking boots with multiple people. Maybe we could talk about it after my life got straightened out and I was no longer in mourning and probably going to end up homeless in my very near future. Then again, maybe not.

Since they were both still laughing and completely ignoring me, I figured it was safe to escape them and their utter madness. I turned and ran. Ran away from them, ran away from their laughter, their particular brand of crazy. If I ran fast enough maybe I could make it to the door and lock myself inside so I could go back to avoiding them because they were all fucking crazy.

I was half way across the lawn when something slammed into my back and I was tackled to the ground. I let out a shriek right before my body hit the ground. A heavy weight landed on top of my back and I ended up with a mouth full of grass.

I spit the grass out and coughed. What the hell?

"Get off me," I yelled and tried to buck the heavy weight of someone's body off of me. It was no use.

"Shh," Tyson said from his place on top of my back. "If you don't stop yelling, Mr. Cole is going to come out here and think we are trying to murder you. He'll probably shoot us."

I ignored his suggestion, and yelled, "If you don't get off me right this second, Tyson Alexander, I am never, *ever* going to speak to you again. And, I'm a girl so I know how to hold a mean grudge."

Before this thing with Chucky, I'd actually never held a grudge against anyone in my whole life and had no intention of Tyson being the second person on my grudge hit list, but he didn't need to know that.

His weight left my back and I was able to pull in a full breath for the first time since he tackled me. Hands grabbed ahold of me under my armpits and I was hauled to my feet.

"What the fuck do you think you're doing?" Quinton's voice vibrated with rage. "You could have seriously hurt her, you fucking idiot."

The person holding me, which I realized was Quinton after he'd spoken, shook me so hard my teeth rattled and my head snapped back and forth with the force of it.

"Are you okay, Ariel?" he asked and his voice was a whole lot gentler than it had been a few seconds ago. And he was calling me by my first name again.

I thought about his question. Was I okay? My body wasn't injured, or at least I didn't feel any injuries. I looked down at my body just in case I missed anything important and I realized I had grass stains on my knees. Other than that, I was fine.

Tyson moved so that he was standing in front of me.

He bent forward so that our faces were almost touching and whispered, "Did I hurt you? I didn't mean to hurt you. I swear it, Ariel. I would never intentionally hurt you."

I shrugged and told him the truth, "I'm not hurt."

But I was baffled. Why in the hell would he chase after me and tackle me from behind? We weren't playing football. We hadn't been playing at all.

Quinton finally let go of me and I bent forward to brush off my knees and forgot Tyson was standing so close to me. My forehead smacked into his and we both jerked back.

"Ow," he whined.

I rubbed at my forehead with my fingers and thought about just how absurd this whole night had been. It had started with me trying to escape a terrifying nightmare. Then I'd seen part of some kind of full moon ritual. I'd then went on to see three of my friend's boy parts. Afterwards, I'd thrown a rock at scary dude Uncle Quinton and bloodied his nose. Then, Tyson got crazy and tackled me. And now this.

I couldn't help myself. I started laughing. I laughed so hard my entire body shook with it.

Weeks, I had spent without them and even though I had had Mr. Cole with me almost constantly, it had still been what seemed to me like some of the loneliest weeks of my whole life. Yes, my depression had been a direct result of what had happened with my mother. But the loneliness had nothing to do with her death. I'd had but a small taste of their friendship, Tyson's friendship the most, and I had been empty of emotions without it, without them. I had no idea how I had allowed it to happen.

I stopped laughing. It didn't seem appropriate anymore.

I swallowed down my emotions, took a deep, shaky breath, and looked Tyson in the eyes. It was now or never. I had to put myself out there. I had to stop holding myself back. Had to stop pretending they weren't as important to me as they were.

"I missed you," I whispered hoarsely, honestly.

It was one of the hardest truths to ever come out of my mouth. To admit I missed him was to admit I needed him in some way. And I did not like needing another human being. Not in any way. It had just been me for so long, with only myself to look after, only my own feelings and welfare to care about, I didn't really know how to go about doing it for someone else. I had already messed it all up by running away from them. What if I messed up worse than that after I let them in? What if I ended up all alone again? I didn't want to be alone, I was honest enough with myself to admit that. But if I opened myself up to one of them they expected me to open myself up to all of them. With them, it was all or nothing.

The problem was, I didn't want all of them.

Only some of them.

And I feared that wouldn't be enough.

Chapter Six

QUINTON HAD BACKED off the moment Tyson wrapped his arms around me in the tightest hug I had ever experienced. I thought about asking him to ease up a bit, but, truthfully, the hug felt nice. I had missed him very much.

"I'm sorry, girl," Tyson whispered, "but you tried to run from me. I missed you so much and I am so tired of watching you run away. Don't run away from me anymore, Ariel. I don't think I could stand to watch you do it again."

The pleading and sorrow in his voice broke my heart.

I pulled him in closer to me, as close as he could get and I clung to him for all I was worth.

"Missed you," I whispered fiercely. "Thought about you every day. Thought about calling you just so I could hear your voice. I'm so sorry for-"

"You don't have anything to be sorry about," he whispered back just as fiercely. "I can't even begin to imagine what you've been going through. It's killed me not to be there for you when you needed me. You have no idea. So I'm not letting you run away from me because I can't handle it."

Guilt ate at me from the inside like a vicious thing. I hadn't meant to hurt anyone, I'd just needed some space to make sure I didn't fall apart and to get myself sorted.

"I'm not running," I murmured.

"Girl, you just tried to."

Since he was right, I didn't try arguing with him.

He rubbed his face against my hair and inhaled deeply.

"Do you want to go back to the clearing?" he asked me.

Did I want to go back to the clearing? Where the Salt and Pepper twins were naked and Julian, Damien and Dash had just arrived and were probably naked under their robes too? Yeah, I didn't think so.

Quinton was suddenly there, hovering over me. He placed his hand on Tyson's shoulder and pulled him away from me.

"It's late," Quinton said. "Ariel needs to get inside where it's safe and she needs to go to bed. What she doesn't need to be doing is gallivanting through the woods with you in the middle of the night. She's had enough of that for one night. Now, she's going to bed. Alone."

Tyson's face darkened and he scowled ferociously at Quinton. There he was, I missed him. I grinned at the both of them. Time's like these made it easy to tell they were related, they both shared the same scowl, the same dark looks. A lesser person would have backed away from that dark look on Tyson's face. Quinton gave one of his own in return.

"You know what I find interesting, Uncle Quint?" Tyson rumbled scarily. It was the same voice he'd used on me the first time I accidently ran into him.

"What?" Quinton ground out.

"We all agreed to give her space, we thought she needed it after everything she's gone through and we didn't want to scare her off. Now I see you out here with her and the other day I caught you leaving her house. How long have you been sneaking over there to see her behind our backs?"

Quinton took a step closer to Tyson and I quickly moved my body between them.

"He hasn't been sneaking over to see me," I rushed to assure Tyson. "I had an issue with Chucky showing up at my house out of the blue and he was weird and a serious jerk. Quinton came over to rescue me. And I went into the woods on my own. I followed you and the twins. Quinton followed me to make sure I didn't get lost or something."

I left out the part about Quinton sticking his tongue in my mouth. I didn't know how Tyson would take that.

Tyson studied my face and his angry glare softened then faded away altogether.

"I also appreciate that you guys gave me space," I murmured. "Thank you, I needed it. But I let it go for too long and I'm done hiding now, done running away. So you don't have to worry anymore. Okay?"

I felt this bottomless need to assure him I wasn't going anywhere in hopes of getting rid of some of the guilt I had been burdened with when he told me how much he'd missed me. It would likely take a whole lot more than a few reassuring words on my part. It would take time. With time, he would learn I meant it when I said I wasn't going to run from them anymore. I had made my decision and I would stick with it. I could go with Mr. Cole and avoid all of this boy drama that the seven of them represented but I couldn't do it. I didn't want the fresh new start to life that Mr. Cole offered me. I wanted to stay with my coven. Well, some of them. And they wanted me. Well, some of them. So I wasn't going anywhere. Not unless they decided they no longer wanted me.

That thought caused a ball of dread to form in the pit of my stomach.

"Why was Chucky at her house?" Tyson asked.

I didn't like him asking Quinton instead of me when I was right there and fully capable of answering for myself. It had been my house Chucky showed up at, me who had just told him about it, me who he should have asked. Not Quinton.

I opened my mouth to tell him just that when Quinton squeezed my shoulder gently and spoke before I could. It's like he knew I was going to tell Tyson off. Quinton the mind reader. Scary thought.

"He's in love with her," Quinton said and he sounded amused. "And he missed her because she hasn't been going to school. Can you blame the poor guy?"

"He's only in love with me because you used some crazy love potion on him and forced him to fall in love with me. Which, in case you missed it," I snapped sarcastically, "I'm not happy about it *at all*."

I moved out from between the two of them and turned so I was facing them both head on. Quinton bit his bottom lip while he watched me like he was waiting for me to do something crazy.

It was Tyson who spoke and he did so sounding tired.

"I'm sorry, Ariel girl. There's no stopping him. I used to try but stopped when I realized there was absolutely no point and it was a wasted effort. With Uncle Quint, it's best to simply let him do his own thing and always expect the unexpected. You'll get used to it. You might never get used to *him,* but you will get used to expecting crazy shit from him."

Quinton shrugged, unrepentant.

"I already told you," he said. "This is who I am and what I am. There's no changing me."

I didn't want to change him. I didn't want to change any of them.

I sighed, suddenly tired. It had been a very long night for me and I was ready to go back to bed.

"What were you doing outside?" Quinton asked me in a serious voice, changing the subject abruptly. "You never told me before and I want to know. Don't lie to me and tell me you just felt like taking a walk because I won't believe you and it will piss me off if you lie to me."

I thought about how to answer him. I wanted to lie but at the same time I didn't want him to be mad at me.

When in doubt, tell the truth. Or something close to it.

I rubbed my fingers across my temple and closed my eyes, wishing I were already snuggled in my bed underneath my warm, comfy blanket.

"Leave her alone, Uncle Quint," Tyson rumbled angrily.

I sighed. Again.

I wasn't interested in listening to them bicker with each other. Why were they always fighting? I couldn't remember ever seeing them get along.

"I couldn't breathe," I blurted. Quinton's mouth pinched tight and he scowled at me. Tyson's brow pinched together and he frowned at me.

"What the fuck are you talking about?" Quinton growled at me. "Did someone hurt you? Where the fuck was Marcus?"

"No, no," I said hurriedly. "Nothing like that. I dreamed I was drowning. I dreamed she-"

I snapped my mouth shut at the sight of the matching scary looks on their faces.

"You, what?" Quinton whispered in a dark voice.

"Have you been… Have you," Tyson stammered. "Have you been having these dreams this whole time?" He swallowed thickly and looked away from me.

I dropped my gaze to the grass and wrapped my arms around myself tightly.

"I wake up and I can't breathe," I whispered without raising my eyes from the ground. I didn't want to see the pity on their faces. "The room always feels like the walls are closing in and they are going to crush me. I can't go back to sleep because all I can think about is her hand on my head, shoving me down into dark, icy water. My lungs burn, my chest feels like it's going to implode. In the dream, I die. When I wake up, it still hurts, I can feel it like it happened in real life. I wake up and it hurts and I can't breathe."

I sucked in a great big gust of crispy night air because I could and because it felt good to do so. Talking about the dream brought it back to life and I shivered, not because of the chill in the air but because I remembered the hopelessness, the helplessness I had felt when I drowned.

"Fuck," Quinton swore harshly. "Ty will go inside with you and he will sleep with you tonight so that you don't have to be alone. I would do it myself but I don't think you'd be comfortable with me sleeping with you just yet. And, honestly, when I get you in a bed and it's just the two of us I have no intention of keeping my hands to myself."

"I can do that," Tyson said quickly.

God. Quinton was not to be believed.

"You can't just demand I sleep with someone," I snapped, "and expect me to do it. That's absurd."

Quinton was suddenly no longer standing three feet away from me but he was *there*. In my space and in my face. His quick movements and the look on his face frightened me. I stepped back, to get away from him and the look on his face but didn't get very far because I backed into a hard, hot, male body.

I let out a loud, shrill, terrified shriek as I turned my head to the side and looked back.

Tyson stood behind me with Quinton in front of me. They'd caged me in. I was trapped and I didn't want to be trapped in between them. Well, maybe I did, but not like this and not with Quinton looking at me like that.

"You don't fucking get it," Quinton snarled in my face and my breath caught in my throat as I looked into his dark, burning eyes. I had never seen him this intense before.

"Get what?" I squeaked out in a voice three times higher than my normal one.

"You are not alone anymore," he ground out between clenched teeth. "You don't ever have to be alone again. In fact, we would prefer it that way. You have got to stop acting like this, like it's you against the world when that's absolute bullshit. I've told you, Tyson has told you, the goddamn twins have told you. Fuck, Ariel, Julian's probably said it in front of you. You're mine. You're Ty's. You're ours. If you were anyone else you would be able to choose your own coven, but you're not just anyone. You're you and you're mine. You're not going anywhere. I don't care if you don't like it, it's just the way it's gonna be. You don't get to choose another coven. You don't get to walk away, ever. You don't get to run away and hide anymore. We are through with all of that nonsense. You don't get to walk away from us, not a single one of us. I don't give a fuck if you think some of the guys don't like you. Maybe you're right. Maybe you're wrong. It doesn't fucking matter either way because you're ours and eventually they will grow to love you, if they don't already. The point I am trying to make is that your self-imposed isolation has come to an end. You are with us which means you actually need to be *with us*."

He raised his hand to silence me because I got over my fear of him and opened my mouth to tell him just how crazy I found him but his raised hand had me snapping my mouth shut.

"I don't mean sex when I say you need to actually be with us. Sex isn't everything. Do we want to have sex with you? Yes, absolutely. Is that how this relationship is going to go with you and all of us? Again, yes, absolutely. You can be a prude and young and naïve all you want, knock yourself out. But that doesn't mean there isn't only one outcome to this situation. And that's *you* with *us*, all of us.

"You're a female witch. You're our female witch. I'm trying to be cool with you because you're new to this and weren't raised to know what to expect, but my patience only goes so far. Your time alone is over. Get used to it, babe, and don't try to fight it. Don't try to fight me. It won't do you any good. Nobody walks away from me unless I want them to and I think I already shared with you why you aren't gonna walk away from me.

"You brought her up before, Annabell. You are not her. You are nothing fucking like her. But, unfortunately for you, you get the us we are after her. It's not going to be easy, I get that, I even understand it. But, you are gonna have to suck it the fuck up because you are the only girl for the job. Don't fight it. Now, Tyson is going home with you. If you don't like it, feel free to pick someone else and I will get them for you."

He backed off and stared me down, watching my face.

"Yeah," he said after a few seconds of watching me. "That's what I thought."

He turned his back on me, started to walk away, and said over his shoulder, “It’s your night, nephew. Take care of her.”

Chapter Seven

I STOOD IN the middle of my bedroom feeling incredibly awkward. I hated feeling this way. After the horrid first day of school, I hadn't been anything but comfortable around Tyson. He had the potential to become my best friend. Leave it to Quinton to put a wedge between us while he was actually trying to drag us closer together.

The door clicked shut softly, announcing Tyson's arrival. He'd gone home to put some clothes on over his underwear. After Quinton's little speech, the fact that Tyson was so scantily clad had seemed to bother him more than it had bothered me. He'd insisted on going home to change.

"You don't actually have to stay with me," I said quietly without turning around to look at him. "I will be fine on my own."

Gentle but warm hands landed on my shoulders. He pulled me back into his solid chest. His hands slid down my arms until they met with my hands. He leaned against my back as he tangled our fingers together. He rubbed his cheek against the top of my head as he snuggled into me from behind.

"Ariel, Ariel," he murmured. "Do you want to be alone? If you want me to go just say so and I will go. I won't like it and Quint will probably try to kick my ass but if it's what you want then I will go."

I shook my head. If he left me I would probably cry and I definitely wouldn't be able to go back to sleep. I only said it because I didn't want him to feel like he had to stay because his Uncle told him to do so.

"I want you to stay with me," I told him honestly. "But I don't want you to be here because Quinton ordered you to be here. He's so bossy and he's always trying to control everything. I don't want him to control who I spend my time with and I certainly do not want him to think he can get away with telling me who I'm going to sleep with in my bed at night. That's ridiculous and I'm not going to let him get away with that."

His body started shaking, shaking mine with it as he laughed softly.

"You want to tell him he's too bossy and that you're not going to let him order you around." He laughed harder. "I'd pay good money to see that. I'm sure we all would. You let me know before hand and we'll all gather around to watch you tell him off and put him in his place."

I was pretty sure I didn't want an audience for that would-be conversation. A conversation I would likely never have because I wasn't quite brave enough to tell Quinton off and I had no idea what his place was so I could put him there.

"I'm tired," I said. And I was. So very, very tired. Since the dream had started up I hadn't gotten a whole lot of sleep. I needed to sleep.

Tyson squeezed my hands before letting go and stepping away from me. I immediately missed his heat.

"Then get into bed," he ordered. "Do you want me to get your computer and set up *Friday Night Lights* for us? Or have you been watching it without me?"

He sounded disgruntled at the end and warmth spread through my entire being. I loved that he sounded like he didn't want me to watch it on my own. As much as I had wanted to continue watching the show so I could find out what happened, I didn't want to watch it without Tyson. It didn't seem right to me to watch it without him. It was our thing we did together.

As much as I wanted to cuddle up with Tyson on my bed while we watched our show I didn't think I would make it through a whole episode without falling asleep.

"Sure," I said. "If you want to watch it then go ahead and get it ready. But I'm not going to watch it. I'm going to sleep. I'm so tired."

"Is that what you're sleeping in?" He asked me quietly.

I didn't even bother to look down at the tank top and short-shorts I had started out the night in in what felt like forever and a day ago. It would feel nice to put on fresh clothing but then I would need to take a shower first and I would likely fall asleep standing up if I did that.

"It's fine," I muttered as I moved towards the bed. It was a sloppy mess from sleeping in it. I usually took better care of my things and always made a point to make my bed when I got out of it. I guess it didn't really matter when it wouldn't be my bed for much longer.

Without bothering to straighten out the mess that was my sheets and blanket, I crawled into my bed.

"I'm going to use the bathroom," Tyson said. "I'll be right back. Get yourself comfortable."

I laid my head down on my pillow and dragged my comforter over my head. I hoped he would turn the lights off when he came back from the bathroom.

I had uncovered my head and was starting to drift off when I heard him moving around the otherwise silent room. The bed moved, the blanket shifted and then his body curved around me, his front to my back. One of his arms slid underneath my pillow, below my head. His lips kissed the top of my head. He leaned into me, pushing my side and part of my belly into the bed as he pushed his knee in-between my legs. His front melded into my back as his free hand slid up my side. His hand stopped just shy of my breast and his fingers curled into my ribs.

"Umm…" I mumbled, unsure of how to feel about this position he'd put us in.

His hand slid back down my side until he met with the hem of my tank top. Skin against skin, his hand smoothed its way up my stomach. He didn't stop going until he moved between my bare breasts and passed them. He stopped just below my neck where he splayed his fingers wide and pushed on my chest, pulling me back against his body as tight as I could get.

"Tell me something," he whispered in my ear.

I couldn't think straight with him wrapped all around me so tightly.

"What?" I croaked out. I cleared my throat and tried again. "What do you want me to tell you?"

"Tell me about these," he said as he ran his fingers across my scars.

I sucked in a sharp breath, suddenly wide awake and clear headed. Twice in one damn night.

"Where did they come from?"

I shook my head.

"How old were you?"

I drew in a deep, shuddering breath.

"Did your mother do this to you?"

I tried to pull away from him but he refused to let me go. Instead, he pulled me in tighter even though I didn't think it was possible to get any closer.

"Why won't you tell me?"

Oh, I don't know. Maybe because I didn't think he needed to know every hideously horrible and humiliating thing there was to know about my life. He didn't share messed up stories with me about his past and I didn't ask him to, nor would I.

"Girl, you know you can tell me anything."

I sighed. I did know. I had no doubts when it came to trusting Tyson. That wasn't it. It was about rehashing it, bringing it back to the surface when I'd buried it so deep that I rarely thought about it. Denial and ignorance were my friend. Also, there was always that little thought in the back of my head telling me to keep it to myself, there was only so much bullshit a person could take before they started to look at you with pity in their eyes and then they bailed on you. I knew, I freaking *knew* he wouldn't bail on me and the pity wouldn't stay there forever. In reality, I knew that. But in my head, it was a whole different story.

"Fuck it," he grunted. "Forget I said anything and go to sleep."

The hurt in his voice pierced my chest like a flaming hot sword, threatening to kill me.

My silence had hurt him. All he was trying to do was get to know me better. I had scars that I didn't want to talk about but, unfortunately for me, they were in an extremely visible place and everyone who looked at me got to take in an eye full. It was also unfortunate for me that most people were nosy and felt the need to ask questions. Tyson wasn't asking to be nosy. He asked because he cared. I'd had a lifetime of people not giving a shit about me. Now that I had someone to care, I didn't need to mess it all up by being an A-hole and hurting their feelings and pushing them away from me.

I sighed heavily and placed my hand on top of his hand on my chest.

"She didn't do this to me," I whispered so quietly I almost didn't hear my own words. I pressed down on where my hand covered his when I said it so he would know exactly what my words meant.

"I was maybe eight when it happened and I don't even remember what his name was because he wasn't around long enough for me to need to remember it. Or maybe I don't remember it on purpose. He came home with her one night and acted like he had no intention of ever leaving again. He was a jobless loser she'd picked up at the club where she was working at the time. I don't think anyone ever told her she wasn't supposed to bring her work home with her. Anyway, a few days after he showed up, I had to leave school early because I got some horrid flu bug. I remember it being awful. My stomach hurt so bad and I couldn't stop puking. When there was nothing left to puke I kept right on dry heaving. I had to walk home from school because my mother didn't answer when the school called and nobody came to pick me up. It was a two mile walk in the cold and I had a fever and still don't remember most of the walk home. But I made it and that's the important part. I could have fallen down into a ditch and froze to death or something but I didn't. I made it back to the apartment."

I paused in my story to squeeze his hand to my chest tightly, probably too tightly. But if I hurt him he didn't complain.

"She had been home when the school called and hadn't bothered to pick up the phone. She'd been there when they left messages on the machine and had not cared even the tiniest bit. She had a man to entertain and coke to snort, nothing else had mattered. At the time, I hadn't minded because it meant I could slip into the apartment unnoticed and hide out in my bedroom. I took some medicine that I found in the bathroom cabinet and passed out in my bed afterwards. I woke up hours later with him looming over me, demanding I get my ass out of bed and make him some dinner. I didn't argue, I knew better. I went to the kitchen and made him some eggs and toast. The eggs… Well, the smell made me sick to my stomach. I ended up throwing up in his lap when I sat his plate in front of him on the kitchen table. He hit me once, right after I puked on him. He backhanded me. I blacked out when I hit the kitchen floor. I woke up when he put his cigarette out on me like I was his personal ashtray. He stuck around for a week longer and I got more of the same. I don't even know why he left."

I expected Tyson to say something when I stopped talking, like apologize to me or something equally stupid, but he didn't say a word.

I forced my body to relax into the bed and against Tyson, not realizing how tense I had gotten while talking to him.

Talking about my feelings and my horrible past experiences hadn't made me feel any better at all. Weren't most girls supposed to enjoy talking about that shit? I apparently didn't enjoy it and worried I now had a whole new set of nightmares to worry about having tonight.

"That bitch is lucky she's already dead," he rumbled menacingly, making me jump. I thought he might have fallen asleep but, apparently, I had been wrong.

"What?" I asked quietly, not believing he'd just said that.

"If that bitch wasn't already dead, I would hunt her ass down and kill her myself. It wouldn't be no damn accident and she would suffer greatly. For hours and hours. She got off way too easy and I fucking hate her even more for it."

I couldn't believe he just said that.

She was dead. What did it matter if she had suffered or not?

"Tyson, I-"

He kissed the top of my head. "Sleep, my sweet girl. I will watch over you and tomorrow I will go and get you a dreamcatcher and hang it up for you."

"It will be pointless to hang it up in here," I said sleepily.

"What?"

"Mr. Cole is moving. He wants me to go with him. I told Quinton that I am not going with Mr. Cole. I want to stay here but I don't want to be homeless. I want to stay with you."

"What did Uncle Quint say?" he asked me stiffly.

"That he'd take care of it and that he'd take care of me," I slurred sounding half asleep because I mostly was.

"Good," he breathed out in relief. "Now go to sleep, sweetheart. Just go to sleep. I will be here with you, to watch over you and chase away your bad dreams."

I did as I was told and I drifted off to sleep held tightly in the safety of Tyson's arms.

I dreamed of nothing.

I also missed it when Tyson pulled out his cellphone to call his Uncle Quinton.

They talked about me and I didn't hear a single word of it.

Probably for the best.

Chapter Eight

I WOKE UP alone in my bed. The early afternoon light spilled into my bedroom through the window. I had been sleeping in later and later every day. It was a weekday and I should have been in school. I didn't miss getting up and ready for school in the mornings. To be honest, there wasn't much I missed about school. I didn't miss the asshole teachers like Mr. Franklin. I didn't miss the asshole students. And I certainly didn't miss the food or the homework. It's not like they were teaching me how to cure cancer or anything of equal importance.

I stretched and sat up in bed. I needed a shower so I could wash off the grass stains on my knees. And I desperately needed to get out of these clothes that I felt like I had been wearing for a year but in reality, it had only been half a day.

The sound of male voices coming from downstairs caught my attention, drawing me away from the contents of the book I was reading. Since the funeral, Mr. Cole hadn't had many visitors, and he hadn't invited anyone into the house.

Curious, and I'll admit it, nosy, I moved towards the stairs, trying to see if I could make out any of the voices.

I moved down the stairs on silent feet. I'd had plenty of practice in being quiet thanks to my mother. I'd learned to try my hardest to stay out of her way for fear of what she'd do to me if she took notice of me. It was never good.

When I hit the bottom of the stairs, I put my hand on the wall and slid along it until I was standing right outside the formal living room. My mother had loved this room. All the expensive furnishings had really done it for her. I didn't get it. The furniture seemed too fancy for me to dare take a seat on it. And it looked uncomfortable and stiff.

Mr. Cole murmured something too quiet for me to hear and I crept a little bit closer. I froze at the sound of Quinton's voice. What in the hell was he doing here talking to Mr. Cole?

I had a bad, bad feeling about this. Was he going to tell Mr. Cole that I had been wandering through the woods last night and then I had Tyson sleep over? I would kill him if he did.

"You're bailing on her," Quinton accused harshly. "She needs you and you're fucking bailing on her."

"My family needs me more right now," Mr. Cole snapped back. "You don't understand what they're going through. You don't understand what I'm going through. And how dare you come in here and get in my face without knowing what's going on."

I held my breath, wishing to be anywhere but here, listening to this conversation. Nothing good ever came from eavesdropping, I knew this. If I were smart, I'd walk away right this second and not look back.

"Bullshit, Marcus," Quinton bit out. "You're telling me you don't think of that girl as family? Remember who you're talking to. I've known you most of my life, don't lie to me. Are you in the habit of buying girls who don't mean shit to you brand new cars? I don't think so. For fuck's sake, you even made her go to Kurt's funeral with you. You took her to your brother's damn funeral. She means something to you and right now she needs you."

I took a step back, ready to flee, but couldn't force myself to move any further than that one step. They were talking about me and I wanted to know what they had to say. If they had been discussing someone else I probably would have walked away. I liked to think I would have walked away.

"Of course I think of Ariel as family. I'm not an asshole, Quint, but it's time for me to move on. You boys are old enough to take care of yourselves. You don't need me to watch over you anymore. And, I offered to bring her with me but she didn't seem interested in moving."

Calmly, like he wasn't just about to drop a major bomb, Quinton said, "She's like us, Marcus. My brothers and me and you. Ariel is exactly like us. You try to take her away from us and you won't like the way it turns out. And, no, I'm not trying to threaten you, I'm simply being honest with you. We'll fight to keep her with us. Even the two she thinks don't like her very much will fight to keep her with us." He paused and I inhaled sharply. Holy crap, he was unbelievable! "And, baby, I know you're there. You might as well come out and join the conversation."

Busted. Again.

I seriously sucked at this eavesdropping thing. First, Addison caught me. Now, it was Quinton. Damn.

I took a deep breath and stepped away from the wall. It was wrong to listen in on conversations that weren't meant for me to hear. But, at the same time, they shouldn't have been having this conversation without me.

"She what?" Mr. Cole sputtered. "That's impossible."

Slowly, I entered the room. I rubbed my damp, sweaty palms down my bare legs. I wished I'd worn something other than short-shorts so I could wipe my perspiration off on something other than my own skin.

I was nervous and my hands shook because of it.

Why would Quinton do this to me? He was supposed to be on my side! And, what the hell? Mr. Cole knew about magic? He knew that the guys were witches? How was that possible?

Neither were sitting on the fancy looking furniture like I had expected. Instead, they both stood on opposite sides of the room, their arms were crossed over their chests and they glared at each other. Poor Mr. Cole. Quinton was so much better at glaring than he was.

Mr. Cole had his shirt sleeves rolled up to his elbows and the top two buttons of his shirt were undone. He wore black slacks and his feet were bare. Casual was a very rare look for him. I'd only ever seen him in his pajamas once, and I'd never seen him in jeans before. I think he only owned tennis shoes because he liked to run.

Quinton, on the other hand, didn't seem to have a problem with jeans. Tight, hip-hugging, ass-cupping, dark blue jeans. He wore black combat boots and a plain black t-shirt. The flames slithering up his forearms were on display today.

I liked the cowboy boots way more.

A muscle in his cheek twitched as he clenched his jaw. I didn't know why he was so mad, it wasn't like he was the one parentless and soon to be homeless. Those dark, bottomless eyes locked on me and I realized he wasn't simply mad, he was furious. Furious on my behalf.

God.

What did I ever do to deserve someone like him in my life? Yeah, he freaked me out and he certainly scared the beejezus out of me at times, but I knew he'd never, not ever, do anything to truly hurt me. But he would hurt someone else on my behalf. I shouldn't like him for it but I couldn't help myself.

Quinton was growing on me.

Like fungus.

I smiled at him really big and said, "Hey, Uncle Quinton. So good to see you again."

His nostrils flared angrily as he directed his hostile glare at me.

"That's not even funny," he growled at me. "Don't joke about something like that. I'm not a fucking pervert."

Well, he wasn't exactly normal either. He wanted me to have an intimate relationship with him, his friends and his nephew. But, no, oh no, he was no pervert.

Please.

I held my hands up in front of me in surrender.

"Sorry, sorry," I said with a small, innocent smirk on my face.

He opened his mouth, likely to bark something awful at me but Mr. Cole's voice stopped him.

"Excuse me," Mr. Cole said sharply. "Would either of you care to explain to me what in the hell's going on. You can't just tell me she's got magic and then act like nothing big just happened."

I shuffled across the carpet, moving closer to Quinton. I couldn't help but be drawn to him.

"She has magic," Quinton said softly as I slid up beside him. I wanted to reach out and touch him.

Why did I want to touch him so badly? I didn't know the answer to that but I desperately wanted to run my fingertips across the pretty colors covering his arms.

"Tell him, babe," Quinton said quietly. "Tell him you have magic."

I shook my head.

Absolutely not.

No way in hell.

No way was I telling Mr. Cole I had magic. He'd think I was crazy. He probably thought Quinton was crazy. Heck, I knew he was. I didn't think we should go around blabbing about being witches when they were, at one point in time, burned at the stake simply for existing. It didn't seem like a smart idea to me. And I didn't appreciate him telling my secret to Mr. Cole.

There were very few people who meant something to me and he was one of them. I did not want him to ship me off to the loony bin because I thought I was a witch. No, thank you.

Quinton frowned at me. “It’s okay, baby. He knows about us. He grew up with Tyson’s dad. They were best friends and they were in the same coven together. He’s one of us.”

My mouth dropped open in shock. The same coven? He was just like us? Did that mean… was he trying to say… Did Mr. Cole have magic? Was he a witch? How could I have lived with him all this time and not known that he had magic?

“I need a drink,” Mr. Cole mumbled.

Quinton rubbed at the back of his neck with his hand and said, “I could go for a drink right about now, too.”

Nobody needed a stupid drink, it was early afternoon for goodness sake. They didn’t need a drink, but I sure needed an explanation.

“You have magic?” I whispered in shock. I’d been living with him for months and I had never noticed anything, I felt stupid.

“I’m not practicing anymore and haven’t been for years.” He said shortly as he walked out of the living room.

I looked at Quinton to see him scowling at the doorway Mr. Cole had just walked out of.

What just happened? Mr. Cole seemed fine one second then upset the next. Maybe he didn’t want his secret out there either. I could relate.

Like a whisper on the wind, there one second and gone the next, fingers gently traced down the strap of my tank top.

"Come on," Quinton murmured.

He pushed harder on my shoulder, herding me towards the door. As we walked down the hallway, following the noise, Quinton's hand slid down until it rested against the small of my back. The heat from his palm warmed my entire back and I fought the urge to shiver while he guided me towards the kitchen where I assumed Mr. Cole was.

Quinton's lips brushed my ear as he whispered, "He's not gonna want to talk about magic with you so don't push him. It'll just piss him off. I'll push so he doesn't get mad at you."

I did not like the sound of that.

Why would talking about it upset him? Magic was what made us special. Why would he stop practicing? I didn't have a very good feeling about this and a knot formed in the pit of my stomach. I didn't think I wanted to know if Mr. Cole had lived through some kind of tragedy. I could handle no more heartbreak. Not when it came to the people I cared about.

We walked into the kitchen in time to see Mr. Cole pour himself a glass full of amber liquor.

I swallowed past the lump in my throat as I watched him throw back the entire contents in three long gulps. I had never seen him drink before and I wasn't so sure I could handle seeing him drink now.

Watching him chug down his drink reminded me too much of my mother. She'd drink a whole bottle of vodka and then she'd get mean.

My hand, as if it had a mind of its own, raised to my forehead. I ran my fingertips lightly over the small scar there. The last time I had been around my mother when she'd been drunk she had thrown her glass at my head and her aim had been spot on. That had been the last time she'd hurt me while intoxicated, but not the last time she'd hurt me. It happened almost every time she got drunk and I had the misfortune to be alone with her. The last time she had been completely sober. Just crazy.

Seeing Marcus Cole work towards getting drunk in the early afternoon did not sit well with me.

"I'll take one of those, Marcus," Quinton said from beside me.

My body tensed, and I had to fight the urge to flee from the room.

Quinton must have felt me stiffen because he crowded me. He was just suddenly in my space, all around me. He had a habit of doing that.

"What's wrong?" He breathed into my ear.

I wasn't going to go there with him. I hated being asked that godforsaken question. My life was chaos, always. I didn't need to spell it out for him, he was smarter than that. And, he'd been there for most of the recent chaos.

Mr. Cole filled another glass half way full of amber liquor and slid it across the counter towards us.

Quinton wrapped his arms around my shoulders and walked me over towards the counter where the half full glass sat. One arm left my shoulders, so he could pick up his glass.

"Babe..."

I shook my head. Now was not the time for him to be relentless and push me. This one time I would be unbendable, and I would not break.

"My sister was a witch," Mr. Cole surprised me by saying. He stared into his newly refilled glass with a lost look on his face.

I leaned back into the solidness of Quinton's body and tried to relax. I didn't know either of them as well as I would have liked to, but I was smart enough to know neither of them would hurt me. They weren't my mother, they weren't going to get drunk and abuse me.

"My dad tried to hide her from the world. Not just from our community but from the whole world. Her name was Lana Ray." Mr. Cole paused to take a drink from his glass. "Shaun, Tyson's father and Quinton's brother, he was my best friend. We'd grown up together since we were children. All of us grew up together, me, Shaun, Felix and Rick. But none of them ever knew I had a sister. Not even the Elders knew she existed."

He let out a shuddering breath before draining the rest of his drink.

My mind was full of thoughts of a little girl being locked away in a room the size of a closet her entire life simply for being born with magic. I couldn't imagine being locked away and hidden from the world. I stayed away from people because I preferred my own company and never really wanted to invite other people into my life so they could see what a mess it was.

A thought occurred to me. Mr. Cole had children. Did that mean they were witches too? And one of them was even a girl.

"Wait a minute," I said. "Are your kids…"

I snapped my mouth shut. I really shouldn't just go around blurting out every thought that ran through my mind. It made me seem nosy and pushy.

"Adopted," he murmured into his drink and without looking in my direction. "I can't have children. They don't know anything. I gave up magic to live a normal life with my wife and my children. I couldn't have that around them and keep it a secret at the same time. After what my sister went through and what my father put the whole family through to keep her a secret from the world. I hated what I was, and I hated anything to do with magic and covens. It's hard to hide magic from your wife and children, hard to hide what you are. I didn't want that for my family. So, I stopped practicing altogether, that way I didn't have anything to hide. And, I got a beautiful, non-magical family as a result."

So, he gave up using his magic to have a normal family. Call me selfish, but I didn't think I would be willing to give up my magic for anything, not even for a shot at a normal family. Then again, I had yet to meet a person who meant anything to me and resembled the word normal.

Quinton sat his now empty drink back onto the counter. He wrapped his free arm around my stomach and pressed his face into my neck.

My face heated. What the hell was he doing? And in front of Mr. Cole no less. We weren't at a place where I was comfortable with him touching me in such a way in front of other people. Heck, I wouldn't be comfortable with him touching me like this in private.

I couldn't think of a way to escape his arms now that wouldn't further embarrass me.

"They found out about her anyway. Even after all the trouble our father went through to keep her a secret. The Elders came to our home and took her away, claiming they wanted to keep her safe. My father wanted her to have a choice in life. He didn't want her to be forced into the roll we've placed our women in. He wanted her to have a choice."

Quinton's arms around me tightened almost painfully but I didn't care. I was too busy running Mr. Cole's words through my head. He made it sound like women didn't get a choice in the way they lived their lives. Quinton made it out to sound different. Like it was your choice and your choice alone. But he also made it sound like you wouldn't want anything other than what your coven had to offer and if, by some chance, you did want something else they'd step aside so long as you were happy and safe.

I was so confused.

"What happened to your sister?" I asked quietly.

I had to know. He talked about her like she was gone, like she'd been lost to him for a long time now and it hurt him simply to talk about her. I wanted to know why.

"She…" he paused to take another gulp of his drink. "It didn't work out for her. She couldn't take the pressure. She… She ended it herself."

Quinton squeezed me again and I remembered what he'd said about taking the lead with asking the questions. I didn't mind because Mr. Cole's revelation about his sister had rendered me speechless.

"Did she meet anyone else yet?" Mr. Cole asked changing the subject abruptly. I didn't like being talked about like I wasn't even here.

"Nope," Quinton answered.

"You should keep it that way."

"Not gonna do that and you know it," Quinton shot back. "Not gonna hide her from anyone. Nothing good ever comes from that, and you damn well know it. Hell, you basically just said that same exact thing but with different words."

"You'll take care of her?"

"Yeah. We all will," Quinton bit out angrily. "You should stay and do the same."

I sighed. Did I want Mr. Cole to stay and take care of me? Hell yes, I did. I finally had a parent who gave a crap about me. I couldn't do it, though. I couldn't handle moving and leaving when I finally had friends and a place I felt relatively safe in. But I wouldn't try to guilt Mr. Cole into staying for my sake. I wouldn't be the person who held him down and kept him from getting what would make him happy. It would break my heart to watch him walk away from me, but I'd do it with a smile on my face so he'd never know how much it killed me on the inside. After everything he'd done for me I could easily do that for him. Well, it wouldn't be easy but no one but me would ever have to know about that.

"We have obligations to-" Quinton started to guilt Mr. Cole some more, but I quickly cut him off and talked over him.

"No," I said forcefully. "Nobody has obligations to me because I have magic and I'm a girl." I pulled out of Quinton's arms, stepped away from him and turned so I could face them both down. "I don't care how it's supposed to be and I don't care about how it's done with the other girls. Those girls are not me. Nobody owes me anything."

I paused to let in a shaky breath. I did not ever want to be considered anyone's obligation. How horrible. It sounded like something my mother would have called me, right along with being a burden.

I squared my shoulders and looked from one man to the next. They were so different in looks but had more in common than I had ever imagined. And they both cared a great deal about me.

I looked Marcus Cole in the eye and, voice soft, said, "I'm staying here but I understand why you need to leave. I hope you can understand why I need to stay. So much has happened in my life in such a short period of time that I really need to find a place to settle, a place to call home and a place that feels safe for me to be in. The past few weeks that has been here with you. But now you have to go and I have to stay. Your family needs you right now and you need to be with your family for you, too. You don't need to be dragging me along with you right now. You are all hurting so much right now and you don't need to be dealing with me, my problems and trying to hide the fact that I'm a witch at the same time. That sounds exhausting, even to me."

Mr. Cole put his glass down on the counter top none to gently. He ran the back of one shaking hand across his mouth.

"Ariel," he said in a rough voice. "I-"

"I already talked to the guys," Quinton said. His voice had changed to something gentler than normal and a whole lot sweeter. "They've got no problem with her moving in with us. She'll have her own bedroom and even her own bathroom. Ty, Addison and Abel are already living there. She'd be safe there with us and we want her there."

My breath left me in a rush.

No. No. No.

I did not want to live in that house. *She* was buried there. In the basement. If I moved in I would never escape her.

"If it's what Ariel wants then I will have to be okay with it." With that Mr. Cole walked out of the kitchen. I tried to catch his eyes with mine, but he refused to look at me.

My heart sank.

In trying to do the right thing I'd hurt him. Hurting him had been the last thing I had wanted to do.

It seemed the only thing I was capable of anymore was hurting the people around me.

My bottom lip trembled as I dug my fingernails into my palms. I needed the pain to make the tears go away.

Damn.

I did not want to cry again.

A tear slid out of my eye anyway.

Chapter Nine

"I THINK WE should-"

"Go away, Quinton," I said softly.

"Baby," he murmured.

He touched my shoulder and I jerked away from him like his touch had stung me. I had no desire to be comforted by his words or his touch at the moment.

"I want to be alone right now," I told him before turning and walking quickly out of the kitchen.

I hoped he knew this wasn't me running away from him again. I knew it was absurd, needing space when I'd just been alone for weeks, but I didn't want to be around other people when I was hurting. I wasn't any good when it came to sharing my feelings and I really didn't want someone to hold my hand while coddling me and telling me everything would be okay. I didn't think Quinton would be very good at coddling, but he'd likely make me more of those promises he and Tyson were so fond of. And, going on how touchy feely he could get, I knew he would for sure hold my hand.

I walked away and this time I did it without feeling guilty doing it. I would make a point to go over and see him later or I could get his phone number off of Tyson and I could text him to let him know I was okay. I had a feeling Quint wouldn't expect an apology or an explanation from me, but he would want to know about my wellbeing.

I made it up the stairs and to my bedroom in record time. I didn't want to stay in the house with Mr. Cole, I had to get out of there. But first, I needed a shower.

I made my bed before going into my closet to pick out clothes. I pulled a black, short-sleeved t-shirt off of a white, plastic hanger. The front of the shirt said *Go Float Yourself* in white cursive lettering. I had found it for a steal online after becoming obsessed with the television show *The 100*. I hadn't read the books yet, but I did order the first one when I got the shirt and had every intention of reading all of them. The shirt and the book had only arrived days ago, and this would be the first time wearing it.

I dug through a black laundry basket on the floor that had my folded clean clothes in it that I had yet to put away. I found a pair of black leggings and a purple bra with matching panties. I grabbed a rolled-up pair of fuzzy purple socks to match the underwear. Not that anyone would see my underthings or care that they matched my socks. Because I planned on spending the rest of my day alone, of course. Not that that would matter.

I left the closet, tossed my fuzzy socks onto my nicely made bed and went into the bathroom. I went to shut the door and hesitated. I had been using the bathroom down the hallway to shower ever since the… accident. Did I really want to shower in here now?

I stared blankly at the counter and could see her head bouncing off the corner like it was happening right in front of my face again. I saw her head hit the floor and the blood start to pool out around her. And her eyes. Those dead, sightless, achingly familiar eyes.

I drew in a deep breath and shook my head, trying to shake free of the memories. It was just a shower in a normal bathroom, I could manage that.

I avoided the counter and moved towards the shower.

I stopped when I caught sight of myself in the mirror and had to take a second to stare at my reflection.

I looked different than I had a month ago. I now had dark circles under my eyes and my tan had faded immensely. My skin would darken again and quickly if I spent a few days outside in the sunshine. Something I needed to consider doing because my face looked unhealthy without the tan.

My shoulder length, ash blonde hair looked a frightening mess from having slept on it and not shampooing it for a few days and also not having brushed it since yesterday morning. Not a pretty look for me. And I had gone downstairs and faced Quinton and Mr. Cole like that. I'm surprised neither of them had run from me or, at the very least, laughed at me.

My green eyes were dull and lacking in any kind of emotion. It scared me, and I remembered why I had been avoiding looking in the mirror.

I dumped my clean clothes on the closed toilet seat, stripped out of my day-old pajamas and got into the shower. I didn't linger under the hot spray of water. I did my thing and was out in less than ten minutes. I also didn't linger in the bathroom. I quickly dried off with an oversized bath towel and dressed in the clothes I had picked out. I wrapped a towel around my wet hair so my hair wouldn't soak through my t-shirt and make me uncomfortable.

I left the bathroom with an armful of dirty clothes and my used towel, I planned on dumping them in the dirty laundry basket in my mostly empty, gigantic closet.

The clothes slid from my fingers, falling to the carpet as I stood in the open doorway taking in my bedroom.

A smile spread across my face as I bent over and picked up the clothing I had dropped. My smile grew bigger as I moved across the room to the closet. I dropped it all in the basket and walked back into my room.

Addison and Abel, the Salt and Pepper twins were both sprawled out on my bed. My mood immediately lifted at the sight.

The watched me step out of the closet with an intensity I was only used to coming from Addison. Abel was the sweeter of the two. Not that Addison couldn't be sweet or that Abel couldn't be intense or serious because they could be. I just wasn't used to getting intense vibes off of both of them at the same time. They usually balanced each other out, one light – one dark. Unless, of course, they were being playful.

The light and dark that balanced out their personalities could also be applied to their looks. They were twins and, for the most part, they were identical. But there was a reason I called them the Salt and Pepper twins.

They were the same height and that height was *tall*. At least six foot two, that tall. They were the same build. Muscular, with broad shoulders, wide hips and thick, tree trunk like thighs. They were huge, but not fat. Extremely muscular, but not to the point where it was overboard and made them scary looking.

Addison was my Salt twin. He had hair so blonde it was close to being considered white. His eyes were pale and light blue.

Abel was my Pepper twin. His eyes were a bright, vibrant green that practically glowed. His hair was black, so black you could sometimes see shades of blue in it.

And they were both absolutely lovely to look at. High cheekbones, firm, strong jawlines, kissable lips. Lovely.

They even dressed similar and I was convinced they shared clothes. Today, they wore white, long-sleeved Henley's. Dark blue jeans. Black belts with silver buckles. And they were both barefoot.

"So," Abel drawled. "Quint tells us you saw our dicks at the full moon ritual. And you didn't want to stick around so you could play with them? You disappoint me, pretty girl."

His deep, rough, gravelly voice washed over me like a comforting blanket and not even the embarrassment brought on by his words could kill the smile on my face.

"I'm heartbroken," Addison said from beside his brother on my bed, in the same voice.

"Me too, twin," Abel said. "Maybe if she came a little closer she could kiss the hurt away and make it all better?" His voice sounded hopeful, but it did nothing to remove the seriousness in his eyes.

"Mmm…" Addison murmured non-committedly. "I don't think so, twin. From the way things are looking from where I'm sitting, it's our girl Ariel who could use some TLC."

"Yeah, what gives, pretty girl?" Abel asked me. "You look like you haven't slept in a week and you've lost even more weight. Weight you couldn't afford to lose in the first place. We talked about this already."

I fidgeted under their scrutiny, twisting my fingers together in front of me.

"Apparently, you don't listen very well," Addison rumbled harshly. "We wanted you to gain some weight, not lose more of it. Is it too much to ask that you take care of yourself? I realize you have been going through a lot, and I sympathize with you, I really do, but it's no excuse for your appearance. Asking you to take care of yourself, to eat, to sleep, to try and be healthy, that's not asking for too much. It's something every person should just do on their own. You can be sad, you can be angry even, but you still need to eat."

He shook his head angrily and ran his hand through his white hair.

He was angry with me and I was glad for it. Abel didn't seem much happier with me than his brother at the moment.

I remember Abel telling me that the only family he and Addison had left after the death of their parents was

Tyson, Quint and the rest of the guys. And now they had me and Addison very much thought of me as family. He had from the very beginning. He also had serious abandonment issues since their parent's death and he was extremely worried I would just up and disappear on them. Something I had actually gone and done to them.

If it were them who had disappeared on me I wouldn't have been angry, I would have been hurt. I had a feeling Addison was hiding his hurt behind his anger, so I wouldn't see that I hurt him.

"Have you not been eating?" Abel demanded to know.

I unwrapped the towel from my hair and let it drop to the floor. I couldn't have a serious conversation with my hair wrapped up in a towel on top of my head. It seemed ridiculous and I had already filled my quota of conversations with bad hair for the next month or two. Probably even longer than that.

I picked the towel up off the floor and tossed it in the direction of the closet. I was usually much cleaner than this, honest.

"I've been eating," I told them as I moved towards the bed, towards them. I hadn't lied, I had been eating, just not as much as I should have been. "And, I do sleep. Or, at least I try to sleep. I just…"

"Have been having that awful dream." Abel said softly.

I didn't know why I was surprised, I shouldn't have been. Nothing about me seemed to be a secret between them. I didn't like that very much.

If everyone knew about my reoccurring nightmare, then did they already know about the kiss I had shared with Quinton? I hoped not. I would like for some things to remain private between the whole lot of us.

"We know about the dream," Addison confirmed in a soft voice that mimicked his brothers. "Tyson told us this morning."

I bit my bottom lip, unhappy at hearing this news. I imagined it had been Quinton who blabbed, I never thought it would have been Tyson. His potential BFF status dropped a notch at hearing this news. Best friends weren't supposed to share your secrets, even if it was only to family. They were supposed to take your secrets to the grave. Or was that only with girls? Were there different rules because he was a boy and I was a girl? I didn't know, I had never had a best friend before, boy or girl.

I couldn't think about it, it would give me a headache.

"We also know about Marcus moving," Addison said, keeping the information flowing.

He sat up on my bed and scooted down until he was at the bottom of the bed and he hung his long legs off the side. His bare feet touched the floor and he leaned forward to rest his elbows on his knees. Hunched over like that, he looked older and, for the first time since I walked out of the bathroom, I noticed I wasn't the only one with dark smudges under my eyes.

Addison had them too.

"And we know about you moving in with us," Abel said as he moved down the bed until he sat beside his brother. He leaned back into the bed on his elbows and crossed his feet at the ankles.

Why weren't they sleeping?

And why did they never wear socks or shoes?

I stood in front of them and crossed my arms over my chest.

"Why haven't you been sleeping?" I asked them both quietly. "You know why I'm having problems. What's your excuse?"

Addison stood up suddenly and loomed over me. Out of the corner of my eye I caught Abel sitting up straight on the bed. His eyes were all for his brother and he looked worried.

I had to crane my neck back to look Addison in the eyes. I wasn't short, but I wasn't *that* tall.

"There's this girl," Addison rumbled angrily. "She means everything to my family and she means everything to my brother and me. But she's been going through some shit and she's shut us out. I don't like being shut out. I don't like seeing the hurt and the worry in my twin's eyes. I don't like it at all, Ariel. And I really don't like that it's there because of you."

Direct shot, straight through the heart.

He raised his big hand and cupped my cheek gently. His hand was warm and felt so nice I couldn't help but close my eyes and lean into his touch.

"If you're hurting, we are hurting," he whispered fiercely, his voice full of some dark emotion. "That's how family works. But it's different with you because you are a girl. It's worse because you're a girl. There are so few of you female witches and after Annabell we never thought we would get one of our own. Now we have one, we have you, and it was supposed to be different."

I sucked in a sharp, pain filled breath and would have moved back, away from him, but the hand not cupping my jaw curled around my hip and he forcefully pulled me into his massive body. I didn't want to be closer to him. I wanted to get far, far away from him *and* his words.

"No, no," he said hurriedly. "Don't take that the wrong way. It wasn't meant to be taken like that. We're supposed to watch over you. We're supposed to take care of you."

He let out a shuddering breath as he slid the hand on my cheek down to my neck and back. His hand moved back until he palmed the back of my head and tangled his fingers into my wet hair.

"Since meeting you, we've messed everything up. Hell, we messed everything up *before* we met you. I think you know that before we actually met you, before you and your mom moved in with Marcus, that we all shared a dream about you. We all knew you were coming and we all knew what that meant, what that meant for us on the whole. Yet we left for the whole summer anyways. You were left alone with that woman for months while we were off on some bullshit male bonding trip. Quint was right to want to stay here because of you. But we didn't stay because he was outvoted, and it kills me to think about what you went through when we could have been here for you but weren't. Then we're back all of two days and you're bleeding from a goddamn head wound caused by that awful woman. What kind of messed up things did you go through that we missed while we were gone for the summer?"

His nostrils flared angrily as he sucked in a deep breath.

His light, light blue eyes, eyes I could easily lose myself in, filled with tears and unspoken words. He closed them tightly and when he opened them again the tears were gone. He'd successfully pushed them down and away.

I wished this was a skill he could teach me because I would love to learn.

"We were supposed to take care of you," he whispered.

My breath hitched at the raw emotion I heard in Addison's voice.

God.

God.

Fucking *God.*

What had I done to them when I walked away and refused to see them or take their calls? No, let's be honest here, when I ran away from them? Admittedly, running away had been a natural reaction at the time, but I hadn't thought about them and how they would feel when I did it.

"Addison, I'm…" My voice caught in my throat, forcing me to stop speaking. Not that I minded, I honestly had no idea what to say to him. I could apologize but I had a feeling that wouldn't have meant a whole lot to him. Actions spoke louder than words and my leaving them for weeks on end had spoke louder than any apology I could utter now ever would.

He released me abruptly and stepped back, leaving me alone and cold. So very cold without his warmth wrapped around me.

My eyes burned and my throat convulsed as I watched him pull a shutter down, covering his eyes and hiding his true emotions from me. My heart beat wildly inside my chest as I bit down hard on my tongue, tasting sweet copper. I winced, knowing I'd made myself bleed. Blood was a whole lot better than tears.

"Abel is going to stay with you tonight," Addison told me in a gruff voice. "I just really need to be alone right now."

I bit my lips, blinking rapidly.

"Addison," I choked out.

"Let him go, Ariel," Abel said in a quiet, subdued voice.

Addison moved past me, heading towards the door.

I couldn't leave things the way the were. I couldn't let him walk away from me, not like this, not upset and angry, not with Abel looking so concerned for his brother.

Good, good, grief. I did not do well with this emotional stuff.

I thought about what to do.

Then, I thought to hell with it.

I spun around and flew after him, running. I caught up to him in the hallway and didn't stop until I crashed into his back. I pressed the side of my head into the middle of his back, wrapped my arms around his middle and held on for dear life.

A deep breath shuddered out of me. I did not want to let him go. If Addison left now, I did not want to be left alone with Abel. I knew Abel wouldn't blame me, but I'd seen his face when his brother had said he needed some time alone. Abel, the look on his face, he'd been crushed by his brothers need to be alone. As far as I knew, the twins did everything together. One of them had even gotten upset when they found out the other one couldn't sleep at night and hadn't bothered to wake up their twin. I didn't want to be the reason they stopped doing everything together. And I cared about the both of them, so very much. I needed Addison to stay, for both Abel AND myself. I knew I deserved to see him walk away from me like I had done to him, to all of them. But, the look on Abel's face had told me he couldn't handle watching his brother walk away.

I needed to make it right. I would do anything to make it right between us.

"Please," I pleaded in a quiet voice. "Stay. Stay with Abel and me. Spend the afternoon with us. And, if you really, *really*, want to be alone, then you don't have to spend the night with us. But, please, I beg of you, just spend the afternoon with me and with your brother. The three of us, we haven't gotten to spend much time alone together. I would like to spend time with you."

I held my breath, waiting for his response. I had put myself out there, something I usually avoided doing at all costs. What would putting myself out there cost me this time?

I held my breath and I waited.

Chapter Ten

ADDISON REMAINED STIFF in my arms, unmoving and making my heart sink to depths I did not even know I carried inside of me.

Now I'd really gone and done it. By putting myself out there with Addison, I feared I had only succeeded in making things worse.

Addison's big body relaxed against me. His arms came up and he placed them atop of the arms I had wrapped around his middle. His big hands covered my small ones and he laced our fingers together.

"Alright," he murmured. "I'll stay with you two. I'm going to run home real quick, then I will be back. Okay?"

Hmm…

If I said okay, then I would be forced to let him go. If I let him go, he might run away and not come back again.

Decisions, decisions…

I let him go and stepped back.

He was mine. Both Addison and Abel were mine in whatever way I wanted them.

He'd come back to me. Even if he didn't, I knew Abel wouldn't leave me and Addison wouldn't leave his brother for very long. He'd be forced to return.

I wasn't left with much of a choice.

"Okay," I agreed in a quiet, defeated voice.

I backed up a step, then two. My shoulders slumped, and without looking at him, I turned and walked back into my bedroom. I closed the door behind me, locking it for good measure. If Addison came back, he would be forced to knock on the door. I wasn't trying to lock him out, promise. I simply did not like being in my bedroom with the door unlocked anymore.

"What's going on?" Abel asked me in a guttural voice. "Where did Addison go? Ariel, tell me what in the fuck is going on. Right now."

He looked agitated, upset and angry all at the same time. And he usually never talked to me like that.

"He told me he was coming back," I whispered in a broken voice.

"Come here, Ariel," Abel ordered.

He held his arms open to me and I ran into them. I crawled into his lap and he wrapped his arms around me.

One of his arms rested low around my hips, above my butt. His other hand ran up and down my spine, in a soothing gesture.

His forehead rested against mine and he murmured, "If he said he was coming back then he will come back. Have some faith. My twin isn't a liar. If he said he'd do something, then he will come through."

I nodded my head against his, letting him know that I believed him. No one knew his brother better than he did, if Abel said Addison would be coming back then I believed him.

With me still seated in his lap, he scooted back until his back met with the headboard.

He shifted around, grabbing hold of my thighs and moved me where he wanted me to be. I ended up facing him with my legs on the outside of his, straddling him. My chest was mere inches from his own.

This had not been what I was expecting. He'd taken advantage of the situation, not that I blamed him. I couldn't blame him; the twins were playful and had no problem being touchy feely. I couldn't harp on him for being who he was.

"Thank you," he murmured appreciatively. "Thank you for going after my brother and trying to stop him. I feel like he needed that from you. Like he needed you to reach out to him, to let him know you actually cared about whether or not he left. Sometimes it's hard to tell with you, you're very closed off and sometimes I think that gets to him. But, don't worry, he'll come back to us. Please, don't worry. And, stop looking so sad."

Don't worry.

Easy for him to say.

I worried about everything. Every stupid, little thing.

I snuggled into him, pressing my front to his. Abel was so easy to be around that I felt comfortable touching him.

"What do you want to do today?" He asked me.

I had no idea and didn't think I was going to figure it out while sitting on his lap like this. I couldn't think.

"I don't know," I mumbled.

"Do you have a hair dryer?" He asked me.

I nodded my head against his.

"Will you go and get it and a hair brush for me?"

I lowered my arms and scooted back, off of his lap. I swung my legs down off of the bed and stood up.

I found the hair dryer in the linen closet in the bathroom. I had to untangle it from a whole mess of cords that were connected to a hair straightener and a curling iron. It was a frustrating mess and I almost gave up on it, but I got my hair dryer free. I felt like throwing my arms up in the air in victory. I did no such thing because Abel could see me from his spot on the bed and I didn't want him to think I was a crazy loon. The hair brush I found on the counter. Both I brought back into the bedroom and held up for his inspection.

He crawled off of the bed and took the hair dryer from me. He plugged it in in the outlet by the window seat and sat down.

"If you sit on the floor in front of me I will dry your hair and brush it out for you."

I stupidly hadn't put two and two together when he'd asked me to get the brush and the hair dryer. What else was he going to do with them?

He spread his legs and I hesitantly moved to sit on the floor in between them. I sat up straight, forcing myself to sit still. With gentle strokes, he ran the brush through my hair. Over and over again. Then he turned the blow dryer on and got down to drying my hair. Half way through someone knocked on the door.

I popped up and sprinted across the carpet, nervous about Addison's return. I unlocked the door and pulled it open.

Addison stood there with his hand raised, ready to knock again. He had a book bag in his other hand.

“What was that noise?” He asked me.

“Hair dryer,” I explained.

He grinned at me. “I leave you alone in your bedroom with my twin and you decided to do your hair. I bet he loved that.”

“Actually,” I told him, “it was his idea.”

He chuckled. “He’s losing his touch.”

I shook my head and moved out of the doorway, letting him inside. Once the door was shut and locked, I moved back to where Abel was sitting and plopped back down on the floor in between his legs.

As soon as I had my butt on the carpet, Abel turned on the hair dryer and got back to work.

Addison sat down on the floor by my legs and unzipped the black back pack he had in his hands. He dug through it and pulled out a coloring book. Next came a box of crayons and then a metal tin with colored pencils in it.

“What are you doing?” I asked curiously. Had he really gone home to get a coloring book and crayons? That was absurd.

“We, Ariel girl,” he said. “It’s what we are doing. You wanted to hang out and spend time together. We’re going to do it while coloring. I got some sweet adult coloring books off of *Amazon.* One of them has got swear words in it. I’ve got an *Alice In Wonderland* one. A doodle one with weird animals in it. I love to color, it’s relaxing. And, I don’t know if you’ve noticed, girl, but you really need to relax.”

The blow dryer shut off and Abel tapped me on the shoulder with the hair brush. “You’re all done now.”

"Thanks," I muttered, at a loss for words. They'd both robbed me of speech. One wanted to play with my hair while the other wanted to color with me.

I picked a picture out of the swearing book. Coloring in naughty words? Sure, why not. I figured I could maybe give it to Quinton later, he seemed fond of swear words. I used them as well, but I tried to keep them in my head where people wouldn't judge me for using them.

Addison colored in a picture of a fox and Abel colored a picture of wild flowers. It was cute, ridiculous and probably one of the best afternoons I had had in a very long time.

Chapter Eleven

"WHERE ARE WE going?" I asked as we turned onto a dirt road. We weren't far from home and I had no idea where we were going.

It hadn't occurred to me to ask Quinton where we were going when he'd asked me if I wanted to go for a ride with him and he hadn't talked the entire drive.

He also didn't bother answering my question as we came to a stop in front of a cute little cottage.

The only thing around was trees. Trees, trees, and more trees.

The square, two-story home had a washed out stone front. There were two windows on either side of the front door and both had weathered flower boxes overflowing with some type of hanging vines. The shutters around the windows were painted black as was the front door. The chimney sitting atop the cottage had smoke billowing out of it, giving it a charming look. The over grown plants and the black paint on the door and shutters, not so much.

A stone walkway lead up to the house. There was another one off of it that lead around the side of the house, where it disappeared from view. It probably lead to the back yard.

The front yard wasn't much to look at. The grass was cut short. The dirt driveway, which I thought had been a road, ended in a huge circle that met the grass and the stone pathway that ran to the cottage.

Overall, it was cute, if a little isolated. I half expected Snow White and her dwarfs to come walking out the front door.

"Quinton?" I asked softly while looking around, taking in the scenery. "Who lives here?"

"Dash," he said without looking at me.

Both my eyebrows shot up as my head whipped around to stare at him.

Why would he bring me here? Dash was not one of my favorite people. Outside of spying on him in the clearing, the last time I'd seen him had been the day my mother died, and I distinctly remembered him calling me a stupid girl. I think that had been the nicest thing he'd said about me. Well, he did say I had a sweet ass. I was not impressed.

I asked a better question. "*Why* are we here?" I'm afraid it came out snottier than I had intended. If he'd shared our destination with me I never would have gotten in the damn car with him in the first place. And he knew it.

Quinton shut the car off and turned to face me. For the first time, I noticed he hadn't bothered to put his seat belt on. I frowned at him, bothered by this knowledge. I needed Quinton in my life. What I didn't need was for him to end up a mangled mess if he got into an accident and flew through the windshield, all because he was careless and didn't take the time to buckle his seat belt.

His face lost all seriousness when he caught sight of my frown. His eyebrows drew together, and he looked confused.

"What's the matter with you?" He asked.

He wanted to know what was the matter with me? How much time did he think we had? The list was long.

I sighed and said, "You're not wearing your seat belt."

He blinked before his lips curled up in a smug smirk. "Look at you," he taunted, "all cute and caring. You give a shit about me. Already. That bond's only gonna get stronger. First, you're concerned for my safety. What's next, are you gonna wash my dirty socks and scrub my back in the shower?"

My face burned, and I knew it would be an unattractive shade of red. What I wanted to do next was strangle him with the seat belt I had earlier wanted him to put on.

Wash his dirty socks? Please. Wasn't Julian his little man servant? He could wash Quinton's dirty clothes. I wasn't even going to think about a naked Quinton in the shower. At least not while I was around him. I was surely embarrassed enough as it was. I did not need to ever think about a naked Quinton. That would be bad. I'd probably end up cross eyed if I did… Right?

Shit.

I unclicked the seat belt and reached for the door handle. My intent was to escape the vision of a naked Quinton with droplets of water gliding down his body. The problem was, this vision only existed in my mind. How does one escape their own mind?

Quinton gently grabbed ahold of my left arm, the arm closest to him, stopping me from trying to open the door.

His face was suddenly back to serious. I liked amused better.

"Dash is a moody bastard," he said. I blinked, having forgotten that we were sitting parked in front of Dash's cute cottage. "Always has been, as far as I can remember."

I wasn't sure I needed to know anything more than I already knew about Dash. And I didn't know why Quint was sharing.

"He has room for you," he rushed out. "You need to live with one of us. You're uncomfortable with staying at the house right now and I get it, I do. I don't like it, but I get it. Julian and Damien live together but their house is out. It's too small for another person because it's only got two bedrooms. That leaves us with Dash and, thankfully, he's got room for you. And, he also doesn't mind you staying here with him."

I opened my mouth to protest or maybe shout at him, he saw and hurried to get out the rest.

"You've got a room at the house. It's yours and will be waiting for you, whenever you're ready. All the guys have rooms at the house, so it's not a big deal that you do too. I'm gonna be honest with you, Ariel. I want you to live with me. I want your permanent home to be with me, wherever I am. I get why you don't want to stay there right now, but I'm hoping this arrangement with Dash doesn't take too long."

I sat there staring at him with my mouth hanging open. He was crazy if he thought he could just move me in with Dash without asking me if I even wanted to live there in the first place.

I did not want to live with Dash. I didn't want to be homeless, either. And, I really, really did not want to live at the house with Quinton and the guys. I needed to come to terms with my mother's death before I could live there. What choice did I really have?

I sighed heavily and sat back in the seat.

"He hates me," I mumbled. I didn't want to live with someone who hated me, I'd already done that for most of my life.

Quinton let go of my arm. He placed his warm hand on top of my thigh and his fingers curled in.

"He doesn't hate you, baby," He said. "I told you, he's moody. He's lived a life of heartbreak and that leaves a mark on a person. His dad died when he was a little boy and his mother made yours seem sweet in comparison. After his dad died, his mother moved them here, to this cottage, to live with her mother. She wasn't very nice either. He grew up with a woman who told him on a daily basis he should have been aborted. Then, he had a grandmother who beat the shit out of him. She'd whip him, trying to get the evil thing inside of him out. They both died when he was in his late teens, but he put up with their bullshit until then. It did something to him, warped the way he see's women. He goes through women like they are disposable and he sleeps around a lot. He once had four girlfriends at the same time, none of them knew about each other and they didn't get the chance to figure it out because he didn't keep them around for longer than a month. He fucks them and when he's had enough of them, he moves on to the next one." Quinton paused to draw in a deep breath. "He can't do that with you even if he wanted to. You're different, special. You're one of us and he'd never hurt you. He's worried you're going to be the one doing the hurting and he's scared to death of you."

I didn't want to care. I tried to harden my heart against feeling anything. I failed. Miserably. I, too, had suffered at the hands of a hideous person who was supposed to love and care for me. My heart bled a little for Dash, it couldn't not.

Though, none of this made him any less of a dick.

"Why did you tell me this, Quinton?" I asked quietly. I felt like it hadn't been his place to share even part of Dash's story with me.

Quinton grinned at me. "I can see your heart in your eyes, you're that easy to read now. No way are you not going to give him even half a chance after hearing that. I'm not opposed to guilting you into giving me what I want. And, make no mistake, Ariel, I want you to give Dash a chance. In time, I want you to give them all a chance. They want it too. We all do. Even if some of them are going to fight it, deep down they want it, want you, they won't be able to help themselves."

I shook my head. He didn't have to tell me what he was capable of, I already knew.

I'd give Dash a chance, maybe. But I would make no promises.

They were all insane, especially Quinton. He had the hots for me, clearly, and yet he wanted me to have romantic relationships with his nephew and all their friends.

That wasn't going to happen. At least, not today it wasn't.

"So," I cleared my throat. "We're here to what? Check out my potentially new home?"

"Yeah," he grunted as he opened his door and climbed out of the car.

He was annoyed.

I think it bothered him that I never responded aloud when someone brought up the sharing bit. I wished it would stop coming up in conversation, and I didn't respond because I didn't think he would really enjoy hearing what I had to say on the matter.

He moved around the front of the car to come around to my side, so he could open the door for me. I shoved the door open and quickly scrambled to my feet. I wasn't entirely helpless.

He pursed his lips, unhappy with me.

I bit my lip hard, so I wouldn't laugh at him. He wouldn't like me laughing at him.

He turned his back on me and casually strolled up the stone pathway. He wore the same black, scuffed up cowboy boots I'd seen him wear recently. Dark, blue jeans were tucked into the boots. A light gray belt had been slipped through the belt loops on his jeans. His outfit had been topped off by his usual long-sleeved button up shirt. This one was a rich forest green and he had the sleeves rolled up almost to his elbows. The color went well with his tanned skin and dark eyes.

Quinton knocked on the door as I made it to his side. There was no doorbell in sight.

I stood there nervously while we waited for Dash to open up the door.

I had no idea what lay behind the black door. The only expectations I had weren't good ones.

Chapter Twelve

IT TOOK QUINTON banging on the door a few more times with his fist for Dash to open the door. The longer it took, the more nervous I became. Finally, when the door opened, I had my hands clenched together in front of me and my palms had started to sweat.

I felt like an actress, auditioning for a part in a movie I wasn't sure would either make or break my career. Time to quit my day job.

The door opened inwards and Dash filled the empty space. His shockingly bright red hair and beard were the first thing I noticed about him. His beard had grown fuller, longer since I had seen him last.

I noticed his eyes second and I did not linger on them in my perusal of him. His eyes were light gray and best described as haunted. The depth of the horrors he'd lived through shined bright at the surface, for all to see. His eyes told me he had plenty of demons, and they wrestled on the daily.

I wondered if he recognized the horrors in my eyes as similar to the ones shining so brightly in his own. Could he tell I had demons as well when he looked at me?

I didn't think he looked at me long enough to notice.

His outfit surprised me because I felt like I should have noticed it before all else.

He stood barefoot with his pale, naked legs practically glowing in the sunlight. He wore what looked to be a woman's robe that was black and looked like silk. The sleeves were so long they hid his hands from view. The robe was short, stopping mid-thigh, leaving an obscene amount of skin on display.

Was this how he normally greeted company? I hoped not. The chances of me living here with him for even a small portion of time were becoming slimmer by the second.

"What are you doing here?" he asked Quinton in a quiet voice.

He seemed genuinely surprised to see me. What were we doing here indeed? I wanted to give Quinton the stink eye but didn't bother because I figured it would be lost on him. His dirty looks were far superior to anything I might be able to conjure up.

I was having a hard time keeping my eyes off of Dash's ghostly pale legs. Did he have anything on under that robe? I shook my head. I didn't need to know.

"If I had known you were bringing her here, I would have put some clothes on, damn it," Dash grumbled. "Make yourself at home, Ariel. I'll be right back," he said without looking at me and then he and his fancy black robe disappeared into the house.

Quinton pushed past me and moved into the house. He looked at ease, relaxed. How dare he be relaxed when I was anything but.

I followed him into the house reluctantly.

He sighed heavily as he shut the door behind us. “What’s the matter with you now, Ariel? You’re frowning again. Why are you always frowning? Your life isn’t really so terrible at the moment that you feel the need to frown all the time, is it? If you’re not careful you are going to end up with permanent wrinkles.”

He was insane. That’s all there was to say. He should have told Dash we were coming, at the very least. And, honestly, I think he frowned more than I did. He was always so serious, so scary. Which meant he had no room to talk.

“I think my presence at his home has made him uncomfortable,” I told Quinton. “I have no desire to make anyone feel uncomfortable, Quinton.”

And, for goodness sakes, you should have called ahead to tell him you were bringing me here.”

“Ariel, Ariel, Ariel,” Quinton said, groaning. “You need to learn to take that stick out of your ass every now and then, and you need to relax.”

My mouth dropped open.

Oh no, he did not just say that to me.

I was going to kill him.

“Quinton,” I said slowly, making sure he heard every word I had to say. “If you don’t shut your stupid mouth right this second, I am going to super glue your lips shut while you are sleeping. I might even stuff something in there before I do it, too. Something that will leave a bad taste in your mouth for all of eternity. Something you might even choke on. Like a turd. *Then*, I’m going to super glue your lips shut. Honestly, of all the nerve. And you seriously expect me to want to hang around so I can what, put up with all of your bullshit? I don't *think* so. Fuck that. You're crazy."

I shook my head and muttered angrily, "Stick up my ass. I'm so sure. What a dickhole thing to say to someone."

"Wow," Dash said from close behind me. "She's swearing. The twins say she rarely swears. What did you do to her?"

I whirled around to find Dash standing not a foot away from me. I hadn't heard him creep up on me. Something to remember, Dash was apparently light on his feet. Good to know.

And, he was a fast dresser too.

He'd put on black cargo pants, the kind with pockets on the side. He had on a white, V-neck t-shirt covered with an unbuttoned black and gray long-sleeved flannel. He'd forgot to put socks on. They all seemed to forget about socks.

His head tilted to the side as he studied me. I could just imagine what he saw. A crazy girl with cheeks flushed from anger with a squinty eyed look on her face. Not a pretty picture. Weirdly, he didn't look appalled. He looked serious, but then again, I was pretty sure that's how he always looked. But I was surprised to see a hint of curiosity on his face that matched his voice when he asked Quinton what he'd done to me.

Without taking my eyes off of Dash, I pointed behind me, in Quinton's direction, and hissed, "He thinks I have a stick up my ass. Do *you* think I have a stick up my ass?"

“What I think,” Quinton said, “is that it would be unwise for me to answer that question.”

“What?” I hissed angrily.

Dash thought I had a stick up my ass, too!

Quinton started laughing.

“To be fair,” Quinton mused when he stopped laughing, “telling someone you’re going to super glue their mouth shut after you put a turd in there makes you seem a whole lot less uptight.”

“I thought Tyson said she was shy and quiet?” Dash asked, completely ignoring me and my anger.

I bowed my head and practiced deep breathing. I desperately needed to calm down. I didn’t know what was the matter with me but lately my emotions had been all over the place and I was quick to anger. Before, I tried really hard not to get angry about anything and I would have been mortified by how I had just spoken to Quinton. I still kind of was and felt like maybe I should apologize to him for it, but I had no intention of actually doing so because, at the same time, I knew he deserved it. If I didn’t speak up he would bowl right over me and I would eventually turn into his puppet. Nobody wanted that, well, at least I didn’t want that. Who knew what Quinton wanted.

“I think,” Quinton said, “our Ariel is coming into her own skin and isn’t going to be as shy and quiet as we all thought her to originally be.”

“Glad to hear it,” Dash muttered. “And I’m seriously enjoying watching it.”

I hated them.

Both of them.

They were devil's spawn and I hoped they both choked on turds.

I clenched my hands into fists at my sides and took another deep breath. What in the hell was the matter with me?

A phone started ringing. It rang three times before Quinton answered. Of course, he was rude.

"What?" Quinton growled. I shook my head, that was no way to answer the phone. "You're joking... They can't be here right now... Do they know about her? Were they at Marcus's house first? Shit, yeah, I'll be right there."

He hung up without saying goodbye.

"Who was that?" I demanded to know. "Was who at Mr. Cole's house?"

Quinton looked nervous as he slid his phone back into the back pocket of his jeans. He squeezed the back of his neck and closed his eyes.

"Dash, can she stay here with you for a few hours?" Quinton asked in a strained voice. "Just until I can get rid of them, then I will be back for her."

"She can stay the night," Dash told him.

Yikes.

I wasn't ready for a sleepover with Dash.

"I'll go with you," I said as I walked towards Quinton. "You can drop me off at home."

I stopped in front of him and still he did not open his eyes. Something was seriously wrong here.

"Who was on the phone, Quinton?" I asked quietly. I wanted to know what was going on, why he looked suddenly defeated.

He dropped his hand from the back of his neck and his eyes snapped open. His dark eyes bored into mine, attempting to crawl into my soul so he could have a look around and see what was inside of me.

I took a step back, to get away from him and that look, but his arm shot out and he grabbed ahold of my forearm, stopping me mid-step. He jerked on my arm, pulling me forward until I collided with his chest. His big, warm hands pressed into the middle of my back, caging me in.

I was trapped in Quinton's arms and this time I didn't really want to be there.

"What's happening?" I asked in a small, panic filled voice.

His eyes bored into mine, still searching for a way into my soul. I had an urge to close my eyes tight and hide from him.

"Do you trust me?" He asked in his deep, rough voice.

The question surprised me, but I didn't even need to think about the answer and I wasn't surprised by it.

"Yes," I told him honestly and without hesitation.

His eyes lit up and he grinned at me.

"Thank fuck," he said with feeling. "Some Elders showed up at Marcus's house, probably just to check in on him. He's been going through a lot lately with the death of his brother, your mother's disappearance and now he's moving away from where he's lived with his family for years. They don't care that he pulled away from them years ago. If you have magic, whether you want to be a part of our world or not, whether you want to be in a coven or not, the Council of Elders keeps tabs on you. Best case scenario, they are here to offer him condolences and a place back in the fold. Worst case, they are here because they know about you and want to meet you."

"But-"

"No," he said firmly. "No buts. You heard what Marcus said the other day about his sister and why his dad kept her secret and how the Council took her away from her family. What he didn't tell you, what he left out because he didn't want to scare you, was that the Council was trying to convince her to join with a coven. They had covens come to meet her, to offer her things. Money and shit, you name it and they probably offered it to her. She didn't want any of it. How could she have when she had been raised in hiding by her father and told that the covens way with girls is wrong, sick even. My father met her once and he told me she was a fucking head case, Ariel. The thought of being in a coven full of men terrified her. The Elders didn't care, they wanted her in a coven, even if it was one they had to hand pick for her. They thought if she joined a group, it would be the safest place for her and the best way to introduce her to our way of doing things. She freaked, slit her wrists and bled out in a bathtub. We're not supposed to talk about it because the Council doesn't like to be reminded of that black mark against them. But it happened, Ariel. They took her from her home, a teenage girl, tried to force something on her that she did not want, and she killed herself to escape it. I'm not saying that's going to happen to you, I'm not saying that situation is anything like yours, and I'm not trying to scare you. But you need to know what we are up against here and you need to listen to me."

My mouth had gone dry while he was talking. I swallowed, tasting the bile that had slowly made its way up my throat.

Please, don't let me puke on Quinton.

I had known the ending of Mr. Cole's sister, something I knew had been kept from me for a reason, had been tragic and heartbreaking. But nothing had prepared me for this. Poor Mr. Cole, my heart broke for him. Letting him go, after hearing this, was going to be so much harder now. I wanted to stick with him, keep him close so I could keep him safe. He needed someone to protect him from himself. Obviously, he made horrible decisions when left on his own and he gave too much, too freely.

I took in a deep, shuddering breath as I pushed all thoughts of Mr. Cole to the side. There was a time and a place for everything and this wasn't the right time for me to be worried about him. I would do that later when I was alone and not afraid to cry.

Right now, there were more important things to stress about. Like this Council of Elders. I felt like the guys had been lying to me about these people.

"But, you said-"

Quinton leaned down, getting in my face.

"No buts," he growled. "And, honestly, Ariel? What would you have done if you were us? Scare you with the truth about these people? I don't think so. We wanted you to want to stay with us, not run away screaming."

He kissed my forehead and abruptly let me go. He stepped back, taking his heat with him.

Looking over my shoulder, he completely ignored me and spoke to Dash. It was like he said what he had to say to me and now I was dismissed, he was moving on. Quinton could be quite a jerk at times.

I did not like being ignored which was something I was just now learning about myself.

"She's yours, for now, but I will be coming back to get her later. Since she's moving in with you, you've got no room to bitch at me for coming back to get her. Tell her whatever you want to about the Council and you better damn well make sure nothing happens to her."

Dash and I both scowled at him as he walked out the door.

Chapter Thirteen

FINGERTIPS TRAILED LIGHTLY down my spine, making me jump. I let out an embarrassing squeak, loud and girly. As soon as it left my mouth I desperately wished I could stuff it back inside. It was a sound that should never, not *ever* come out of me when in the presence of other people.

Placing my hand on my chest to slow down my beating heart, I shuffled to the side and whirled to face him. I think he sniffed my hair before I could put some space between us. How weird was that?

"What are you doing?" I breathed out.

Some of them were getting far too comfortable with touching me. Dash shouldn't have been one of them. He didn't even like me and he had no business touching me.

"Hey," he said in a low voice as he held his hands out in front of him, palms towards me. "I didn't mean to scare you and I'm sorry that I did. You don't have anything to be afraid of while you're here with me. I promise. I'm going to be the perfect gentlemen."

If I wasn't so embarrassed by that hideous noise I had made I would have rolled my eyes at the word promise. Here was another one. And I didn't know this one well enough to trust his word yet.

"You startled me," I whispered, which was the truth. Did I tell him not to touch me again? No. Did I tell him

I had embarrassed myself? Nope. Not his concern on the last and I didn't want to be mean with the first.

"I'm sorry," he repeated.

He looked harmless and contrite standing there with his hands up and the worried look on his face.

I was beginning to feel bad about my reaction to him touching me. It wasn't that he'd touched me. Honestly, I had forgotten about him even being there. It had more to do with someone coming up behind me without me knowing they were there and not hearing them approach. It had freaked me out.

"Are we good?" He asked as he lowered his hands.

I nodded, silently telling him that, yes, we were good.

He scratched his jaw, itching at his beard in what looked like a nervous gesture. I was glad to not be the only one uncomfortable in this situation. Not nice, I know, but it was the absolute truth.

"Are you hungry?" he asked awkwardly as he continued to play with his facial hair.

I shrugged a shoulder casually and said, "I don't know."

"How can you not know if you're hungry or not?"

"My stomach is in knots," I told him honestly. "That's the only thing I can feel in my belly right now."

His hand dropped from his face as he crossed his arms over his chest. His arms were covered in freckles. They were cute.

"Do you want to see the house?" he asked me.

I nodded, enthusiastically.

"This way," he said as he turned and walked away.

"Do you really think the Council would take me away from here against my will?" I asked quietly as I followed close behind him.

My eyes took in as much of his house as I could as I followed him.

The front door opened into a small, mud room. The walls were painted a warm, inviting gray. The walls were empty, no shelves, no hooks for hanging up your coat, nothing decorative at all. Two pairs of shoes were on the floor, pressed up against the wall. Guys flip-flops, black with thick gray straps. And black, lace up the front ass kicking boots. I needed a pair of boots like that in my life.

He talked as he walked.

"Honestly," he said, "they aren't as scary as all that. What happened with Marcus's sister was not a normal happenstance. I agree that it was a horrible, tragic thing to have happened, but it's not like the Council killed her. Quint shouldn't have made it out to sound like that."

He paused inside a cozy living room, giving me time to take in the sights. The walls in this room were painted the same gray of the mud room. A fireplace with a black, marble mantle had a fire blazing brightly in it. In front of the fire place sat a black couch, covered in orange toss pillows with a bright orange ottoman in front of it. The hardwood floor was sadly devoid of rugs, but I thought it could use some. A large, flat screen television had been mounted above the fireplace and was currently off. Black shelving ran around the entire room, right below the ceiling. It was stuffed to bursting with both movies and books. The walls in here were bare as well.

When I had seen it all, I looked to him, hoping the expression on my face told him that I wanted him to continue with his speech about the Council.

He didn't disappoint.

"They didn't take her from her home thinking they would cause her any harm. They took her out of there thinking they were helping her. Marcus's dad was not entirely right in the head. I mean, who has a child and hides them away from the whole world? That's crazy."

I followed him out of the cozy living room as he kept talking.

"She was messed up in the head from being sheltered and hidden away like that. Hell, Ariel, her own brother wasn't even allowed to breathe a word of his sister's existence. It must have been some serious threat that kept him from speaking up about her. Can you imagine?"

I shuddered at the thought. Yeah, I actually could imagine the kind of threat that would keep a person from speaking out.

Dash didn't point out what room we were standing in for this tour. He simply kept on with his story, pausing long enough in each room for me to take everything in.

The more he talked, the more I relaxed around him.

The room after the living room was the dining room. Same gray paint. Same hardwood floor with no rugs in sight. The table surprised me. It looked antique. It was huge, dark wood, and I counted ten heavy looking chairs. Four chairs on each side, one on each end. The walls were barren in this room as well.

"When girls are born, and it's determined they have magic, in our world that's a reason to celebrate, a reason to throw a party. And the Council wouldn't have taken her away from her parents, they don't do that if your parents have magic. And, in some cases they will leave you with the parent who doesn't have magic if something unfortunate should happen to the other one. That's what happened with me. My mother petitioned the Council to keep me after my father died. Anyways, if you have a girl and she has magic, your entire family gets treated like royalty. They would have wanted for nothing."

I followed him out of the room after he noticed I had stopped looking around and had been ready to continue on with the tour.

The dining room lead to the kitchen.

"This is my favorite room in the whole house," he told me shyly.

I wasn't entirely sure why.

The appliances were black and nothing special. The counter top on the small island was wood, butchers block. The rest of the countertop was white tile. The walls in here were painted a dark red. A small, circular kitchen table had been shoved into a corner with three chairs pushed into it. The table sat in front of a sliding glass door. Light gray curtains hung around the door.

I found myself shrugging, I didn't get why this would be anyone's favorite room.

"Only memory I have of my dad is of him sitting at that table, drinking a cup of coffee."

I looked at the table again with new eyes. If what Quinton had told me about Dash's life with his mother and grandmother was true (and I didn't think he had lied to me about that. What would be the point?) then I could completely understand why this was his favorite room if he saw his dad sitting at the table every time he walked in here.

I wanted to tell him how sorry I was for his loss, but I didn't want to change the subject away from the Council and what he was telling me about them. He was giving out an awful lot of information and I wasn't sure when I would get another chance to learn this much about them.

He cleared his throat while he walked across the room to open a door.

"Bathroom," he said as he opened the door. "Pretty standard. Do you want to look inside?"

"Nope," I told him, and he shut the door. I had no desire to check out his bathroom, though, I probably should have checked it out seeing as I would be living here with him soon enough.

"Let's go back to the living room," he murmured.

He got us each a bottle of water out of the refrigerator as I made my way back to the living room. He'd entirely skipped over the upstairs tour. I had no desire to scope out his bedroom, but I was nosy enough to want to know what the upstairs looked like. I mean, come on, that's where my room was going to be, he should have brought me up there and showed me around.

After picking a spot in a corner of the couch, I sat down. I slid my feet out of my flip-flops and drew my knees up to my chest.

I felt bad for having my bare feet on his couch and wished I had socks on.

My mind drifted as I stared into the fire, watching the logs burn while the flames danced around.

I pressed my cheek into my knee and closed my eyes. The next thing I knew Dash was gently shaking my shoulder, waking me up.

"Hey," he said as I sat up and looked around.

How long had he been gone for? It felt like I had only closed my eyes for two seconds before he was shaking me awake.

"Hey," I muttered back in a rough voice. I cleared my throat and scooted further back on the couch. I let my feet drop to the floor and I sat up straighter.

A tray sat on the orange ottoman. Mugs of hot chocolate and a plate loaded with cookies rested on the tray. Ah, so that had been what took him so long.

Without being invited to do so, I picked up a steaming mug of hot chocolate and held it between my hands. I blew into the mug before taking a sip from it. I couldn't remember when the last time I had hot chocolate was. It was delicious, even if it did burn going down.

"Anyway," he said as he picked up a cookie from the tray, carrying on with our previous conversation. "She had problems before the Council tried to get her to join a coven. She didn't like going outside because her father had only allowed her outside at night and even then, she wasn't allowed to leave their fenced in backyard. The whole thing is fucked up and the Council was just trying to do right by her, they'd been appalled by the way she had been treated. And, can you really blame them for taking her out of there and getting her away from that man? I don't. And I don't think it's their fault she killed herself, either. Marcus's father got drunk and drove his car into a tree a week after she died. That whole family has suffered one loss after the next, especially Marcus. First his mother, then his sister, his father, his wife and now his brother. Not to mention this shit with your mom. I can't really blame him for getting the hell out of here."

My eyes filled with tears I refused to shed. I didn't want to talk about Mr. Cole and his sad life anymore. It was making me feel guilty. Guilt for being upset with him for not staying with me. Guilt with myself for not telling him the truth about my mother and keeping this gigantic, hideous secret from him. And guilt because part of me was relieved he was going so that I no longer had to lie to him. The lie was eating at me, festering inside, threatening to poison me. Yeah, I had guilt, I had bucket loads of it. And I really did not want to be talking about Mr. Cole anymore today.

I plunked my mug on the tray and asked, "Do you think they will want to meet me?"

In my head I saw a bunch of wrinkled old dudes wearing suits and huge sunglasses that covered up half their faces. Were there women on the Council? Somehow, I doubted it.

"Shit," Dash exclaimed as he slammed his mug down on the tray. The brown liquid sloshed over the rim of the mug, spilling all over the tray.

"What?"

"With you here I forgot I had shit to do today." He muttered. "Damn. I have to get ready."

He scrambled to his feet and practically ran out of the living room, leaving me baffled as I watched him go.

What the hell just happened?

Chapter Fourteen

"WHAT ARE YOU doing?" I asked Dash curiously.

He was rolling out some sheer black fabric across his large dining room table.

"Prepping for my client who is going to be here in about half an hour," he grunted.

I had found out Dash was excellent when it came to giving out information, even if it was a little awkward.

However, his answer made me blink in confusion because I had no idea what in the heck he was talking about and I expected a better answer than that from him. "What do you mean by client? What sort of client do you have coming?" I asked.

Please don't let him mean date and he said client to try and spare my feelings. He could have sex with whomever he wanted, I just didn't want to be around when he did it.

He looked up sharply and studied my face. Damn, I must have given something away in my voice. I kept my face as blank as I could, going for innocent. I meant it when I said I didn't care who he had sex with, because I didn't. I didn't have those kinds of feelings for Dash, I didn't know him well enough to feel much of anything towards him. I think what bothered me was knowing that he was supposed to have those feelings for *me* and, yet he seemed indifferent. A blow to the ego, that was.

"I have a few clients that have standing appointments, although, this one isn't one of mine," he said carefully. Yeah, he hadn't bought my innocent look. I didn't think I was very good at it because Quinton never bought it either.

I sighed and repeated my question, "What do you mean by client?"

I didn't like repeating myself and wished he had simply answered my question the first time around.

"What is it exactly that you're imagining it is that I do with these clients?" he asked and now he sounded amused.

I bit my bottom lip and looked away from him. Not because I was embarrassed, but because I was starting to get frustrated with him. Lately my frustration quickly turned to anger and then I lost all common sense and threw shit at people's heads, injuring them. I didn't want to cause Dash bodily harm, at least, not yet I didn't.

"I'm a witch, Ariel," he said softly, sweetly.

"As am I," I replied. My reply was neither soft nor sweet. I'm afraid it came out a bit sullen.

Why was he telling me these things I already knew? If not for his tone of voice, I would have thought he was playing with me, laughing at me. But his tone was sweet, so I knew he wasn't.

"I offer my services to people for a fee, and not a small one, either," he said.

"What sort of services?" I asked suspiciously. Was he running some sort of one-man male prostitution ring out of his home? If so, I didn't think I was going to be able to live here with him after all.

He sighed, heavily, sounding for all the world like he was beginning to lose patience with me.

"Damien, Julian and Quinton meet with clients here as well," he shared. Finally, we were getting somewhere. "People come to us, looking for answers, looking for love, wanting riches, wanting all kinds of things. Children, sex, money, murder, love, fame, revenge. You name it and someone will pay money for us to help them get it. They pay for potions, spells, to have their cards read. The Council allows it for some reason, I think it has a lot to do with Quinton. People are afraid of him and we get away with a lot of things because of it."

He finished covering the table in black cloth. He picked a box up from the floor and set it atop the table. Dash started pulling objects out at random. Slim, black and white candle sticks. A white BIC lighter and a deck of cards that was three times the size of a normal deck of cards. The tops of the cards were black with no words or images on them.

Tarot cards.

I pointed towards the deck and said excitedly, "Tyson promised to teach me but there has been no time." I left out that there had been no time because I had been avoiding them.

I eyed the deck of cards wistfully. I had gone on a date once that had taken me to a carnival. I had been fascinated with the gypsy fortune teller woman and if I'd had my own money at the time I would have paid to have her do a reading for me. My date had thought her a fake and had dragged me out of there. I didn't get my reading and I still wanted one. Though, I wasn't entirely sure why. The future could be a frightening, dangerous thing and I was sure my future held some things I absolutely did not need to know anything about until they were happening. But, I was curious. Oh, so curious. About everything, and I wanted to learn. I wanted to learn everything they were willing to teach me.

"Have you ever had a reading done?" Dash asked as he set up the table. Candles in their holders, cards placed neatly off the side in a stack. I wanted to reach out and touch them, make sure they were real.

I shook my head in the negative and his gray eyes raked over my face, taking in my expression. He frowned deeply but let whatever he was frowning about go.

"This lady coming today is a real bitch," he told me as he moved around the table, towards me. "She always asks for Quinton because she wants his cock. He'll flirt with her, let her think she has a chance and she always comes back for more. She lusts after beauty, money and things she couldn't afford on her own. So, she married a very rich old man. That old man died about eight months ago and all his money disappeared when he died. She keeps coming to us, hoping we can help her find the dead man's money. The problem with her is, we aren't a detective agency and we sure as fuck aren't treasure hunters. She gets her cards read every week in hopes that something will change, with her money situation and with Quinton. She's not going to like seeing me today and she really won't want to see you."

"What did I do?" I asked quietly while trying to digest the things he'd just told me.

He stopped in front of me and grinned huge. I blinked stupidly at him. I had never seen him smile before. It did wonders for his face and chased some of the demons out of his eyes.

"Nothing. Like Quinton is going to flirt with some bitch now that we have you," his smile faded away, but the lightness didn't leave his eyes. "You have no idea, do you?"

"No idea about what?" I asked, and he laughed again.

I opened my mouth to question him and he cut me off.

"We will have time afterwards," he said. "I want you to stay and watch, learn something, if you can. After she's gone, I will read the cards for you."

I licked my suddenly dry lips, a nervous gesture. I badly wanted the opportunity to learn something new from them. I had been on my own for a while with my magic except for what I read about in books. I wanted to learn from someone real and not because I read about it in a dusty old book.

I liked Dash smiling at me. I liked this side of him, him wanting to do something nice for me, like taking the time to read my cards simply because he could tell it was something I desperately wanted.

"Thanks, Dash," I said quietly. This time my voice *was* just as sweet as his had been earlier. It embarrassed me, and I imagined my face turning three different shades of red. "I would like that very much." Understatement of the year.

"Quinton was right," he breathed out.

"About what?" I asked, surprised by the sudden topic change.

"We're all fucked when it comes to you," he said as someone knocked loudly on the front door.

Chapter Fifteen

DASH HAD BEEN right about his client who showed up. She made a big deal about only wanting to work with Quinton. Then, when Dash told her that under no circumstances would Quinton see her, she told him she wanted Damien. Personally, I didn't get it, Damien didn't seem like the friendliest choice either. And, why was he better than Dash?

She didn't give any explanations as to why, she simply demanded. If she couldn't have Quinton, then she wanted Damien. End of story for her.

And Dash gave into her demands. I wanted to tell her to get the hell out, but it wasn't my house and she wasn't my client or guest. She was Dash's client and, with a firm frown in place, he left me alone with her to go phone Damien and see if he could come over immediately to take care of her. The immediately had been another one of her demands because her time was precious, and she didn't need Dash wasting anymore of it.

After spending all of two minutes in her presence, I decided I hated her guts.

And, did I mention, Dash *left me alone with her?* Not his smartest move, but I couldn't blame him for escaping her. I wished I could have escaped with him.

She pulled out a chair at the dining room table and sat down with a graceful flourish. She plopped her mammoth sized designer purse on the table in front of her.

I leaned against the wall by the entryway to the living room and I did it awkwardly. I was going to wring Dash's neck for putting me in this position.

"So," she said conversationally as she flipped her long strawberry blonde hair over her slender shoulders. "Who are you and why are you here? They don't usually have guests when I come over."

I didn't like the way she'd said that. So I didn't respond with an answer. Instead, I crossed my arms over my chest and laid my head back against the wall. If Dash wanted me to be nice to her he probably shouldn't have left me alone with her.

"What, are you mute?" she huffed. "No wonder Quinton won't come over here, what with you being here and all. Who could blame him?"

"I'm not mute," I told her honestly. And then I kept right on going with the honesty. I tried to bite my tongue, but it didn't seem to be working so well for me lately. "I'm not mute, I simply have no desire to hold down a conversation with someone who is, clearly, an asshole."

She stared at me a moment, looking completely dumbstruck before giving an enraged shriek and pushing to her feet. The chair flew back, clattering to the floor in a heap.

I should have kept my mouth shut.

"What did you say to me?" She screeched.

I winced at the horrible, high voice that came out of her mouth. I seriously hoped I never sounded like that in my whole life.

"Answer me, you little bitch," she screamed. Thankfully, this time her voice wasn't as high as it had been before.

Pounding footsteps were coming from behind me. Dash was running to get here. He was going to strangle me. This wasn't a very good way to convince him to like me, by enraging his client.

"I'm sorry," I said in a rush, in an attempt to smooth things over before Dash got here.

"How dare you call me an asshole," she seethed.

I shrugged. To hell with her. I had tried being nice and apologized. What more did she want from me?

"What the fuck is going on in here?" Quinton asked from the doorway.

He stood in the doorway, not a foot away from me. Dash stood next to him. Both stared at me in what looked like sick fascination.

"I think I'm ready to go home now," I told them in a quiet, embarrassed voice.

"Oh, no you don't," the woman raged at me. Her small hands were clenched into tight fists at her sides. Her extremely vulgar cleavage heaved up and down with every enraged breath she took in. She looked about two seconds away from tackling me to the ground and trying to rip my hair out after she clawed up my face. "You owe me an apology, you little brat."

The urge to flee, to run and hide from her and this situation was strong. When fight or flight hit the scene I had always chosen option number two and ran whenever I could. The person who took option number two and ran was no longer the person who I wanted to be. No more running like a scared little rabbit for me.

Moving away from the wall, I stood up straight and squared my shoulders.

"Oh, fuck," Quinton muttered under his breath. "Look at her face."

"I see it," Dash said, and his voice shook with laughter.

I didn't find anything amusing. Not one tiny, little thing.

"She called me an asshole," the woman accused. She pointed her clenched fist at me and spit out, "I paid good money to be here and I will not put up with this disrespect from you or anyone else while I'm here."

"You are an asshole," Quinton said in a bland voice.

She flinched as if he'd struck her. She must not have ever seen this side to him before. Dash's words from earlier came back, flooding my mind. This chick had the hots for Quinton and if he were unavailable, she had no problem working with Damien. Then Julian. She would probably make a better coven member than me because she had no problem with latching on to more than one of them.

She switched tactics immediately. In the blink of an eye she went from high screeching to low pleading.

"Quint," she whined, "you don't really mean that."

"Get out," he snapped at her in a harsh voice.

I had a feeling Ms. Prissy Pants had never seen the real Quinton come out to play before. She was in for a real treat.

"I'm not leaving until I get what I paid for," the lady whined as she stomped her foot angrily, like a naughty child.

My lip curled in disgust as I watched a grown woman get ready to throw down a massive temper tantrum.

She stomped her foot a second time. With her hands on her hips she leaned forward and hissed at Quinton, "You owe me a reading. I already paid for one and I'm getting what I paid for. I've been coming to you amateurs for months now. Months! And you've yet to really give me what I've paid for. If you aren't going to give me what I want then I demand a refund! I want it all back, every cent I have spent here." She stomped her foot several more times, and screamed, "I want it and I want it now."

In the silence that followed her screaming came an unexpected sound. A pathetic sounding meow from a cat.

Nobody had said anything about there being a cat.

Another pathetic sounding meow came as a dainty little black cat strutted into the room, coming from the kitchen. He was adorable!

"Oh my god," I squealed and clapped my hands gleefully, forgetting the drama going on around me and focusing solely on the cat. "What a pretty little kitty cat."

I had always thought it would be awesome to have a cat. They napped a lot, purred when you petted them, liked to laze about in the sunshine, had serious attituded problems and a superiority complex. They were adorable little creatures and this one was cuter than most. He was mostly black with a little splash of white on one of his front paws.

I walked towards him, ready to pet him, not caring in the least if he turned out to be a feral little beast and snapped at me, showing me his claws and teeth.

Two steps in on my journey across the room and I came to jarring halt as an open palm slammed into my cheek. My head jerked to the side as pain exploded in my cheek.

I blinked in shock as I cradled my injured cheek with both hands. Someone had struck me, slapped me across the face.

"You stupid bitch," I heard Quinton growl before a feminine voice cried out in pain.

I couldn't bring myself to care about what he did to her to make her cry out like that. The days where I allowed someone else to hurt me were over and I was glad for Quinton's interference because I honestly had no idea how to respond to what she'd done to me.

She cried out again and I heard sounds of a struggle. I looked up in time to see Quinton had her in a headlock with his arm around her throat. She was spewing out profanities and clawing at his arms as he dragged her out of the room.

I closed my eyes as my shoulders slumped forward. I was more than ready to go home.

Note to self, don't ever get in the car with Quinton unless you know your destination and the purpose of the trip ahead of time.

This was all his fault.

What an A-hole.

Chapter Sixteen

SOMETHING SOFT BRUSHED against my ankle, making me jump. I opened my eyes to see the dainty black cat rubbing up against my ankle. He weaved in between my legs, rubbing up against the other ankle.

Bright green eyes blinked up at me adoringly as he started to purr.

"Pretty boy," I cooed as I lowered my hand from my stinging face.

I squatted down, brining myself closer to the little beast. His bright eyes watched me with an intelligence no animal I'd met before possessed. I rubbed my hand over his soft fur, scratching behind his ears and making him purr louder.

"He likes you," Dash said quietly from behind me. I didn't jump or flinch at his sudden appearance.

"He's a cute kitty."

A zip lock bag filled with ice cubes appeared in front of my face. I took it from him with a mumbled thanks and pressed it to my cheek. The cold made me flinch, but I didn't pull it away. I didn't want a swollen cheek for the rest of the day or all of tomorrow.

"He hates Abel and Addison." He shared with me. "I don't know why but when those two come over he goes into hiding. He doesn't like Damien, either. He doesn't hide when Damien comes over though, instead he comes out and makes a point to hiss at him."

I would have said the adorable little cat probably didn't like people who sucked but the Salt and Pepper twins didn't suck. However, Damien did.

"What's his name?" I asked as I continued to scratch the cat behind the ears.

"Binx."

I paused in petting his cat so I could tilt my head back and look up at him.

"Like the cat from Hocus Pocus?" I asked in a surprised voice. When he nodded I couldn't help the giggle that escaped me. "You named your cat after a cat in a witch movie."

"It's a Halloween movie, actually," he replied. "And that cat kicked ass."

I agreed with him a hundred percent. It was still kind of funny.

"She should never have touched you," he cursed under his breath. "If she wasn't such a bitch, I might feel sorry for her."

"What do you mean?" I questioned him. She didn't get her cards read and Quinton had wrestled her out the front door and that had been that. Right? That didn't sound like something to feel sorry for her over, she'd had that coming.

Dash looked at me oddly, like he'd never seen me before.

"I like this," he blurted.

I tilted my head to the side and frowned. "Like what?" I asked in confusion.

"This," he declared as he waved his hand towards my body, making me catch my breath. "How sweet and innocent you are. I haven't had a lot of sweet and innocent in my life. I'm thinking my luck has finally changed and I couldn't be happier about it."

I gaped at him.

He liked me?

Dash? Dash Flynn liked me?

Could this day get any weirder?

Answer: yes. Always. I should never ask that question. You would think I'd know better by now.

Binx rubbed his head against my still hand, demanding my attention once more. I gave his head a little pat and stood up.

Dash hovered over me, too close for comfort. I took a step back. He took a step forward, invading my space.

"Do you like it here, in my home?" He demanded to know.

I took another step back and cleared my throat. "Yes," I answered him honestly in a thick voice.

What was going on here?

I took another step backwards, hit wall and all the air left my lungs in a rush. This was fast becoming a familiar situation for me and I wasn't sure I liked it all that much.

If he kissed me right now we were going to have a serious problem.

"Let's go," Quinton barked harshly from the doorway. He shot Dash a dirty look and crossed his arms over his chest. "What the fuck are you doing?" He growled at Dash.

For once, Quint and I were on the same page, it was definitely time to go.

I stepped to the side and further away from Dash before quickly scurrying to Quinton's side.

I pulled the bag of ice away from my face and tossed it in the direction of the dining room table. It landed on top with a clatter and slid a foot before coming to a complete stop.

I waved lamely at Dash and knew my poor abused face was flaming red.

"Thanks for, um, hanging out with me today," I babbled awkwardly.

"See," he teased, "sweet."

"She hit me in the head with a fucking rock," Quinton grumbled. "That's not very sweet, if you ask me."

No one was asking him anything.

"Time to go," I groaned. We were not talking about the thing with the rock. I still felt a little bad about that one.

"Jesus," Quinton grumbled. "What is it with you? There's never a dull moment when you're around."

I shook my head. I wasn't going to do this with him, not in front of Dash. When he wasn't speaking, Quinton and I got along so well. When he opened his mouth, that's when things started to go south for us.

"I'll meet you in the car," I told him as I turned and stormed out of the room.

How long did he plan on throwing that rock incident in my face? Probably for forever.

I walked out the door and headed straight for Quinton's black car. His car surprised me. I could see him behind the wheel of some black muscle car or a sleek Mercedes like what Mr. Cole drives. In comparison to those cars, Quinton's car looked normal, boring even, something a regular, every day person would drive. It didn't suit him at all. Maybe that's why he drove it, because it fit in and didn't draw attention in the least.

The locks beeped before I made it around to the passenger side and I knew he had followed close behind me. Good. I wasn't in the mood to sit out in the car like a child and wait for him to come out so he could drive me home.

This time, he didn't bother walking around the car to try and open my door for me.

As soon as he had the car started and rolling down the driveway, I started in on him with my questions.

"What did the Council want?" I demanded to know. I kept right on firing them out at him one after the other, not giving him a chance to respond just yet. I knew if I let him open his mouth he wouldn't let me get another word out and the conversation would go on to be a one-sided affair after that. "You weren't gone for very long. Did you even see them? Why were they at my house? How many of them were there? What's going on, Quinton? I have a right to know and you have no business keeping things like this from me. It's not right and it will make me angry."

I crossed my arms over my stomach as I rested my forehead against the cool glass window. The trees blurred as we sped past them.

Fabric rustled, and I assumed he was moving around in his seat. I was too tired to turn and look so I could see what he was doing. It had been a long day and when I got back to Mr. Cole's house I was going straight to bed. It wasn't just today; this week had been utterly exhausting. Hell, this entire month had done me in.

Quinton placed his hand on my thigh and gently squeezed.

"They weren't here because of you," he said in a tight voice. "They came because they are concerned about Marcus, so they reached out to him. He turned them away at the door. I don't know what's going on with Marcus, but I feel like it's got to do with more than just your mother and his brother dying. They seemed very concerned about him."

My breath fogged the window, but I was far too tired and lazy to reach up and wipe it away. I wasn't really paying attention to the landscape anyways, the trees all looked the same to me.

I thought about what Quinton had just told me. Did the Council really, honestly, have reason to be concerned about Mr. Cole? Right after his brother had died, I might have said yes. But now? No, no I did not understand the Council's concern. To me, he seemed to be doing remarkably well for someone who'd recently lost his brother, thought his lover had run out on him and been left with the sole responsibility of a teenager. He always seemed so calm, so collected. Then again, I now knew what I knew about his sister and that was a bit of a game changer.

Quinton pulled into the driveway to Mr. Cole's house. Both of us had been quiet for a few minutes now. Not an awkward silence. It was more him being quiet and giving me time to digest what he had told me. I appreciated his silence more than he would ever know.

I liked this side to Quinton. I liked most sides to Quinton. Not that I would admit that out loud to him or anyone else.

I unbuckled my seat belt and reached for the door handle.

"Babe," he called quietly.

I looked to him in question and was surprised at what I saw. He looked angry. No, he looked enraged.

What the?

"What's wrong?"

His eyes darted to Mr. Cole's house then immediately came back to me. They were now guarded, he'd put his wall back up, hiding his emotions from me.

"Nothing," he muttered quietly. Then, louder, he asked. "What are your plans for the night?"

What? Change of subject much?

"I'm going to go to bed," I told him honestly.

Like I had energy for anything else. Please.

"Good," he said. Then he demanded, "Now give me a kiss before you get out of my car."

I couldn't help myself, I laughed.

Please.

If he wanted a kiss, he could kiss my ass.

I did not think so.

I opened the door and slid my right foot out, placing it on the cement driveway.

"I will see you later, Quinton," I told him as I climbed out of his car.

Kiss him, he'd said. Like I was at his beck and call. What an asshole.

He put his tongue in my mouth once, and the only way he'd pulled it off is because he'd surprised me. That did not mean we would be doing it on a regular basis.

I walked into the house without a backwards glance. If I looked back at him he might think I didn't want him to leave me and I could really use some time to myself at the moment. I know that sounded absurd because I had had a whole month to myself, but I really needed to catch my breath.

The beeping of the alarm greeted me inside the house and I moved quickly to silence it.

"Ariel," Mr. Cole called from the kitchen. "Is that you?"

"Yeah," I shouted back.

"Come here for a second."

I froze, not wanting to go there. He meant the world to me, but I wasn't sure what to think in regards to him anymore. Too much had happened, and I hadn't had enough time to process it yet.

I walked into the kitchen and stopped short. He stood with a hip against the counter in gray draw string pants and a black short-sleeved t-shirt. His hair was messy, as if he'd been pulling at it excessively. There was stubble along his jaw and he had dark circles under his eyes.

My heart clenched painfully at the sight of him. Was it my fault that he looked so bad? Had he not been sleeping?

"What's wrong?" I asked in a flat voice.

"Nothing's wrong, sweetheart." He assured me. "I wanted to let you know that I have to go out of town for business tomorrow and I will be gone overnight. Perhaps you could have one of the Alexander's stay over here with you? I would rather you not stay here alone. If that's okay with you?"

I nodded, I would figure something ou,t so I didn't have to be alone in the house overnight.

He cleared his throat awkwardly and looked to his feet.

"Have you eaten yet?" He asked in a quiet voice.

"Yeah," I lied. "I'm tired. I'm just going to go to bed, if that's okay with you."

"Night, sweetheart."

After a mumbled "Night" in response, I started to leave the room. Before I hit the hallway, I paused.

"Marcus," I called over my shoulder. His head snapped up and his tired eyes focused on me. "Please be careful on your trip."

Warmth and surprise lit up his eyes and he might have said something, but I left the room before he could.

I couldn't do it.

I was all done with emotional bullshit for one day. I could take no more.

Chapter Seventeen
Quinton Alexander

I BACKED OUT of Ariel's driveway probably too fast and completely furious. My fingers were wrapped around the steering wheel so tightly my knuckles were starting to turn white, if it hurt I was far too numb to notice.

After reversing out of the driveway my car shot forward, faster than I had reversed out of the driveway.

The house was light from the inside, letting me know Ty and the twins were safe and at home, probably conspiring against me. Lately, they had been making complaints about having to go to school. If Ariel was not going to attend public school, then they didn't think they should be forced to attend either. I agreed with them. I hadn't gone to school a day in my life and I had turned out just fine. However, I wasn't about to tell those three idiots that. They had started arguing with me about it and every day they would come up with a new reason they shouldn't have to go, and they proposed it to me. The whole ordeal amused me greatly because I was not the person who made them go to school in the first place. Tyson had started going after his parents died and I think he went to get away from me and our mutual grief. The twins went because Tyson did, and they had been curious about what it would be like. None of it had anything to do with me and they could quit at any time they wanted to.

I floored it, cruising past the house and headed into town.

I picked my phone up out of the cup holder and swiped my finger across the screen without taking my eyes off of the road. The screen lit up and I glanced down. I hit contacts and glanced back at the road. Using my thumb, I scrolled through the names. When I got to the J's, I clicked on Julian's name and put it on speaker.

He answered on the third ring.

"Yeah?" Julian said in greeting.

"I'm coming to get you," I announced. "And I will be there in less than five."

"I figured as much," he grumbled. "Dash called, and he filled us in. Damien's coming too."

I grunted, not liking our third wheel. I hadn't talked to Damien or seen him in weeks. Not since we had words about the way he talked about our girl.

And now he wanted to tag along?

I was immediately suspicious.

"He feels like shit, Quint," Julian snapped at me. "Give him a break."

I looked down at my phone, double checking to make sure I had called Julian and not someone else. Sure enough, I had the right number. He never snapped at me. He was always the calm one and I was the one who snapped at people.

"What gives, man?" I asked.

"Just get here," he ordered before hanging up on me, making both my eyebrows go up in surprise.

Damn.

This wasn't like him at all.

Now worried, I pushed down harder on the gas pedal, damn near flooring it. Speeding tickets weren't an issue for me, if I were to get pulled over I could easily get rid of a police officer. If there was more than one, it would be a bit of a struggle. I could only do so much with magic and focusing on more than one target at a time without something to aid me could sometimes backfire horribly.

I made it to town, blew past the school and turned onto Julian and Damien's street. I parked in front of their house and let my car idle at the curb.

From the street, their house looked like a tiny, one-story shack. The houses on this street were so smooshed together that you couldn't see anything but the front of them. Which was why you missed how long it was.

I couldn't live in a house with small rooms. I liked my space. I liked having a large bedroom and I liked having my own bathroom. Living with three other people and having bedrooms for three, now four, more people, our house needed to be big and have room for us to be alone and in our own personal space when we wanted it and together in different spaces when we wanted that. My house was big and that's how I liked it. This house, though… You couldn't fit all of us in the living room. Maybe if we spread out between the living room and the kitchen we would all be able to fit. There were too many of us to be cramped together like that. I didn't know why Julian even still stayed here when I knew for damn sure he preferred to be at the main house.

Annoyed, I tapped my fingers against the steering wheel. If it wasn't full on dark right now and the neighbors weren't uptight fucks, I would be laying on the horn. I did not enjoy being made to wait even when I was in the best of moods.

What the fuck was taking them so long?

Jesus.

I scowled at the front door, hoping to see one of them walking through it. When nobody came through the door, I sat back in the driver's seat and let out a heavy sigh.

Everything would come together, everything would work out. It had to. I kept telling myself that once Marcus moved, Ariel would have an easier time of it. She had so much obvious guilt eating away at her and I knew a lot of it had to do with Marcus. I don't think she liked lying to him about what had become of her mother, she was usually a very honest and open person, lying didn't look good on her. That month the two of them had together all alone in Marcus's house probably hadn't made the situation any better. It had almost destroyed me, knowing she was right next door and I couldn't get to her because she hadn't wanted anything to do with me. I had never been more afraid of something in my life than I had been in that month, thinking she hated me or was afraid of me. And thinking of her being all alone with Marcus in that big house, the both of them bleeding from an unseen wound…

I shook my head. What I had felt had seemed like nothing in comparison to what the twins had gone through. They had both been absolutely miserable and felt they were to blame for what had happened. They'd let her leave school by herself and something awful had happened to her. Then she'd disappeared on them, on all of us and the twins hadn't dealt well with that because they had some serious abandonment issues. They hadn't been to blame and every single one of us had taken the time to tell them so. They hadn't cared. Addison had retreated into himself and, at one point, he'd stopped speaking to anyone who wasn't his brother. Abel had watched his brother helplessly and the longer it went on, the angrier he'd become.

I hoped like hell that all of it was behind us now.

The passenger door opened, revealing Julian. Right after, the door behind me opened and Damien got in.

As soon as their doors were shut, I was speeding down the road again.

Remembering Ariel's concern from earlier, I told them they should put their seatbelts on.

"What?" Julian asked in disbelief. "Since when do you care if someone wears a seat belt? You're not even wearing one yourself right now."

I looked down and, sure enough, I had forgotten to put my seat belt on when I'd gotten into the car.

Shit. And she hadn't commented.

I reached across my chest, grabbed ahold of my seat belt and dragged it down. When I had it lined up with the slot it was supposed to go into, I pushed down on it until I heard it click, locking into place.

"What's that all about?" Julian asked in a curious voice.

"Ariel," I stated and explained no more. Maybe she wouldn't give a shit whether or not they wore their seat belts. It made me a dick but I kind of liked that thought.

Two distinctive clicks sounded in the quiet car and I had to bite my lower lip to keep from laughing at them. All it took was her name to get them to cooperate.

"What's the plan?" Damien asked from his place in the backseat.

I stiffened in my seat and tried to squeeze the life out of the steering wheel. I didn't exactly have a plan. I'd gotten angry and I always acted out when I was angry, I lashed out and I never took the time to think about it before hand. With Dash, the two of them had been my best friends for as long as I could remember. No one knew me better than the three of them and the fact that Damien would ask me about my plan pissed me way the fuck off. He knew I didn't have a plan, he was just trying to be an asshole.

"Damien will go to the door," Julian rushed out, likely trying to stop me from pulling off to the side of the room and ripping that fuck face out of the backseat and beating on him. "She likes him and thinks he's pretty. If we send him to the door, she'll open it for him because she wants to fuck him."

"She wants to fuck you, too," Damien countered.

He was right. Earlier today, before I had to get physical with her and haul her ass out of Dash's house, I would have said she wanted to fuck me as well. I think my putting my arm around her throat and squeezing might have put a damper on her libido where I was concerned. At least I hoped so.

"After Dash called, I went through what I had at the house and found a potion for her."

Julian. Bless his fucking heart. He came off as the sweet and calm one out of the four of us. He might be the calm one but calling him sweet was downright laughable. I had yet to come across someone more vindictive than Julian. And revenge? Don't even get me started on that one. Julian got some sick thrill out of getting revenge on someone who'd wronged him. I'd stood by his side and watched as he'd stolen fortunes, slipped someone a potion to make them infertile. One client had simply insulted him, and he put shit in her tea that made all of her hair fall out, she'd even lost her eyebrows and eyelashes. Her entire body had ended up bare, completely hairless. And the kicker? It had been permanent. She'd come back to us, asking for help. Julian had laughed in her face and told her to look on the bright side, she'd save a bunch of money on never having to purchase shampoo or razors again. He did shit like that all the time.

I was almost afraid to ask him what he'd come up with.

"If Damien can hold her arms down, I'll need you to get her mouth open, Quinton."

I nodded, I could do that. Easy.

"Did she really hit Ariel?" Damien asked in a gruff voice.

From his voice, I could tell he did not enjoy the thought of someone hurting our girl.

"Yeah," I ground out. "The bitch slapped her across the face. Right in front of us, too. I think she would have kept hitting her if I hadn't dragged her out of there."

"She cornered me when I was coming out of the bathroom at Dash's house," Damien shared. "She got up close and in my space, rubbed her tits up against me and tried to slip her hand down the front of my jeans. She went straight for my dick. Seriously, my boy wasn't even hard and still she went right for it."

After a few seconds of stilted silence, in a sarcastic voice, I asked, "That's it? You're okay with fucking some lady up because she grabbed your dick when it was soft? Un-fucking-believable. I would expect something like that from Julian, but you? No fucking way."

Julian started laughing.

"You don't understand," Damien exclaimed in a taut voice. "I think it's my fault she attacked Ariel."

Julian stopped laughing and, sounding genuinely confused, asked, "What are you talking about?"

If he hadn't asked, I would have.

Without the use of my turn signal, I slowed down and turned right, onto Jackie's street. The houses on this street were the polar opposites to the one's on Damien and Julian's street. These houses were large and had tall fences around them.

I slowed down and switched off my headlights as I pulled up to the curb in front of her house. She'd downsized after her husband croaked and moved into a much smaller house. My house was bigger than the one she lived in now.

"When she tried to feel me up, I stopped her and told her I wasn't interested because I had a girlfriend."

"Yeah, Damien," I bit out. "We all know about your fucking girlfriend. What's this have to do with Ariel?"

A click came from the back, telling me Damien had unbuckled his seat belt. He appeared closer in the rear-view mirror as he moved, leaning in between the front seats. He placed his elbows on the arm rest and propped his chin on his closed fists.

Always striking a pose, was out Damien. Even when no one was looking.

"I described my girlfriend to her. I told her my girlfriend was beautiful. That she had light blonde hair and lovely, mysterious green eyes that reminded me of my brother, Dash's eyes. I told her about how sweet this girl was and how she was everything to me and to the rest of you. In hindsight, I probably shouldn't have shared that last bit but it had just come out. I feel responsible, and I feel like it's my fault Jackie attacked Ariel. I want to make it right, which is why I'm here."

Damien straightened and sat back. He scooted across the seat and opened the door behind Julian. He slipped out of the car and closed the door without making a sound.

My head swiveled to the side and I caught Julian's shocked expression. I imagined I wore a similar one.

"What do you think happened to the girlfriend he wanted to keep around?" Julian asked me.

I grinned at him. “Don’t care. She’s gone and that’s all that matters to me. Now we’re all on board.”

A slow, smug smile spread across Julian’s face.

He didn’t need to say it, I knew what he was thinking because I was thinking the same thing myself. There’d be no more fighting amongst us. If we could bring Ariel around then we’d both get everything we wanted.

I opened the door and got out of my car, closing the door behind me as silently as Damien had. Julian did the same.

We moved closer to the wooden fence, hiding in its shadows.

Damien stood on the wide porch, bathed in the light. He rang the doorbell and we all waited. Jackie’s car was in the driveway, so we knew she was home. Stupid, stupid, stupid. She had a nice and big attached garage, she should have parked her car in there. Especially if she was one of those idiots who didn’t lock their car doors, thinking they were safe because they were parked in their own driveway. Please. I had watched one too many horror movies to swallow that load.

The door opened, and Jackie appeared. Damien immediately reached out and took her by the hand. She didn’t even flinch or try to pull away from him.

After doing some fast talking, Damien was pulled into the house behind her. The door closed behind them and I let out a breath I hadn’t realized I’d been holding. I’d been nervous about this first part not going smoothly. Forced entry and breaking and entering weren't my style. I could usually charm my way into anywhere. Anywhere except for maybe here.

Julian flicked a hand towards the house and I inclined my head. It was time.

We sprinted across the lawn and hurried up the front steps. Julian tried the door and turned to grin at me when the door pushed inwards, opening easily for him. He moved into the house and I followed along behind him. I closed the door behind me and I was smart enough to lock it.

Two steps later and we both came up short.

What in the…

Damien was on the couch, on top of Jackie. Her hands were at his ass, squeezing and holding on for dear life. Damien had her arms stretched out above her, pressed into the arm rest and held on tightly between his hands.

Jesus.

How long had he been in here for? All of three minutes? This had to be some kind of record.

Julian made a weird noise and I moved forward. If he laughed now she might start to struggle before we were ready, and we couldn't have that.

Damien moved on the couch. He straddled Jackie's waist, with a knee in the couch on both sides of her body. He sat up as far as he could while still holding down her arms above her head.

Jackie turned her head to the side and inhaled sharply, trying to catch her breath. That must have been some kiss.

Thankfully, her eyes were closed, and she missed Julian and I creeping up.

I knelt down on the carpet, beside the couch. Julian moved around to stand before the arm rest.

With a nod from Damien, I wrapped my hand around her jaw and squeezed. Her face smooshed unattractively as she made a fish face.

Her eyes flew open in surprise and pain as she gurgled at me, unable to scream with my hand on her face like that. She tried to shake her head but couldn't after I placed my free hand on her forehead, holding her still.

A cork popped, and Julian leaned down, getting in her face. Over and over again her nostrils flared as she drew in angry breath after angry breath. Her eyes were wide, showing too much white.

Julian didn't fuck around and quickly put the clear, glass vial to her lips. He tipped it up and poured the liquid into her mouth. He covered her mouth with his hand and I let go of her forehead in order to plug her nose. Damien jerked on top of her as she furiously bucked her body beneath him.

She made gagging, choking sounds before she swallowed. Once I knew the liquid had gone down her throat I removed my fingers from her nose.

Tears trailed out of her too wide for her face eyes, running down into her hair.

"You can remove your hands now, Quint," Julian instructed me.

Immediately, I pulled my hands away. I rubbed my palms on my jeans in an effort to rub the feel of her skin away.

Ariel didn't know it but she gave off a sweet heat of her own. Now that I had experienced it for myself, I didn't want to have to endure the touch of another female.

"What, are you mute?" Julian mocked in a high voice and I felt my eyes grow wide. What was this now? "No, bitch, but you are now. This is your payment for putting your hands on her. And if you ever, *ever* tell anyone about this, about us being here, your insides will start to rot and there won't be a damn thing anyone will be able to do for you."

Julian straightened, and I stood. Damien crawled off of her now limp body and the three of us loomed over her.

She opened her mouth wide, probably so she could let out an impressive scream, but no sound came out at all.

Silently, she choked as her hands wrapped around her throat.

Julian laughed while we turned away and left her like that. Damien remained silent and I was thoughtful. Thinking on Julian's comment about being mute and watching her clutch at her throat while no sound came out, I realized something. Dash must have filled him in on something he hadn't shared with me and I wondered what else could have possibly been said to my sweet Ariel.

The car ride to their house was eerily quiet, each of us lost in our own thoughts. When I pulled up to the curb, they got out of my car without a word spoken or a backwards glance.

We had accomplished what we'd set out to do and we didn't need to discuss it.

And Ariel never needed to know.

Chapter Eighteen

TIME WAS RUNNING out and this needed to be done. I would rather it be me who did it and not Mr. Cole. But I was smart about it and had made a phone call before coming in here because no way I could tackle this on my own. And, if I were to be honest, being alone with my mother's things made my stomach hurt and my skin crawl.

I looked around the absurdly large walk-in closet and couldn't keep the grimace off my face. My mother must have had a busy summer swiping Mr. Cole's credit card. She certainly hadn't had this much stuff when we'd first moved in. She could have given out fifty lap dances a day and she still wouldn't have been able to afford half of this fancy crap.

I found it interesting that nothing in here belonged to Marcus. Had she kicked him out of his own closet when we moved in here? Where were his things? Who put up with nonsense like that? I didn't think any amount of sex with my mother had been worth getting kicked out of your own space and then paying for her to refill it with brand new things for her. Then again, I'd yet to have sex so what did I know. I could be wrong.

Mr. Cole had not said a single word to me about what he planned on doing with my mother's things. It's like he either didn't think about it at all or he was expecting her to come back any day now. I hoped he didn't think about it at all because no way would she be magically appearing on the front stoop three days from now.

Besides, I didn't want him to have to deal with her stuff, not with everything else he had going on. I had nothing going on and she was my mother, my responsibility. I could take care of it.

I picked up a red, high heeled shoe with a delicate looking ankle strap. We wore the same size shoes. That didn't mean I wanted to keep them for myself. I didn't want anything of hers and planned on donating it all to a second-hand store. I threw the shoe on to the floor, close to where I had gotten it from.

After shaking open a large black garbage bag I had found in the pantry, I tied a corner of the bag around the doorknob to the closet door. It would be easier to work with rather than dragging it around behind me or picking it up off the floor and having to shake it open every time I wanted to stuff something in there.

I latched onto the first piece of clothing I saw and ripped it off the metal hanger. The hanger clanked loudly against the bar and the other metal hangers around it. I didn't even know you could still buy metal clothes hangers, I thought it was plastic or nothing. I didn't even think you could get the wooden ones anywhere. Why was I standing here holding in my hands a dress that had belonged to my mother and thinking about whether or not you can buy metal or wooden clothes hangers anymore?

It was official, I had gone off the deep end and completely lost my mind. What in the hell was the matter with me lately? I felt so far from my normal self that it kind of scared me. The past month, my emotions had been all over the place and I didn't feel very stable *or* sane. Was this part of the grieving process? If so, it sucked. I craved stability and desperately wanted to feel some semblance of normal. Which was stupid because I had no clue what normal even consisted of.

The dress I held in my hands was a deep, dark, wine colored red. The material soft and slinky. I held it up for further inspection and couldn't hold in the small laugh that escaped me at what I saw.

The dress screamed Vivian Kimber, only a better quality.

I held the dress up in front of me, taking stock. She and I had been almost the exact same size.

The dress had two-inch-wide shoulder straps. The skirt hit just above mid-thigh, making the length indecent. The front was so low-cut half of my bra would have been showing were I to actually wear the expensively offensive thing. I couldn't remember ever having seen my mother wearing this dress.

I let it drop to the carpeted floor instead of stuffing it into the black garbage bag.

When Addison walked into the closet twenty minutes later, six more dresses had joined the dark red one in a pile on the floor. The garbage bag remained empty and where I had hung it on the doorknob. Every single dress I had dropped to the floor, my mother had never worn and all of them still had their price tags attached.

"Abel should be here with boxes soon," Addison told me from his place in the doorway.

I held the dark green dress clutched in my hands up for his inspection.

"Do you think this is my color?" I asked him quietly.

"Do you honestly want to wear her clothes?" He shot back immediately.

I shook my head. No, I absolutely did not want to wear anything that had belonged to that woman. Her clothes ranged from the ultimate stripper to slutty Stepford wife. I didn't think either would suit me very well.

"Why do you need the boxes?" He asked in a serious voice. "You don't actually want to keep any of this stuff, do you, Ariel? We should get rid of it all. No reminders of her. A fresh new start for you."

Throw it all away… so much waste. All of it, a massive waste.

When I didn't answer, he pushed it. "What are you going to do with all this stuff? Her stuff?"

"Salvation Army?" I responded and shrugged. "Goodwill? Whatever second-hand store that's closest and takes donations. I don't have a preference. Mr. Cole is going to be all moved out in less than two weeks and all this needs to be gone before then."

"Just throw it away," he insisted.

"No."

He really needed to stop pushing me on this.

Angry, I balled my fist around the green dress, clenching it in my hands and wrinkling the material.

"If you aren't going to keep it then why do you care where the fuck it goes?"

I clutched the dress to my chest as I tried to slow my breathing. My entire body trembled and the lights on the ceiling flickered briefly, off then back on.

He didn't seem bothered in the slightest by the lights going in and out.

"Do you know what it feels like to be hungry?" I asked him in a quiet, strangled voice. "To be starving and open the refrigerator only to find it empty save for a half empty carton of spoiled milk, beer and, if you're lucky, a slice of cheese for you to eat. The freezer's only got Vodka and ice trays in it. The cupboards are bare. What do you do? What do you do, Addison? Do you wake up your mom to ask her for money so you can go to the store and get something to eat? I'll warn you, she's naked and will be extremely hungover when you wake her up. And, as an added bonus, the same will go for the dude she brought home with her. Neither will be happy to see you. So, I ask again, what do you do, Addison?"

He stood with his shoulder propped against the door frame and his arms crossed over his chest. His body looked carved from stone, one little crack and the entire image would crumble, and he'd be reduced to a pile of rubble on the carpet.

A muscle in his jaw ticked as he ground out through clenched teeth, "Did that happen to you a lot?"

He was angry on my behalf. Oh, he was so very angry. Anger was okay, but he didn't answer my question and I think he didn't answer it because he couldn't. He had no idea what being hungry, really hungry, felt like. I hoped he never had to find out.

"You don't wake her up and you don't ask her for anything," I whispered, and the trembling stopped. I hadn't calmed down, the storm still raged inside me, I'd simply silenced it on the surface. "You go to sleep hungry. You get up hungry, and you go to school hungry. You don't get to eat until lunch time rolls around and you get a tray of food provided to you by the school because your family is poor. Then, when you go home at the end of the day, you might have to do it all over again. Unless you're lucky. If you're lucky, your mother will have picked up some packets of Ramen and a box of Saltine Crackers for you."

He straightened, moving away from the doorway and took a step in my direction.

Holding the dress out in front of me like a shield, I barked, "Stop."

Immediately, he stopped moving forward.

Looking pained, and sounding exactly how he looked, he whispered, "You're not ever going to have to go through anything like that ever again. I can promise you that. You'll not ever have to go hungry again and you sure as shit won't be eating Ramen and crackers every day, or ever again. This is exactly what I'm talking about, why you need a fresh start and need to get rid of all this," his arm swept out, waving around the closet, indicating all of my mother's belongings, "shit. We need to throw it all in the fucking garbage."

When he stopped speaking he took another step in my direction but stopped when I took a step back, away from him.

I wasn't backing up because I was afraid of him. I backed up because I wanted to make my point clear before he got close to me and made me think of something else.

"You're missing the point," I said as I glared at him.

"And what is the point?"

Good question.

What was the point? What was my point in sharing all this garbage from my past with him?

I swallowed down the lump in my throat and searched inside myself for some bravery. There was a whole lot in there, just sitting around waiting for me to use it.

"I have never, not once, owned clothes that had not been worn by someone else before me, not until I moved in with Mr. Cole. He gave my mother money and a credit card. When he did that, she threw out all my things and made me buy all new things online. Before moving here, I had only ever owned *one* new pair of shoes, and they had been a gift from one of the men in her life. I have lived my whole life wearing second-hand goods, someone else's castoffs. Old, worn and used things. Things people should have probably thrown in the trash. Those were my things, my belongings. I don't even want to consider what my mother would have dressed me in if weren't for places like the Salvation Army or Goodwill. I wouldn't have had a winter coat or boots to wear in the cold. I would have been dressed in rags. Do you get my point now?"

Yes, I sounded like a bitch at the end of my little speech, but I didn't care. This was something I felt strongly about.

"No," he ground out. "No, I do not fucking get your point. Explain it to me."

That's what I was trying to do.

A sound escaped me, laughter. It was bitter, and not at all friendly.

For the first time since having me the lot of them, I felt a tiny sliver of resentment. We were so different. I know some of them had struggled in their lives, I'd only heard snippets and never gotten the full story on any of them yet. But they had all grown up with money. With nice things and nice clothes and food in their bellies. I didn't hate them for it, I didn't have room for hate in my heart. But they would likely never fully understand me because none of them had any idea what it was like to be me.

"My point, Addison, is, that all this stuff that you are insisting on throwing away could make a whole world of a difference for someone else, someone in need. You don't get it because you've never been that person before, that person who desperately needed something and not been able to afford it. You don't know what it's like and if you did, you wouldn't be alright with simply throwing all of this stuff away. I'm not okay with it, though. I am so far from being okay with it, it isn't even funny. You don't get it because you have no idea what the other side looks like. I can understand that, really, I can. But I'm not going to change my mind about it, and I'm not going to throw this stuff in the garbage. I asked you and your brother to come over and help because I don't want to do this by myself and I missed you, but if you're going to keep up this nonsense then you are going to have to leave and I will apologize to you for wasting your time while you are on your way out the door. I'm not trying to be-"

"Shut up, Ariel," he said, rudely cutting me off, his voice thick with emotion.

He took another step towards me and when I didn't back away from him, he kept on coming.

I dropped the dress to the floor and held my arms out, waiting for him to reach me. His big, thick arms wrapped around me, engulfing me. I was pulled into his wide chest and he pressed his face into my hair.

"Not to be mean, pretty girl, but I don't think I want to hear about how you grew up anymore. It's sad and awful and it makes me angry."

I nodded, my cheek brushing across the soft fabric of his t-shirt. I didn't want to make him feel bad and I didn't want to make him sad and angry. I wouldn't be sharing with him anymore, not if it made him feel that way.

"Okay," I said, agreeing with him quickly. "No more sharing. I promise."

It seemed it was my turn to do the promising.

He sighed loudly and gave me a squeeze.

"I didn't actually mean it. You can share whatever you want to with me and I will listen to every single word you have to say. I want to know everything you have to tell me."

Yeah, that wasn't going to happen. Not after telling me how my memories made him feel.

His chest shuddered as he blew out a deep breath, causing the hair around my head to stir. His arms lowered, moving away from me and he took a giant step back. I missed his heat and had the urge to be the one to make the next step, to step into him and wrap my arms around his middle. I didn't. With Addison, I needed him to make the first move. For now. Hopefully not for forever.

Chapter Nineteen

TEN MINUTES LATER when Abel breezed through the door with an armful of unmade cardboard boxes, Addison and I had an entire garbage bag filled full of dresses. They had been folded and carefully placed inside the bag. Watching the plastic bag fill up made my heart feel incredibly light.

"I've got more in the truck," Abel said as he dropped the cardboard to the floor. "There's also a role of tape out there, too." He clapped his hands, loudly, making me jump. "Alright, pretty girl, where do you want me?"

I grinned at him, making him pause mid-step and blink at me.

"Yeah," he muttered under his breath. "A seriously fucking *pretty* girl."

My grin turned into a flat-out smile. I had no problem with them calling me a pretty girl.

A black, high heeled shoe flew through the air and smacked Abel in the cheek. It clattered to the floor as Abel pressed the palm of his hand against the side of his face.

"Explain yourself, twin," Abel snarled at his brother. "And do it quick or else we are going to have more than words."

"Maybe I just felt like hitting you with something." Addison shrugged, like he didn't have a care in the world, like his twin brother hadn't just threatened him with violence.

Abel folded his arms over his wide chest and scowled at his brother. A visible red mark marred his cheek. His vibrant green eyes heated, lighting from within with a burning hot rage.

The hair on my arms stood to attention as the atmosphere in the room went electric. Power danced along my skin, making me shiver.

Whatever they were doing, I didn't think it would end good.

"Calm down, twin," Addison said as he waved a hand dismissively in his brother's direction. He hadn't even bothered to look in said direction. His entire focus was on the clothes hanging before him and if he felt the atmosphere in the room change he didn't let on. He seemed as cool as could be and completely unconcerned.

Maybe I should pick up a shoe and chuck it at his head? He looked like he could use a good thumping. Then I remembered the look on Quinton's face when I'd hit him in the head with that rock and thought better of it. Addison was here to help me, and I had already gotten crazy on him once, he didn't need to add me injuring him to the list.

If I started assaulting all of them, they would likely contact the Council and see about trading me. Not really, though. They weren't getting rid of me that easily.

Another shoe sailed through the air, this one purple and had a freakishly sharp looking heel about 4 inches long. That sucker could do some serious damage and was probably capable of taking out an eye. It collided with the back of Addison's white-haired head with a smack before dropping to the floor.

I made a rough, disbelieving noise as my head whipped around, seeking out Abel with my eyes.

He stood there with an angry glower on his face, his wide, thick thighs spread apart, feet planted firmly in the carpet. His arms hung loosely at his sides and he looked alert and ready for almost anything.

What he didn't look like was someone who had just thrown a shoe at his brother's head. I should have at least caught his arm lowering.

Hmm… curious.

"Did you… did you just use magic to throw that shoe at your brother's head?" I asked in an excited voice.

"This isn't funny, Ariel," Addison grumbled darkly.

"I'm not laughing," I told him without taking my eyes off of Abel.

Abel ignored his brother and asked me, "Do you want to learn?"

Boy, did I ever.

I clapped my hands together happily and bounced up and down on the balls of my feet.

"Please," I whined in an excited voice. There was no hiding just how excited I was at the thought of learning something new.

"What the fuck?" Addison growled. "He just tried to brain me to death with a hooker shoe and neither of you seem concerned about me in the least. I could be bleeding to death over here from the massive head wound I just received courtesy of my own goddamn brother."

The smile on my face grew bigger by the second and I sincerely wished it had been me who'd thrown the shoe.

"Come here," Abel ordered softly, and I didn't hesitate walking straight to him.

"I don't think this is a good idea," Addison grumbled. Abel ignored him, so I did too.

Still smiling, I stopped directly in front of him. He grabbed me by the shoulders and turned me until I faced Addison and the way I had come from. His heat hit me as he pressed his front into my back. He placed his hands on my hips and pressed his face in my neck.

"Close your eyes and clear your mind," he murmured.

Clear my mind? Was he crazy? He had to be. Clearing my mind sounded impossible with his big body pressed into mine and his heat all around me.

I closed my eyes, I could at least do that.

My eyes flew right back open when one of them snickered, I could never tell which one because they always sounded exactly the same. Still, my money was on Addison. Abel had no reason to laugh at me at the moment.

Abel put slight pressure on my hips, squeezing. "Ignore my brother," he said. "Now, close your eyes and clear your mind. Otherwise, this will never work and we're wasting our time."

Abel's lips, soft and smooth, brushed against the pulse in my throat and I stopped breathing for a second.

"Close your eyes," he murmured against my overheated skin. "Close your eyes and let it all go.

I closed my eyes and let out a deep breath, ready to try it again. I couldn't give up after the first try. Addison could laugh at me all he wanted. Abel could get up in my space. Whatever. I could ignore them both.

I blew out another deep breath and relaxed against Abel's big, warm body. The hands on my hips loosened, he wasn't holding me to him anymore, just touching me for the sake of touching. I was happy to have him standing at my back, it made relaxing my body all the easier.

With effort, I pushed all the garbage in my head to the side. It wasn't easy, and it took some time. I stood there, rearranging my thoughts, for a good twenty minutes before I was able to blank my mind and think of absolutely nothing.

The only thing I saw with my eyes closed was darkness. Until I reached for the now ever-present flame I knew was there waiting for me. It was tiny but grew stronger, burning brighter as I reached out to it in my mind.

"Good," Abel murmured against my ear in encouragement. "Very good. Without opening your eyes, I want you to visualize the object you want to manipulate in your mind. Do you remember what the shoe that hit my twin looks like? Or, even any of the other shoes in this closet. Whatever shoe you pick, I want you to see that, and only that, in your mind's eye. Nothing else. Once you have it in your sight, it's yours to manipulate. Like your flame, it's yours, just waiting for you to do something with it. So, do something with it."

I was concentrating so hard that I couldn't come up with something sarcastic to snap at him. Besides, it would ruin my concentration. I couldn't remember what the shoe that had smacked into the back of Addison's head looked like. But, I did remember a very pretty black one with only a three-inch heel that looked like something my mother hadn't bought for herself but had probably been a gift.

I pulled the image of it into my mind and watched it dance around before my inner flame.

"What now?" I asked in a husky voice.

"Now, you manipulate it," he whispered. "You make it yours and you do what you want with it. You put your energy into it and make it do your bidding. Eventually, you will be able to do this with your eyes open. It might take a while, but you'll get there. For now, you need to keep your eyes closed so you can concentrate."

I thought about what he'd said, really thought about it, and the shoe began to spin in circles inside my head.

From across the room, Addison gasped.

Now that it was mine to do with as I pleased, I actually had to come up with something to do with it. Nothing came to mind and the flame inside my head grew even brighter.

"She's not disciplined," Addison ground out. "You should stop this now. She's not ready for it. She needs to be taught in a contained area. There's too many things in here that could potentially be damaged."

"Nonsense," Abel told his brother in a confident voice. "None of this shit matters. Who cares if she destroys something in here. She's fine. Leave her alone."

"Abel," Addison pushed out in strangled voice I hadn't heard him use before. "You should not have said that. She's a little, um, oversensitive when it comes to throwing things away, I don't think she's going to like hearing you talk about destroying things in here in such a casual manner."

The more agitated their conversation made me, the faster and faster the shoe spun in my mind.

In a disbelieving voice, Abel muttered, "What the hell are you talking about? She's fine. Leave her alone."

"Abel," Addison barked at his brother. "Be quiet for a second."

The shoe spun round and round inside my mind. So fast it started to blur. Thoughts of my mother and why I was surrounded by her things crept into my mind.

I shook my head, trying to shake the negative thoughts from my mind as I opened my eyes.

I shoved the shoe out of my mind, giving it a solid, mental toss. The flame flickered before going out.

I watched in awe as the shoe I had seen in my head flew through the air, crashing into the wall. It bounced off the wall and landed on the carpet with a thump where it immediately burst into flames.

My eyes rounded in horror and I screamed, loud and girly. The fire seemed to grow larger as my screaming grew louder. The flames grew higher, taller, crawling towards the ceiling.

I watched in open mouthed horror. Oh, what had I done now.

"Ariel," Abel yelled in my ear as he placed his hands on my biceps and shook me roughly. My teeth clacked together as my head rattled from side to side.

A harsh beeping started, higher than the beeping of the alarm on the doors and windows. The smoke detector. That horrible sound was the smoke detector in the master bedroom going off.

Shit.

My uncontrolled emotions and the magic inside me that I had absolutely zero control over were going to burn Mr. Cole's house down.

I didn't want that.

What was the matter with me? I couldn't do anything right. And now I was going to burn Mr. Cole's house down when all I was trying to do was take some of the burden off of his shoulders.

"Where's the fire extinguisher?" Abel shouted at me.

I shook my head; how would I know where the damn fire extinguisher was? It's not like I'd ever had to use one before. I didn't just light shit on fire with my mind on the daily.

Addison ripped a dress off of a hanger and started beating out the fire with it. He hit it over and over again until the fire went out. The carpet around the shoe was a charred, blacked out mess and the shoe still smoked a little.

Addison held up the dress he'd used to put the fire out. It had gaping holes burned into it and was completely ruined. "I'm sorry, Ariel," he said in a sad voice. "We're not going to be able to donate this one. I'm afraid it's headed for the trash."

"Girl," Abel said, his voice shaking with suppressed laughter. "You tried to burn down Mr. Cole's house." He snickered, and a laugh escaped.

I whirled around and jabbed my finger at him. "I did not!" I shouted, getting angry.

Addison coughed, and I could tell he was trying not to laugh too.

"This isn't funny," I shouted, my voice vibrating with anger.

They both lost the battle at the same time and burst out laughing.

I shook my head, exasperated. With them and myself. It's not like I had intentionally tried to light anything on fire, but it still happened anyway, and I could have easily burned the house down while I stood by and stupidly watched.

"Oh my god, twin, you should have seen her face." Addison said as he clutched his stomach, like laughing this much had pained him. "She looked like she was going to piss herself when that shoe went up. Priceless. I wish we would have filmed it."

"Yeah, yeah," I grumbled under my breath. "Laugh it up, assholes."

That set them off again and they laughed harder.

Eventually, they calmed down and we were able to finish the job at hand without any more mishaps. They only made fun of me a little for trying to burn down the house, which I appreciated greatly. They spent two long hours with me, helping pack everything up. They never once complained and after the little shoe debacle, they stopped telling me to throw everything in the trash, I think it had something to do with Addison pulling Abel aside, outside of my hearing range and whispering to him. He probably told him not to push the loony girl any further out of fear I might light him on fire next.

In the end, there were five boxes of shoes and ten garbage bags full of clothes. The only things I threw away was her underwear, open containers of lotion and the like, and used makeup. Her bottles of perfume went into a box. Handbags and wallets went into a box. Her jewelry I put in a box by itself and put it to the side, I didn't know what Mr. Cole had given her and if he would want any of it back.

The only thing I kept for myself was a tattered old box I found hidden behind a stack of suitcases. When I opened the box, I found hand written letters from my mother and to her. There was a whole mess of photographs and a few other things in there. Immediately, I closed the box without looking through the contents. Curiosity raged inside me but I didn't want an audience when I looked through it all. I wanted to be alone for that because I had no idea what I would find.

My Salt and Pepper twins were very sweet and, even though I could tell they wanted to ask me about the tattered box, neither of them made a peep about it.

They carried it all out to their truck and loaded it up without me having to ask them to and without me having to lift a finger.

I offered to order pizza but they both claimed they had something to do and needed to leave. I thanked them for the help and was sad to see them go. With Mr. Cole being gone, I was now all alone in the house and wasn't very appealing to me at the moment.

After locking the door behind the twins and arming the alarm, I grabbed the box out of my mother's now empty closet and headed up to my bedroom.

Chapter Twenty

AFTER LOCKING THE door, I slowly made my way over to the bed. I was in no hurry to look through the box.

Locking the door to my bedroom might seem a bit ridiculous considering I was in the house by myself and all the doors and windows leading to the outdoors were locked up tight and the alarm had been turned on. It wasn't ridiculous to me. I couldn't be in my bedroom by myself and not lock the door behind me. Paranoia and fear owned me, I was their bitch when I was in my bedroom and my bathroom. Too much had happened here when I was supposed to be alone.

I sat on the bed and scooted towards the center, dragging the box along with me. When I got to the center of the bed, I curled my legs to the side as my hip and my elbow pressed into the bed. The side of my face rested in the palm of my hand as I eyeballed the box.

I wanted to know what was in there, but, at the same time, I was scared out of my brain and did not want to know. Before today, I had never seen this box, or its contents, in my entire life. My mother had never struck me as the type of person to hold onto things like photographs, letters and keepsakes. The things in the box must have come before my time, or, from when I was too young to remember things. She had never, not ever, kept a photograph of me. There were no school pictures, no baby pictures, no nothing. And now I find pictures she had kept secret for the past however many years, maybe even more years than I had been on this earth.

It made my stomach churn.

She had hated me, honest to goodness, hated me. Her own daughter. What had I done to her to deserve such treatment? Maybe just being born had been enough in her book. It wasn't in mine. If she hadn't wanted to have kids then she should have learned how to use protection and maybe gotten herself on birth control.

I sat up straight, stretched my legs out in front of me and crossed my feet at the ankles.

The box sat on the bed, taunting me.

I could think of not one single person she had cared about enough to keep mementos of. Not one single, solitary human being. Not even herself. I knew how much she'd loved herself and had enjoyed her own image. She'd never even had pictures of herself around.

A small part of me wanted to take the box and everything inside of it out to the yard and light the bitch on fire. A far bigger part of me wanted to rip that sucker open and pour through every single little thing in there like it was my sole purpose in this world.

I sighed heavily as I leaned back against the headboard.

Why did I feel like the secrets hidden inside that box were going to be life altering? Probably because that hateful cow wouldn't have kept the stuff inside the box for years and years if it hadn't meant anything to her.

Since I had never known her to care about anyone besides herself, this was huge.

I had to re-open the box, there was no getting around it for me.

I reached a hand inside and blindly pulled out the first thing I touched.

A folded-up piece of paper. A letter. I wished it had been a picture instead, that might have been easier to take in.

The paper was worn and had clearly been handled a great deal.

With shaking hands, I unfolded the letter and began reading.

My dearest Vivian,

I know you hate me and for that I am sorry. Sorrier than you will ever know. I won't apologize to you because I know you don't want to hear an apology from me and it wouldn't mean anything to you. I understand this. I don't have to like it, but I do understand it.

I have been patient with you. But, time is growing short for me and I need to see her. There are things I have to tell her, things she needs to know. Things only I can tell her.

Please, my beautiful sister, I beg of you, let me see my daughter.

I have money and will pay you, if that's what it will take. I am more than willing to give you whatever it is that you want. Name your price and it's yours.

Please –

I crumpled the letter into a ball in my hands.

My mind was empty, blank.

I had been wrong to open the box and I didn't want to read any more.

Fuck this.

Fuck it all.

I pushed everything I had just read out of my mind. I couldn't deal with it right now. I couldn't do it.

Not now, maybe not ever.

Mr. Cole wasn't coming home tonight, and I really did not want to be alone. But, I didn't want to be here. And, I didn't want to be next door.

Where could I go if I left this place? This wasn't home anymore, and I needed to get out of here.

I tossed the letter back into the box and got up to pack a bag.

I thought I knew where I could go. Hopefully, going there would erase all this bullshit I thought I had just learned from that one letter.

I grabbed my bag and the stupid box, I didn't want to read any more of it but I also didn't think I could leave it behind. I thought it might disappear if I left it behind, then I'd never get answers. I took both out to my Range Rover. The overnight bag, I put in the front passenger seat. The box, I stuck in the far back.

As I drove, I focused on forgetting everything that had recently happened. Thankfully, I was an old pro when it came to pushing things aside and pretending like they never happened.

Chapter Twenty-One

I STARED AT the adorable cottage from inside the safety of my Range Rover and gripped the steering wheel tightly between my fingers.

Back at Dash's house.

Again.

What was I doing back here?

Good Question.

I was back here to spend the night, even though the owner of the house didn't know that yet. I did this so I could judge whether or not I really wanted to stay here after I moved out of Mr. Cole's house when he moved away and it seemed like a far better option than being alone right now. Since I couldn't, wouldn't live at the main house with the guys, I needed another place to stay so I wasn't homeless. Quinton said this was the place for me and I had to take his word for it. So, I was here, taking the initiative. Probably not the wisest solution.

The sun was setting in the sky, the forest around the cottage already dark. All my life I had lived in the city surrounded by tall buildings, constant traffic, and never-ending noise. The first time I had ever even walked into the woods had been the night of the full moon ritual. I had no desire to go exploring in the woods. I had no desire to go bird watching or whatever. I didn't have the appropriate shoes for hiking, so that was out. Camping sounded extremely uncomfortable, not to mention the whole going to the bathroom outside while squatting down next to some tree nonsense. Camp fires looked cool and I would love to roast a marshmallow and eat it. But you didn't need to go into woods to have a camp fire, you could easily have one in a backyard, or at a beach.

Scaredy cat, who me? Never.

I didn't miss the big city and I had no desire to go back, but I would take hanging out in houses over playing in the woods any day.

I blinked, coming back to myself inside my Rover. My knuckles had turned white. What in the hell was I doing sitting in my Rover in front of Dash's house thinking about exploring the forest? Rabid little squirrels. I shuddered in my seat. Beady-eyed, puffy-tailed little weirdos.

I pulled my keys out of the ignition, grabbed my bag off of the passenger seat and opened my door.

Movement in the rear-view mirror caught my eye and I paused with my door ajar. The dome light came on, momentarily cutting off my view of what was happening in the mirror.

Was Dash outside?

A glance to the side showed me the cottage was lit up from within, the chimney smoking. Would he go outside and leave all the lights inside on?

The overhead light dimmed for a moment, then shut off entirely.

The mirror showed that there was no one behind me. Thankfully.

I shut my door and hit the button to lock the doors. A click sounded throughout the Rover, letting me know I was safely locked inside.

I clutched the bag to my chest as I eyed the rear-view mirror.

There was nothing out there.

What was the matter with me? I didn't know but I had a really bad feeling in the pit of my stomach growing larger and more acidic by the second.

If I had Dash's phone number, I wouldn't have hesitated to call him and make him walk out to my car and walk me safely inside.

Something was seriously not right.

I looked at the vehicles I had parked next to and my stomach twisted for a different reason. I had no idea what Dash drove. Did he have more than one car? Was he in there alone? Did he have another client here? A date?

I scrunched up my face as I chewed on my bottom lip. I probably should have called first. I didn't want to interrupt him if he had a date. My throat tightened, and I clutched the bag tighter to my chest. Why did the thought of Dash on a date bother me so much?

A conversation I had overheard floated through my brain.

"She's too young. I'm not ready to give up my social life for a girl I don't even know and am expected to share," Dash had said.

Julian's reply had been immediate.

"By social life, I assume you mean dating and sleeping with random's you bring home with you?"

Even Quint had told me about how much Dash liked to sleep with the ladies.

The black Camaro gleamed shiny and masculine. It looked like something I could see Dash driving. The big, silver, SUV parked beside it could have easily been driven by a male or female.

I should have gotten Dash's phone number from Tyson and called ahead first.

Why did I care so much?

I had no interest in the truth at the moment ,so I left that particular question be.

The mirror showed nothing but trees and the driveway behind me.

This was absurd. I was supposed to be done being afraid.

There was nothing out there.

I squared my shoulders. Brave, I needed to be brave. There wasn't always something lurking around every corner, some great danger, some new torture, waiting to lash out and attack me.

I needed to step away from that mindset, far away from it and start to think positively. If I was constantly thinking unhappy thoughts, then how would I ever find happiness?

Fuck it.

I hit the button and unlocked the doors. If I sat out here much longer, it would be full on dark and I would never get out of the Rover. I opened my door and climbed down quickly before I could lose my nerve.

I slammed the door, looped my arm through the straps of my bag and bleeped the locks on the Rover.

Maybe I should have left the bag in my vehicle. The bag seemed a bit presumptuous but leaving it in the Rover would mean I would have to come back out and get it if I stayed.

I sprinted across the stone walkway. I kept my eyes focused on the black door, my prize. I was too big of a chicken to look behind me, but I felt it. Eyes on me. The hair on the back of my neck stood up as tingles raced down my spine.

There was someone out there, I could feel them, and they were watching me.

What felt like years later, I made it to the door. I slapped my open palm on the door over and over again. My heart sped up to an almost unbearable speed and I was afraid it was going to leap right out of my chest, so it could run away from me.

Slap! Slap! Slap!

What the hell was taking him so long?

I imagined him wearing that ridiculous black robe, sprawled in a chair with his legs spread wide with some faceless brunette kneeling between his open legs. His eyes were screwed up tight, his lips pursed in a grimace and his crotch was hidden from view due to the bobbleheads ministrations. She was a person I had made up in my mind, conjured out of thin air. Nameless. Faceless. Not real. And I hated her.

Holy crap! I needed to get a grip before I lost my mind.

I glanced over my shoulder hurriedly, just to make sure there wasn't really anyone behind me, ready to murder me. There wasn't. The driveway, tiny yard and as far as I could see, remained empty and void of human beings.

I let out a relieved breath and turned back towards the door when I heard it opening.

About time.

He needed a doorbell.

Dash stood in the doorway, frowning down at me.

Slutty bastard.

At least he had more clothes on than his little black robe, sort of. Black, drawstring pajama pants. Bare feet. Naked chest on display. He wasn't wearing a shirt. And his nipples were pierced. Like Quinton's. Black barbells decorated each nipple, and I was staring.

Damn it.

I cleared my throat and blurted, "There's someone out here, spying on me. Maybe it's one of your girlfriends."

I winced. I had sounded like a jealous crazy person.

He didn't seem to care.

He grabbed my free hand with one of his and pulled me into the house. His eyes scanned the driveway right before he slammed the door shut.

"What are you talking about?" He hissed at me.

Okay, maybe he did care that I sounded like a crazy jealous person. Or, maybe it was the small fact I had showed up at his house out of the blue and hadn't bothered to call first and let him know so he could get rid of his date. Wouldn't want your little high school soon-to-be life partner (or whatever) to show up and cramp your style so you couldn't get your rocks off.

Again, slutty bastard.

He shook my arm roughly.

“Ariel,” he hissed my name. “Talk to me.”

I sighed and told him the truth. Not the part about me imagining him getting frisky with some faceless bimbo. I kept that part to myself. I didn’t think it wise to share that with him. Not at this point in time. Probably not ever.

“Julian,” he yelled making me jump.

“You are going to stay in here where it’s safe,” he told me in a much quieter, gentler voice. “Julian will stay inside with you while Damien and I go outside and take a look around. If there’s someone out there we will find them. It’s probably just a hunter, though. The assholes are constantly trespassing on my land.”

I loved that he didn’t think I was a crazy person and he was going out to investigate on my behalf. He didn’t have a security panel by his door like at Mr. Cole’s house that let me know there was a security system. I kind of hated the one at Mr. Cole’s house. It beeped at me all the time and made me rush around to do things for it. Punch in the code, activate, deactivate. Beep. Beep. Beep. The thing was bossy and annoying, but it did do one thing very well, which is what it was supposed to do. When it was activated, and all the doors and windows were locked, I felt extremely safe being there. Dash going outside to check things out for me would go a long way towards making me feel safe staying here. Quinton had told me there was a bedroom here for me, I hoped it wasn’t on the main floor.

Feet thundered on the stairs, more than one set. Julian and Damien coming down the stairs. I hoped they didn't have a girl with them.

Dash turned towards the sound of approaching footsteps, exposing his bare back to me.

I gasped in shock at what I saw on his back. My eyes filled with tears as they raked over his skin. Scars. So many scars. Thin, white lines crisscrossed all over the entirety of his back. The scars looked old, the skin raised where it overlapped others, it looked to be several layers deep.

My heart made a valent attempt to crawl up my throat so it could come out of my mouth in the form of a sob. Something I'm sure he wouldn't appreciate hearing.

It looked like he'd been whipped. For years. And years.

I placed my palm on my chest, trying to slow down my heartbeat.

He whirled around to face me, hiding his back from me. He leaned towards me, threateningly. I backed up until my back met with the door. My bag slid from my arm, crashing into the floor.

With a face full of thunder, he snarled, "Not pretty enough for you, princess? What's the matter, don't like what you see? Don't worry, Ariel, you won't ever have to touch me."

With that, he turned around and stormed off, further into the house. I stared after him with a world of heartbreak in my eyes and tears trailing down my cheeks. I hadn't done anything wrong and yet I'd still managed to mess everything up.

I swallowed thickly, painfully. I didn't want Dash to hate me.

Who had done that to his back? Quint had said that Dash's mother and grandmother had treated him horribly. Were they responsible for those horrific scars on his back, hadn't Quinton said something about his grandmother whipping him? I couldn't remember exactly what Quinton had said to me about it. Did he have more somewhere else I hadn't seen? I hoped not. Somehow, it would seem a whole lot worse if his family were the one's responsible for it. It would also make what happened between my mother and I seem just a little bit less horrible. Which didn't make me feel very good to think but I kind of liked that I wasn't the only messed up one in the bunch. It made fitting in with them seem a whole lot more realistic.

"What the hell was that?" Julian asked cautiously.

He and Damien stood across the room, watching me, both looking extremely upset.

I sighed, completely forgetting about the creepiness outside due to the fact I had so much bullshit to deal with inside.

Boys.

You really didn't need more than just the one. More than one was a headache.

Chapter Twenty-Two

I DIDN'T KNOW Julian or Damien very well. One seemed nice and had always been sweet to me. The other one had a nice, non-complicated girlfriend who had sex with him whenever he wanted her to and she was older than me.

Both had seen me naked and neither would I consider a friend.

And, right now, both of them looked worried.

I didn't want to deal with this. Which seemed to be the story of my life now.

"Ariel," Julian prompted.

Julian had honey blonde hair that was buzzed extremely close to his head. He was tall and thin, but somehow still muscular. He had light brown eyes and a gold lip ring on his bottom lip. He wore blue jeans and a plain black, short-sleeved t-shirt. He didn't have any socks on either. If you took the lip ring out, and with the right clothes, Julian looked like he could fit in anywhere. If not for the magic, I wondered if Julian would still be best friends with Quinton, Damien and Dash. His personality didn't seem to fit in with the rest of theirs. Quint was Scary. Dash was angry. Damien seemed haughty. And Julian, well he seemed sweet.

Damien hadn't made a very good impression on me, but he was really pretty to look at in a cold, untouchable sort of way.

He had a thin, sharp, angular face. His hair was blonde. Long on top, shaved on the sides. He had light brown eyes framed by extremely thick, feminine lashes. His skin was tanned to golden perfection. He wasn't dressed casual like the others but instead wore black slacks and a dark blue long-sleeved button up dress shirt. He wasn't barefoot either and had black socks on his feet.

People who walked around barefoot were weird. My feet always got cold.

"I think there was someone outside when I got here. Dash was going to go check things out and…" And, what? I didn't know how to stay quiet when faced with someone else's horrible truths.

"What?" Damien asked cautiously. I think it was the first time he had ever spoken directly to me. "Who was outside? There's no one around for miles."

I puffed up my cheeks and blew out a large breath. Now this one, he would think me a crazy person.

"Julian," Dash said coldly as he walked back into the room. "You stay inside with her. Damien and I will check things out outside, make sure there's no one creeping around."

He wouldn't even look at me. Holy crap. Panic threatened to choke me. This was not good. We weren't friends yet, but we were going to get there, I knew we were going to get there. And I liked him. His quiet intensity and the depths of darkness in his eyes. The way he watched everything, always so serious. The fact that I had only seen him smile the one time and it did funny things to my heart. All things I found endearing about him. He was closed off, guarded, and he reminded me a whole lot of myself.

And I knew myself, I knew how this was going to go if I didn't fix it now. If I didn't find some way to fix this now, it would fester and nothing good would come of it.

Think, Ariel Kimber, think.

I completely understood why he'd snarled at me and had had a similar reaction when someone took notice of my scars.

That was it, the key to solving this problem.

I stepped around my bag and walked directly towards where he was standing, avoiding me. I unzipped my black hoodie as I walked the last few feet to him, not stopping until I was directly in front of him.

He watched me with caution. Yeah, I didn't blame him one little bit. I definitely shouldn't have come here. Too late to turn back now.

"What are you doing?" He asked quietly. This time he met my eyes easily, curiosity shining bright in them. Also, there was fear in there. Fear of what? Me? Were they all afraid of me on some level? What the hell.

"Give me your hands," I ordered as I held my hands out to him, palms up. I waited patiently for him to place his hands in my open, outstretched ones.

He didn't make me wait long.

Without taking his eyes off of me, he laid his hands gently in mine. I let out a relieved breath. Honestly, I hadn't thought he was going to do it.

Before he could change his mind and pull away from me, I stepped closer, getting into his personal space.

Before I could think better of it, I lifted his hands in mine and placed them against my chest. His warm palms rested against my skin, covering my collarbones.

Covering my scars.

He stiffened as his gray eyes bored into mine.

"What are you doing?" Damien asked curiously from beside Dash. I was glad to hear he only sounded curious and not like an A-hole.

Dash ran his thumbs across my collarbones and I closed my eyes tight to ward off the light that had started shining bright in his eyes. Compassion and something far, far sweeter.

"What did this?" he murmured.

Interesting choice of words. What, not who.

"Doesn't matter," I whispered back. I stepped back, and his hands fell away. Quickly, I zipped my hoodie back up, covering my scars once more. "I just wanted you to know that you and I aren't so different and as long as my scars don't bother you, yours won't bother me."

"Ariel-"

I cut him off. Whatever he had to say, I was sure I didn't want to hear it.

"Quinton told me that you have a room here for me. I thought I would try it out, if that's okay with you. I don't mean to impose, and I probably should have called first. But Mr. Cole went out of town on business and I don't want to be in the house alone. I don't want to stay in the big house with the guys because… Well, I haven't been over there since… you know." I shrugged helplessly. Understanding filled his eyes and I knew I needed to explain no more. "So, do I have a room here or what?"

Rude. I could be so unbelievably rude when I was uncomfortable.

His face was incredibly soft, and he seemed completely unaffected by my rude tone.

"Yeah," he said softly. "You've got a room here. It's upstairs. Julian will show you the way. We'll be back in no time."

He raised his hand and gently brushed my hair back, tucking it behind my heavily pierced ear.

He stepped around me and sauntered towards the door. He'd put on a flannel shirt he hadn't bothered with buttoning, but it did the job of covering up the scars on his back. And he was still barefoot.

"Come on, Damien," he called over his shoulder before opening the door and walking outside. I almost smiled when he didn't bother closing the door behind him. Maybe my habits were catching.

Damien scooped up a pair of shiny black dress shoes and then he was out the door behind Dash. He actually managed to close the door behind him.

That left me alone with Julian.

He walked right passed me with a small smile on his face. He picked my overnight bag up off the floor and ushered me out of the room. He herded me through the house and up the staircase.

"Up you go," he mumbled as he placed his hand on the small of my back and he ushered me up the stairs.

I wanted to snap at him that I didn't need his assistance in walking up the stairs, I could do it myself.

I chewed on my lips to stop the words from coming out. His over friendly manner rubbed me the wrong way. He was the nicest person all the time. It was absurd. What did he have to be so nice and friendly about?

I was in a bad mood. It was based off of several things. Being here with people I wasn't entirely comfortable with, feeling like someone had been watching me, making my skin crawl, Hurting Dash's feelings. And, lastly, but certainly the most important, exposing part of my history to Dash in hopes of making him feel better. I shook my head angrily. First Tyson, now Dash. Who was next, Julian?

I did not think so.

I stomped up the stairs, shaking off his hand and made it to the landing before he did.

There were three doors, all of them closed.

He gestured to the left and I moved to the closed door he'd directed me to.

His hand curled around the doorknob and he paused. His lips curled up in a boyish smile, a smile that said he had a secret and it was a good one.

"Something for you to remember," he said. "Tyson never forgets anything. Not one single little thing."

Julian turned the knob and pushed the door open. He stepped into the room with me coming in directly behind him. What he'd said about Tyson didn't really register until after I had stepped into the spacious room.

It *was* a spacious room for a normal sized house. Which meant that it was half the size of my bedroom at Mr. Cole's house. The perfect size for a bedroom because the room I had at Mr. Cole's house was way too big for me, I would never be able to fill it with stuff and the space was wasted on me.

The floors were a gleaming dark wood and looked recently polished.

The walls were a sweet, sunny, canary yellow that made me want to laugh and cry at the same time. Now I got it about what Julian had said about Tyson. Canary yellow was my favorite color and I had only told Tyson, it had been on the second day of school.

There was one window facing the front of the house and the driveway. The window was framed by black, gauzy, see through curtains.

I stood in the middle of the room, moving in a slow circle, taking everything in.

The bed looked to be Queen size and the metal frame was painted a light, girly purple. The comforter was black and covered with yellow, open bloomed roses. Not all that different than the comforter I had on my bed at Mr. Cole's house. Tyson really had been paying attention. I wanted to know what color the sheets were. There was a pile of black and purple pillows at the head of the bed. One of the black ones even had silver sparkly sequins on it. Sparkly wasn't really my thing but I appreciated the attempt towards girly that they had made for my benefit.

A wicker love seat sat alongside the wall beside the window. There was a white padded cushion on the seat and the love seat was loaded down with more black, decorative pillows. At least there were no sequins or sparkles this time. It didn't make up for there not being a window seat and if I stuck around I would probably trade out the pillows for my own girly ones.

A thick, black, hand woven circular rug lay on the floor in front of the love seat. Everything had looked brand new until I got to the rug. I didn't much care for the thought of them spending money on me. I had a bed and a dresser at Mr. Cole's that were more than perfectly suitable for me and they could have easily been moved here. Now what would be done with them? Perhaps they could move it to Quinton's house so Mr. Cole wouldn't have to do anything with it.

There was another matching rug laid on the floor beside the bed.

A tall dresser was against the wall opposite the bed. A black framed oval mirror hung on the wall above the dresser.

My eyes skirted through my reflection in the mirror and I took in the rest of the things decorating the walls. A black and white Bad Religion concert poster had been framed and hung on the wall. It made me smile. I had never hung up posters of the things I liked up on my walls before. A framed Boondock Saints movie poster hung up on different wall. Norman Reedus stood shoulder-to-shoulder with Sean Patrick Flanery and they looked brutal but delicious standing together.

A tall, black bookshelf was pressed up against the wall behind the open bedroom door. A few steps closer showed me that half the bookshelf was empty, and the other half was filled with books about magic, the history of witchcraft, rituals, candles, spells, you name it. Some of the books looked old and worn and I wondered where they had come from.

Julian remained silent as he stood back, silently watching me take everything in. I appreciated him standing back, giving me space. If it had been Quinton or my Salt and Pepper twins they would have been in my space and drilling me with questions and the twins wouldn't have been able to remain quiet. Tyson would have probably been able to give me silence, but he wouldn't have given me space, I knew that much.

Julian was a different, rarer breed of male. One I liked a whole lot at the moment.

I would investigate the books on magic and whatnot at a later time, when I was alone and had the time to thoroughly examine them, when I could give them the time they rightfully deserved.

I looked away from the bookshelf to give the room another onceover and gasped in shock when I made it back to the bed. My lips parted, and my wide eyes were unsurprisingly wet.

Oh my god.

They didn't.

They couldn't have.

Why would they?

I blinked rapidly as I curled my fingers inwards, balling my hands into fists. My fingernails bit into my sweaty palms, likely leaving the indents of half-moons into my skin. The sharp bite of pain always served well to chase away my tears. I had scars more than on the area around my collarbones. My palms were covered in scars. At least these ones I had inflicted upon myself.

The scars were well worth it. Unshed tears had sometimes been what stood between me and a whole world of physical pain. A safety mechanism I no longer needed. I should probably look into a healthier way to deal with my emotions and to stop my tears. I didn't see it happening in this lifetime. Maybe in the next one, I wasn't really all too interested in breaking old habits in this lifetime.

"Do you know what these are?" Julian asked quietly, breaking the silence between us. I had kind of forgotten about him.

Perhaps I had been too hasty in my earlier assessment of him. Apparently, he couldn't keep quiet.

I nodded in answer, words had escaped me. My eyes never left the two beautiful black and white pen and ink drawings that were framed and hanging on the wall above the bed.

"Are you sure you know what these are?" Julian asked hesitantly.

I got his hesitancy. Those two pieces of art hanging over my new bed were priceless heirlooms that belonged to the Alexander family. They were beautiful black and white ink drawings, the details impressive. A true artist had created them.

They were giant, poster size tarot cards.

The Magician and The Moon.

The Alexander family had once owned an entire deck of poster sized ink drawings of tarot cards. They were over three hundred years old and the family had lost the majority of them in a fire years ago.

Only eight of the deck remained. Tyson had four and Quinton had the other four.

The Magician had come from Tyson and The Moon had come from Quinton.

This left them each down to three.

Do you know how many cards are in a full deck of tarot cards? Seventy-eight, that's how many. And they had a whole eight of them left between the two of them.

And they had each given me one of theirs. I had a hard time wrapping my brain around it.

I had looked up the cards and their meanings after seeing them on Ty's wall and him telling me which one's Quint had. The Magician card could mean two things. The first meaning represented control, taking control over your life and having a certain level of success. The second meaning had to do with being creative and talented. Since I wasn't very creative or talented, I liked the first meaning a whole lot better.

The picture showed a bald man in a cape standing in the center of a pentagram. He held a sword in one hand with the tip pointed towards the ground. In his other hand he held a cup raised high in the air. The words *The Magician* hung in the air above his bald head.

Because it represented taking control of your life, I loved that they had chosen that card to give to me.

The Moon is the card of intuition, dreams and the unconscious. I found this choice in cards interesting because of the dreams I always had. They meant something, and I couldn't always figure out what.

The card showed a moon glowing high in the sky. Wolves were on the ground with their heads thrown back, howling at the moon hanging high in the sky.

They were both awesome, but I liked The Moon more.

This was important. These drawings were important to Tyson and Quinton.

Why had they given them to me?

I wasn't certain sure, but I thought I knew.

And what I thought scared me.

Chapter Twenty-Three

"ARIEL," JULIAN CALLED, making me jump.

As nice as he was, I needed him to go away.

I wanted to be alone to explore my new bedroom. Or one of my new bedrooms. Quinton had said they had a room for me at the big house. I had no intentions of seeing that one.

I turned in time to see Julian drop my bag at the foot of the bed.

"I'm going to go make dinner," he said. "That's what I was planning on doing before you showed up. You take as much time as you need, honey. Get comfortable in your new space and come down when you're ready."

He smiled kindly at me as he left me alone in the room.

My space. I liked the sound of that. Mr. Cole would be gone for good in just a few short days and I needed a new place to call my own. If I could get over being jealous and crazy, this place might actually work for me. It was cute, and I liked how they had set it up for me.

I closed the door and froze.

"What in the…"

On the back of the closed door was a white poster with a unicorn covered in glitter. Below the unicorn in dark purple lettering and all caps read: YOU ARE ABSOLUTELY FABULOUS!

I stood there frozen and with my mouth hanging open as I stared blankly at the offensive thing. It had to go. If I stayed, I was getting rid of that thing for sure. There were far too many glittery things in this room.

Yikes.

There was one door other than the main one and I had a feeling it didn't lead to the bathroom. After sticking my head inside and pulling on the string hanging in front of my face, the light came on. I was right. There was no bathroom. The space was a tiny closet the size of a coffin.

I couldn't keep the stupid grin off of my face. Now here was a closet that was more my size than the giant monstrosity I had now. I could fill this one up with my clothes and still have room to spare. It was going to get colder, perhaps I could fill the rest of the space with hoodies or sweaters and the floor with some fabulous knee-high boots. I didn't have any knee-high boots, but I could see myself sporting some and looking fantastic in them. I needed to get a job to pay for all the crap I wanted.

With a sigh, I left the closet, closed the door and made my way towards the bed.

I picked up my bag off the floor and tossed it on the bed. The contents spilled out across the pretty comforter. I really needed to get a big bag that had a zipper on it. This one was black with thick, wide yellow straps. I think it was meant to be a beach bag for towels, sunscreen and whatnot. It was new, and I had no intentions of using it for a beach bag. It was my overnight bag. I had to buy a new one because the last one was left at Tyson's when I spent the night with him. I had left it there with all my clothes inside it and never gone back to retrieve it. The next one I got would come with a damn zipper so my clothes wouldn't spill out of it all the time.

Since I figured it would be more than likely that I moved in here, I decided to unpack my bag.

I dumped the bag upside down and everything fell onto the bed. Bra and panties, red and matching. Black cotton short-shorts with a matching tank top. They were covered in tiny white stars and were my pajamas. Two pairs of leggings. One black, one red. A black tank top with a green army tank on the chest. A red, short-sleeved t-shirt with a gold and black crown on the front. Two pairs of fuzzy socks. One black, the other one light blue. A hairbrush with a yellow handle. A tube of sparkly lip gloss (I liked sparkles when they came in my lip gloss!). A leather-bound journal and a black ink pen. And my toothbrush. I hadn't packed any makeup, not that I had much. And I hadn't brought a whole lot of clothing with me. I wasn't sure I was staying more than a night at the moment. I wanted to be home when Mr. Cole came back from his trip so I could spend some time with him before he was gone for good. I could bring the rest of my stuff with me after he was gone.

I grabbed my pajamas and re-folded them. I piled my bra and undies on top with the black fuzzy socks and walked them over to the dresser. I clutched them to my chest as I opened the top drawer.

There were brand new fuzzy socks in there with the tags still on. Red, orange, yellow, green, leopard print, zebra striped, pink, white and purple. The animal prints were cute, and I immediately wanted to put on the black and white zebra striped ones. Someone really had been paying attention. And they'd probably gone through the bag I'd left at the big house.

I dropped the small pile into the empty side of the drawer and pushed it shut. Thankfully, there weren't underthings in there too. That would be crossing a line.

Out of curiosity, and because I would be putting the rest of my clothes in there, I pulled open the second drawer. This one only had one thing in it and it was silky. Purple and silky. I pulled it out of the drawer and held it up in front of me for examination. It was a robe like the one Dash wore but longer. This robe would likely kiss the floor when I walked in it. I brought it closer to my face to read the tag. Silk, it was made of silk. Had Dash gotten this for me? How kind. And overly priced. I folded the piece of clothing carefully and put it back in the drawer. When I got some clothes hangers, I would hang it up in the closet. It wasn't something I would normally wear but I think I might have to wear it anyways so there weren't any hurt feelings. I wasn't sure purple was even my color, but someone sure seemed to think it was.

I opened the next two drawers to see if there were any more surprises waiting for me and couldn't tell if I was disappointed or relieved when there weren't. The rest of my clothes went into the second drawer alongside the pretty robe.

My hairbrush, phone and charger, I put on top of the dresser. My now empty bag, I placed on the floor in the coffin sized closet. The journal and pen, I placed on an empty shelf on the bookshelf.

I had been writing in the journal since my mother's death. I wrote about everything other than how I was feeling. I wrote about the books I read, the magic I learned, what I hoped to learn, any questions I had. But never about my feelings. Those had been too raw even for me to put down on paper. Maybe now I would be able to get it all out of me and in my journal.

I was sifting through the books on the shelves when there was a soft knock on the door.

"Are you coming down for dinner?" Damien called through the closed door.

I looked around the room frantically, searching for anything that would give me an excuse to not have to talk to Damien. I had never spoken to him before and he was kind of a dick.

He knocked again.

"Ariel?"

Shit.

There was no way out of this one.

After a quick glance at myself in the mirror above the dresser, I moved to the door. I opened it a crack and peeked out.

Damien looked down on me with a blank, emotionless face and bored eyes. The sleeves on his dress shirt had been rolled up and his arms were crossed over his chest.

He did not look impressed.

Well, two could play that game.

I crossed my arms over my chest and tried to make my face look as bored as his did. I think I failed because he frowned at me.

Whatever.

Maybe he was just wondering what I was doing behind the door. Yeah, that was it. Because it was only open an inch or two and he couldn't exactly see me.

"Can I help you?" I whispered.

Shit.

I should close the door in his face and put myself out of my misery.

"Are you alright?" he asked carefully, and I noticed he no longer looked bored but concerned. He probably thought I was a moron.

Great. Just what I needed, one more reason for him not to like me.

"I take it there was no one outside," I said to change the subject and take the heat off of me.

"No," he said firmly, and his eyes bored into me making me fidget behind the door. "No one was out there."

If he said so. I wasn't sure I believed him. They hadn't been out there for very long and we were deep in the woods. I would have to let it go. I fingered the doorknob without taking my eyes off of him and was relieved to find the little button to lock it. Not that it would do me much good, but it was better than nothing.

My pulse sped up as he continued to stare at me. What was this, some sort of test? I didn't much care for being tested. I licked my dry lips and refused to be intimidated by him. I would not fail this test, and I would not blink first.

He shifted his weight from one foot to the other and pursed his lips, looking very displeased. Hopefully not with me because I hadn't done anything wrong, not to him.

He cleared his throat and looked away first. Score! I won, not that I had the slightest clue what I was winning. No one had explained the rules or the name of the game to me.

"Dinner is ready," he mumbled awkwardly before rubbing his hand over the back of his neck. He seemed nervous all of a sudden and would no longer look me in the eye.

These people were so freaking weird sometimes.

Without another word he turned and walked away. Down the stairs he went, and I was surprised by how quiet he was. He didn't make a sound as he went down. Huh. He and Julian had sounded awfully loud when they'd gone down them earlier.

Dinner with Dash, Damien and Julian… I didn't think I was ready for that. It was bound to be incredibly awkward. If I had known the other two were going to be here I don't think I would have come.

My phone chimed from its place on top of the dresser. I practically skipped across the wood floor to get to it I was so thankful for the distraction.

I picked it up, swiped the screen to unlock it and opened up my messages. There was one from Tyson.

Tyson: Where are you? The house is locked up tight and it looks like no one is home. Are you over there?

I frowned at my phone. I probably should have told someone where I was going. I would probably have to do that from now on. That was going to get old real fast. I texted him back quickly before he could question me anymore.

Ariel: I'm at Dash's.

I put the phone back on the dresser and, after a quick look through the room, I walked to the door. I didn't bother to shut it behind me. There was no one up here and I didn't think they would go pawing through my things so soon. And if they did, whatever, it's not like I had a whole lot of things here for them to go through.

Trust was important when living with someone and if I was going to live with Dash fulltime then I would need to trust him. He had to be able to trust me too, that was important to me, which is why I didn't open up the two closed doors and peek inside. Though, I very much wanted to. I hoped a bathroom lay behind one of those closed doors. It would suck to have to go down the stairs every time I had to go to the bathroom or wanted to take a shower.

I made it half way down the stairs when I stopped. I turned around and went back to my room.

I kicked my flip flops off and sat down on the edge of the bed. I put the light blue fuzzy socks on my feet even though I really wanted to put on one of the brand-new pairs.

Then I went downstairs, and I was just as quiet on the stairs as everyone else had been.

"What's she doing here?" I heard Damien say when I made it to the bottom of the stairs.

I stopped cold at his words and my heart squeezed painfully in my chest. I did not want to hear this crap.

"Shut up," Julian snapped. "She should be coming down here and minute now and she doesn't need to overhear this bullshit and take it the wrong way."

The fist wrapped around my heart loosened just a little bit.

"I didn't mean anything bad by it," Damien shot back. "I just figured Quint or Ty would have said something about her coming over here. What's wrong? Why did no one call to tell us she was coming? Why is she here?"

Since eavesdropping did me absolutely no good and I had learned my lesson the hard way, I took the last step off the stairs and woodenly walked to the kitchen.

"She's moving in, which means this is her home now," Dash growled darkly. "I want her to feel welcome in her own home. I want-"

"Nobody knew that I was coming," I said into the now silent room. I looked at Dash, ignoring the other two for the moment. "If they had known, they would have let you know, I'm sure. And, I realize I absolutely should have told you I was coming over, but it was kind of a spur of the moment thing. Mr. Cole had a last-minute business meeting pop up that he had to go to. It's a overnight trip and I really didn't want to be alone." Here's where things were going to get awkward for me but to hell with it. "It's really depressing being there with all the moving boxes everywhere and I just had to get out of there. I couldn't go next door because… well, to be honest, I am still avoiding going over there. But you already know about that because that's why I'm moving in here and not there."

And, oh god I was rambling. My fingers were tangled together in front of me, twisting every which way. I was incredibly nervous and all three of them were watching me like hawks. Even Damien eyeballed me.

Dash moved away from the counter and opened a drawer. He rifled through things until he came out with a silver key on a little circular key ring. He held it up for my inspection before tossing it my way. I caught it in mid-air.

"Key to the front door," he told me. "It's yours because this is your home too. You can come and go as you please and you don't owe any of us an explanation for showing up out of the blue."

I shifted from foot to foot nervously as I clutched the key to my chest. "Yeah, but I wasn't supposed to move in yet and I really should have called." Which I could not have done because I didn't have his phone number. Best to leave that part out.

"Doesn't matter."

I frowned at him. Why was he being so easy about this?

"Thanks for the room," I rushed out in my most sincere voice. "It's lovely."

The corner of his lips twitched, and I stopped breathing. He wanted to smile at me.

"Take your house key upstairs while we take the food to the dining room," he ordered.

I did as I was told. I usually did.

When I got back down the stairs after placing my key on top of the dresser they were all in the dining room, waiting for me.

I hesitated in the doorway as I took in the scene.

Chapter Twenty-Four

THE THREE OF them were seated at the large dining room table. Dash at the head with Julian and Damien sitting across from each other. That meant I had to pick between Julian and Damien to sit next to. No brainer. I picked Julian, he was the safer bet, the nicer bet.

. They watched my every move as I strode up to the table. I pulled out the chair beside Julian and sat down.

An empty plate appeared in front of me. I grabbed it out of the air and sat it down with a clunk on the table.

"Dig in," Dash ordered gently.

I looked up to see him watching me and I gave him a hesitant, half smile. My palms were sweating fiercely, and I was thankful I had already set the plate down or it would have probably slipped from my fingers and that would have been embarrassing.

Dash tipped his head towards the food on the table and continued to watch me. I noticed no one else was eating even though they already had food on their plates. I hoped they weren't going to watch me eat because that wouldn't help at all with my nervousness and I would likely choke on whatever it was I was attempting to stuff in my face.

There were dishes on the table filled with food. A bowl with salad mix in it. Four different kinds of salad dressings. A plate with a pile of breadsticks on it. A casserole dish with what looked like creamy chicken alfredo in it. The table was littered with things. A plastic bottle of parmesan cheese. Salt and pepper shakers that were cute little ceramic cats, one black and the other white. I could guess which one was the salt shaker and which one was the pepper shaker. A half empty roll of paper towels and a small pile of silverware.

Who was supposed to eat all this food?

When I continued to sit there stupidly staring at all the food, Julian picked up my plate and started filling it with things. He skipped the salad entirely and piled the plate high with alfredo. He plopped two breadsticks on top of it and smothered the whole thing in parmesan cheese. The plate thunked down in front of me and I stared at it in open mouthed horror. I couldn't eat all that.

He placed a fork on the edge of the plate and pushed the ceramic cats towards me.

"Uhh…"

"Eat," Julian mumbled. "You're too skinny and you've lost even more weight over the last few weeks. Are you eating every day? Are you eating at all?"

I tore off a hunk of a breadstick and dipped it into the alfredo sauce before stuffing it in my mouth. I chewed as I thought about how to answer his question. After I ate the first bite, the other three picked up their forks and stated eating. They had been waiting for me to take the first bite.

I ate without taking my eyes off of my plate. The rest of them were quiet as they ate too.

Had I been eating properly these past few weeks? I thought I had been but now I wasn't so sure. I had been sleeping through breakfast, eating a piece of toast for lunch with a cup of coffee to chase it down and eating dinner with Mr. Cole on most nights which was usually some kind of take out. Huh. Guess I hadn't been eating as much as I should have. I didn't think one crappy meal a day and a piece of toast were going to cut it with them.

Before we had moved in with Mr. Cole I would have been more than happy to be able to eat a takeout meal, toast and coffee every day. It would have been a decent change from the normal of ramen and crackers that I ate almost every day.

I chose not to answer Julian's questions and he didn't ask again. It wasn't any of his business how much I ate every day.

"So, Ariel," Damien said quietly. "When are you planning on going back to school? You've missed what, three weeks now? You're going to fall behind."

I choked on the breadstick I'd just taken a bite of and had to take a few sips of water to get it to go down.

School.

I coughed.

Of all the things he could pick to talk about and he wanted to talk about school. What would he think if I told him I had zero intentions of going back to school. Being a high school drop-out wasn't something I thought they would find cute or endearing.

How was I going to explain to them that I wasn't going back to school? How would Quinton and Tyson take the news? Should I really not go back to school? The thought of going back had me cringing in my chair. The GED test was sounding better and better by the day.

"Hey," Tyson shouted from the front of the house. "Where is everybody?"

I sat back in my chair and breathed out a sigh of relief. Saved by Tyson. Now I wouldn't have to answer any uncomfortable questions.

"What's he doing here?" Damien muttered angrily. He was staring into his plate of food with a scowl on his face.

"Brother," Julian said in warning.

"Are you brothers?" I asked curiously. They didn't look to be related and no one had said anything about them being brothers. I would have heard about it by now.

Julian winked at me. "We're all brothers. It doesn't matter that the only blood brothers are the twins. We're all family and sometimes the family we make for ourselves is the best kind."

I wrinkled my nose at him and asked in a serious voice, "Does that mean you're going to start calling me sister?"

"Wha… What?" He sputtered.

"Sister," Damien spit the word out on a disgusted sneer. I didn't know what he had to be so disgusted about. He had a girlfriend and didn't see me like that.

"Please, tell me you're joking," Julian whined.

This was by far the most awkward dinner I had ever been a party to. And nobody had really said anything. I sincerely hoped Dash wouldn't expect me to have dinner with him every night. Then again, it was bound to be different with just him and me.

Tyson's heat hit me. His chin rested on top of my head as he moved into me. He wrapped his arms around my chest and squeezed gently.

"When you didn't answer me back I got worried," he mumbled. His chin rubbed against the top of my head with every word he spoke.

Tyson squeezed me tighter and swayed from side to side, rocking us slowly.

"I left my cell phone upstairs," I told him. "If I had thought you were going to come over here if I didn't text you back right away, I would never have left the thing upstairs."

"Do you like your bedroom?" he asked quietly, ignoring our avid audience and changing the subject.

I, for one, was having a very hard time ignoring our audience. Looking through the people seated around the table, I noticed all of them were watching Tyson and not me. Dash's gaze was drawn towards where Tyson's chin rested on my head and the sad look was back in his eyes. Why did seeing me with Tyson make Dash look sad? I didn't understand him. Julian was looking a little higher, at Tyson's face, and he had a thoughtful expression on his face. And Damien, well his eyes were locked on Tyson's arms wrapped around my chest. A muscle ticked in Damien's jaw, indicating he was upset or angry about something. Was he upset because Tyson was touching me? Or, maybe, because I seemed so comfortable with his touch?

Apparently, I didn't understand any of them. Except for maybe Tyson, I knew what he wanted from me. And Quinton, he was a little too forward with what he wanted from me and I understood him all too well.

"It's perfect," I whispered, answering his question about the bedroom that had been put together for me. And this was no lie, the room was perfect for me. Except for that outrageous unicorn poster. I did not like that thing at all. The rest of it was absolutely perfect. Even the tiny, coffin sized closet worked for me. And, I even loved the love seat that had been brought in to replace my window seat. It wasn't the same as what I had at Mr. Cole's but that didn't mean it wasn't amazing. I didn't have much in my room at Mr. Cole's house. Don't get me wrong, every little thing I did have was lovely and I took pains to take care of it, all of it. I could lie and say they were just things, but I wasn't going to do that. I was done lying to myself about anything. When you grow up poor, with second hand everything your whole life, you tend to learn the value of brand new, only ever been yours things. I'm not ashamed to say that by value I sometimes meant monetary value. I always expected Mr. Cole to get tired of my mother and her insane behavior and kick us out to the curb. We would need money to survive in that scenario, so I had made sure I knew what everything I had been given was worth. But another part of me, the better part of me, had always been ecstatic to have something of my own, something nice and new, something bought solely for my use. I loved the things Mr. Cole had gotten for me and I went out of my way to keep them in perfect condition. Not just for resale purpose if it came down to that, but because I simply enjoyed having nice things and wanted to keep them that way. I had been slacking on this lately. Like, I hadn't been making my bed every time I left it and I was developing a really bad habit of tossing my dirty clothes and towels onto the bathroom floor. Maybe that would change now that I wouldn't be having my own bathroom and would be expected to share with Dash?

The room they had put together for me suited me far better than the one I had put together for myself at Mr. Cole's house. I couldn't wait to put more things on the wall and fill my closet floor with things like knee-high boots. And, I wanted to put makeup and lotion and nail polish on top of my dresser.

I could see my new bedroom quickly becoming home.

"It's absolutely perfect," I repeated on another whisper because it was worth repeating. Emotion threatened to rise up my throat and I forcefully shoved it back down. Now was not the time.

"I got you a present," Tyson said. "If you are done eating you should go up to your room and I will meet you up there with it after I get it out of my car."

A gift.

Tyson had gotten a gift for me.

Did I want it? Yes, absolutely.

I looked at my plate which was only half empty. I really could not eat any more.

"Let's go," Tyson said as he moved back, away from me.

Apparently, he didn't require me telling him what I wanted, he simply knew.

"She's not done eating," Julian barked at Tyson.

"You don't get to order her around," Damien said angrily.

They were annoying.

"You're giving me a headache," I blurted and they all snapped their mouths shut. "Dinner was great, really, but I can't eat anymore."

I pushed my chair back from the table and stood up. All three of them were glaring harshly at Tyson. Better him than me.

Tyson smiled broadly at them. It wasn't his normal bright and beautiful smile, but a smug, condescending one.

I pushed on his shoulder as I walked past him.

"You have a gift to go and get out of your car," I said. "Remember?"

I didn't stick around to hear if he replied. I didn't want to hear any of them speaking anymore because they might really give me a headache.

I practically ran up the stairs and to my new room. Tyson had come along in the nick of time and saved me from that awkward dinner and the questions they had started asking me.

I closed the door behind me and let out a relieved breath. Maybe I was better off home alone. No, not home. Not home anymore. I needed to get used to that.

I sat on the edge of my bed and placed my hands in my lap, patiently waiting.

What could Tyson have gotten me? I was curious, nervous and excited all at the same time. Since he got me a gift did that mean I was supposed to get him one in return?

Tyson burst into my room with a white box under one arm. He didn't bother knocking.

"What is it?" I asked excitedly. I was practically bouncing up and down in my seat.

He laughed at me and moved to the love seat. After sitting down, he patted the space beside him.

"Come on, girl." He said. "Get that pretty ass of yours over here and open your present."

I was in the seat beside him in record time. Tyson placed the box on my lap and sat back. He studied my face as I studied the box. I lifted the top off and dug through the white tissue paper inside.

Inside the tissue paper lay the most gorgeous dreamcatcher I had ever seen. The circle was black, the inside intricately woven with silver beads placed sporadically. Silver and black beads were hanging down on long strings ending with black and white feathers. There were white markings and words written around the black circle. I picked it up out of the box and held it close to my face so I could make sense of the tiny markings and read the words.

"What are these?" I asked quietly as I ran my fingers over one of the markings. The words were in a different language, one I couldn't read.

Tyson's fingers curled around mine, stopping my movements. His heat hit me, sending a tingle up my arm.

"It's for safety and protection against all things," he murmured quietly. "Even when you are asleep. Especially when you're asleep." He ran his thumb gently over the top of my hand in a slow circle. "I got this for you a few weeks ago. It took me a couple of days to put the spell together because I had to find the right books for it. The one I needed was hiding under Uncle Quint's bed. I found a lot of interesting things under there."

I cocked my head to the side in curiosity at how annoyed he sounded there at the end.

"What does Quinton have under his bed?" I asked with a burning curiosity and a desperate need to know. What did scary Uncle Quint have hidden under his bed? What would make Tyson sound so disgruntled? I hadn't even seen Quinton's bedroom yet and I was already planning on when I could find the opportunity to go digging for treasure under his bed.

"Ty?" I asked, and his fingers tightened around mine, squeezing gently.

I pulled my hand free so I could put my beautiful new dreamcatcher back into the tissue paper filled box.

"You don't want to know, girl," he said in an angry voice. "You're going to have to trust me on this one, you don't want to know."

He was wrong. I did want to know. In fact, I think it was going to bug me until I found out.

I was learning that when it came to my friends and the people I cared about, I didn't like being kept in the dark and I didn't enjoy secrets unless I was in on them. I wouldn't ask Tyson to tell me again when it was something he clearly didn't want to share with me. I would bide my time and wait until I could find out for myself. Invasion of privacy? Yes, absolutely. Did I care? Nope, not in the least bit. This was Quinton we were talking about. Quinton who spied on me, invaded my dreams, stole my underwear, which I never got back, by the way and he's done numerous other things that made him out to be a certifiable crazy man. He made people sick one second, then the next he made them fall in love. Against their own knowledge or even willingness, mind you. He was unapologetic in everything that he did, and I didn't doubt for one second that he would not hesitate to go digging through my closet at the first opportunity he came across. With Quinton, all bets were off. He had it coming.

"Do you like it?" Tyson asked, breaking into my thoughts and pulling me away from what mysteries his Uncle kept hidden under his bed.

"What?" I asked stupidly.

He frowned at me.

"The dreamcatcher," he said slowly. Then repeated, "Do you like it?"

I grinned at him and nodded furiously. "Do I like it?" I said. "No, I don't like it."

His face dropped, and his eyes filled with hurt and pain.

"I don't like it," I hurried to explain myself so I could take that look out of his eyes. "I absolutely love it. It's beautiful. Really. I've never had anything like it before and I've never been given a gift this lovely before."

I left out the part about only ever being given shoes and pretty headbands from one of my mothers' boyfriends before. That had been the only time I had been gifted with something from someone, but he already knew that story. My mother had never bought me a birthday present or a Christmas present before. Not that I had ever bought her anything either, because I hadn't. It had never bothered me until now. I didn't need to be thinking about my mother and all of the things I didn't have while growing up.

The past was the past and in order for it to stay in the past, I needed to stop constantly thinking about it. I needed to focus on the here and now and being happy.

I looked into Tyson's dark, dark eyes. Eyes so full of fire when they looked at me that it made my breath catch in my throat.

I swallowed thickly, quickly looking away from him.

"Can we hang it up, please?" I whispered.

Along finger touched my chin, pulling my head back towards him. I blinked in surprise. He was a lot closer than he had been before. Too close. I tried to scoot back but there was nowhere else to go.

"What are you doing?"

"Did he kiss you? That's the only thing I can think of that makes sense of his behavior lately." He asked in a dark voice I hadn't heard from him in a while.

My eyes squinted in confusion and I sounded confused when I asked, "What? Did who kiss me? Whose behavior?"

I was entirely confused.

Then it hit me.

Oh man.

The only person who had kissed me was his Uncle. How would he know if Quinton had kissed me? I hadn't told a single person.

My heart skipped a beat.

Had Quinton gone home after sticking his tongue in my mouth and told the others about it? My cheeks instantly heated, and I knew my face was flaming in embarrassment. I would kill him, and he certainly wouldn't be kissing me anymore. Not if he went and told all of his friends.

"I… I…" I stammered. I had no idea how to explain this to Tyson.

"He did, didn't he?" Tyson whispered in awe. "That son of a bitch. He's been a smug bastard for days and I couldn't figure out why. What did he have to be smug about? What did he have that the rest of us didn't? I figured it had something to do with you. Sitting here with you, watching your pretty face, wanting to kiss you… I figured it out, he kissed you and that's what he's been so smug about."

I put my hands up to my face and pressed them against my cheeks, trying to cool them off. My face was on fire. At least I knew now that Quinton hadn't told anybody.

But… Wait. Tyson kept saying he. Did he even mean Quinton?

"Uh…" I said as I moved my hands away from my flaming face. I licked my suddenly dry lips and asked, "He who?"

His lips parted in genuine surprise.

"Has there been more than one?" He asked in a strangled voice. "Have you been kissing more than my Uncle?"

"No," I exclaimed. "And it was just the one time. How did you know?"

"I told you, he's been so damn smug. And he walks around with this stupid knowing smile on his face, like he's got a secret and he's laughing at the rest of us. The twins think you had sex with him, but I knew better. You're not ready for sex but I could totally see my Uncle sneaking in a kiss or two. He's pushy and has absolutely no self-control."

He shook his head and sat back in the love seat with an angry scowl on his face.

Holy crap. The twins thought I had sex with Quinton and they were talking about it with Tyson. That was insane. And absolutely mortifying.

"They think I had sex with Quinton," I breathed out on a horrified whisper. "Oh my god. We didn't have sex. I've never had sex with anyone."

"Whoa," he said in a soothing voice. "Slow down, girl. It's just the twins and I think it was more wishful thinking on their part."

What?

Stupefied, I asked, "Why would the twins want me to have sex with Quinton? I don't understand any of you."

"We made an agreement between the seven of us. To back off, give you space and to build on making friendships between you and us. It was Quinton's idea.

If he's telling us one thing, then going and doing the complete opposite of what he told us we were supposed to be doing, then he's not playing by his own rules and no one else has to, either. All bets are off and you're fair game."

I was fair game?

I didn't like the sound of that. I wasn't sure what bothered me more, being fair game or them talking about having sex with me.

"You know," I told him, "I didn't actually agree to any of this. I didn't agree to be in your coven and I didn't agree to having a relationship with any of you."

Even though all of that was true, I had no intention of ever finding another coven. I had found my place and it was with them, I didn't want another coven, no matter what. But the relationship thing still bothered me. It was unconventional, not normal, and a few of them didn't even like me.

"Please, sweetheart," Tyson's said in a soft voice, "don't lie to me. This is your coven and you aren't going anywhere. You think Uncle Quint is going to let you go now that you let him in there? I don't think so. He's just going to keep coming back for more and he's never going to stop. The twins aren't ever going to let you leave them. They take family very seriously, and you are family now. The rest of it will all fall into place. You sound like we expect you to jump into bed with all of us tomorrow. That's not happening. Shit like this takes time. We're all on board and we all agreed to give you as much time as you needed."

I sighed and slouched back in the love seat. I didn't want to talk about this right now. I wanted to shove it to the side and deal with it maybe never.

"Can we hang up my dream catcher now?" I asked in hopeful voice.

He sat forward quickly, snatching the box from my hands. He held the box away from me and out of my reach. His eyes glittered, full of mischief and he smirked at me.

I had a feeling that light in his eyes and the sexy smirk did not bode well for me.

"Girl," he cooed. "I would love to hang up your dream catcher for you. Under one condition. I want you to do something first."

Yeah, this did not sound good.

"What's this condition?" I asked suspiciously.

His smirk turned into a full blown, blinding smile. I couldn't help the small smile that graced my lips at the lovely sight.

"I will hang your dream catcher up for you, and all you have to do is give me one tiny, little kiss. You don't even have to give me your tongue if you're not ready for that."

The smile immediately left my face.

Kiss him?

Oh boy.

Chapter Twenty-Five

WORDS ESCAPED ME, and I suddenly became fascinated with my hands that were in my lap twisting every which way.

Did I want to kiss Tyson?

No, no I did not. I wanted him to kiss me. I didn't want to be the one to make the first move. I would likely overthink it and mess the whole thing up. I didn't want my first kiss with Tyson to be some sloppy thing I screwed up, but I most certainly *did* want there to be a first kiss. And, if it was good, a whole lot more.

I also wanted Quinton to kiss me again too. If I hadn't known that this was the kind of relationship they wanted, I would have felt completely horrible about myself and weighted down by guilt.

"Sweetheart, look at me."

I turned my head to the side so he could see my face. I imagined my eyes were a little wide in my head and probably full of the fear and the near on panic that I was feeling.

"Fuck it," he muttered, leaning forward. He wrapped a hand around the side of my neck and slid it back, into my hair. His hand moved up and he fisted it gently in the hair at the back of my head.

With his hold on my hair, he tilted my head to the side and his lips crashed into mine. Heat seared into me, like he'd branded me with his mouth.

His teeth nipped at my bottom lip, making me gasp at the sensation. His tongue slipped inside and he took control, control over the kiss, control over me. The hand in my hair tightened as he tilted my head giving himself better access to my mouth. His lips moved against mine as he caressed every inch of my mouth with his tongue. He wasn't there for a visit, he acted like he owned the place, the paint had dried and now he was moving in and he planned on staying a good, long while.

I placed my hands on his warm, hard biceps and I kissed him back. Or, I tried to kiss him back. He wouldn't let me.

I made a sound deep in the back of my throat, embarrassingly close to a moan as his tongue slid out of my mouth and he nipped at my bottom lip again.

My breath was coming in pants as I forced my eyes to open. I hadn't even remembered closing them. When had I done that?

Tyson licked his lips and his burning eyes raked over my face, ending back on my lips. My heart was beating way too fast in my chest, rising and falling heavily with each breath I took. His looked to be doing the same.

"I'm sorry," he apologized in a soft, sweet voice. "I shouldn't have done that. I didn't mean to scare you."

I traced my finger across my lower lip. It tingled and felt swollen to the touch.

Tyson's hand slid out of my hair. The backs of his fingers trailed down the side of my neck, stopping just above my collar bone.

His thumb smoothed over my scars as he asked, “Did I scare you?”

I shook my head, silently telling him no, he didn’t scare me, he hadn’t scared me at all.

Someone knocked loudly on the bedroom door. Tyson and I jumped apart as if we’d been burned. I scrambled off of the love seat and threw myself onto the bed. I scooted over until I sat in the middle of the bed. I pulled my knees to my chest and wrapped my arms around them, trying to make myself look as small and innocent as possible.

I avoided looking Tyson’s way, cleared my throat, and called out, “Come in.”

I wondered if I looked as disheveled as I felt. My hair probably looked like a crazy mess, tossed all over the place from Ty’s hand bunching in it. The door swung open and I was all out of time to fix the crazy mess that was my hair. Discretely, I watched Ty out of the corner of my eye. He sat back in the love seat, sprawled out, arm resting along the back of the couch, legs spread wide, feet firmly on the floor. He looked like he didn’t have a care in the world. I wanted to throw one of the decorative pillows at his head. Preferably one of the ones with sequins stitched into it. Served him right.

“Hey,” Quinton said as he stuck his head around the door. “What are you two doing in here?”

He stepped into the room and slammed the door shut behind him, making me wince. Quinton had a thing for bursting in and slamming doors. I couldn’t even believe he had the decency to knock first. A miracle.

"Nephew," he growled, "I asked you a question and I expect an answer."

"Actually," I responded before Ty had a chance to and things got heated, "you came in here and demanded to know what we two were doing. You didn't address one of us specifically. Perhaps Tyson didn't answer because he was waiting politely for me to go first. Did you ever think of that? Huh? No, of course not. Not you, you who barges in and demands to know things that aren't any of your business. What's up with that, huh, Uncle Quinton?"

His nostrils flared angrily as he glared daggers at me.

"How many times do I have to tell you to stop fucking calling me that?" He snarled at me.

Way to poke the sleeping bear, Ariel.

I couldn't seem to help myself.

"He, Uncle Quint," Tyson said, butting in. "Calm down. You're going to scare her if you keep talking to her like that."

Tyson put his hands on his knees and pushed himself to his feet.

I didn't take this as a good sign.

"It's okay, Ty," I said quickly as I scooted towards the edge of the bed on Quinton's side. "And, I'm sorry, Quinton, really, I am. I know how you feel about me calling you that and I should have left it alone. Instead, I said it and I had to pick at you. I'm sorry, honest. And, I won't do it again."

The last part was a lie and had me hiding my hand behind my back so I could cross my fingers. Not that it would do me any good, but I felt the need to do it anyway.

Quinton scowled at me. It wasn't a pretty look for him and a few weeks ago it might have scared me. Quinton didn't frighten me anymore with his dark and intense looks. I could be afraid of him looking at me like that when I actually did something to wrong him. Then, and only then, would I have a reason to worry. Now he was just full of it. All piss and vinegar.

"What were you two doing in here?" He repeated the question he had originally asked when he'd come in here.

I didn't mind him repeating the question, and I really didn't mind going back to our original topic.

But…

"What are *you* doing here, Quint?" I asked instead of answering his question.

He sighed, and his shoulders slumped forward. He ran a hand over his short, buzz cut hair, back and forth.

"You're here," he said simply.

I raised both my eyebrows and titled my head to the side, waiting for him to continue. When he didn't, I twisted at the waist to look back at Tyson. I shot him a questioning look.

"Do you know what he means by that?" I asked Tyson.

"Babe," Quinton said in a patient voice and I turned back to face him. "Why do you think Ty's here?"

When I didn't answer right away he shook his head sadly.

"Ty's here because you're here," he informed me. "Do you think he'd come over here to hang out at Dash's house just because? Um, no. I can't even remember the last time he came over here on his own and without me telling him to do so. Same goes for the twins who are, right now, downstairs. They aren't here to hang out with Dash or Damien or even Julian. Ty's here because you're here. I'm here for the same reason. The twins don't do well with being alone, they hate it. But if everyone had stayed in tonight, they still would have left to come here. Because this is where you are and, in case you missed it, we want to be where you are."

My hand rose, outstretched on its own accord, reaching for him. It was like I couldn't stop myself. When Quinton was around I had a hard time not touching him. I pressed my hand to my chest instead, stopping myself from doing what I really wanted to do. If we were alone I would have reached for him. But we weren't alone. Tyson was here and not five minutes ago we were trading our most intimate secrets, via mouth to mouth.

"It's true, sweetheart. I'm only here for you. Dash isn't exactly my favorite person on the planet. He's family, yeah, but that doesn't mean we're besties. You and me though, girl, we are going to be besties. Besties who swap bodily fluids on the daily."

I shot Tyson a look that his words rightfully deserved, a seriously nasty look. He chose to ignore it and, unfortunately, continued speaking.

"Even if it means I have to come here to the sour puss's house." Tyson shrugged. "As long as you're here then this is where I'm going to be. I would move into your room here with you if I thought Uncle Quint wouldn't lose his damn mind."

"Don't even think about it," Quinton ground out. "It's bad enough I have to deal with her being here, I don't need you running off on me too."

I folded my arms over my chest and tried to defend myself. "I didn't run off on anyone. I told you why I couldn't stay in the big house with you. You understand why, I know you do, and you aren't even really mad that I'm staying here. You wanted me to get to know the rest of them, so much so, you even encouraged me to stay here. With Dash. So, don't even try to whine about that. It's your jealous insecurities coming out to play. Get over it. Now," I put my hand out to my side, gesturing to Tyson, "Ty promised me he'd hang up my dreamcatcher for me and we are going to have to go to the store to buy some kind of hook or something to use to hang it from the ceiling with. I don't know, that's not my area of expertise. I'm sure Tyson can handle it. Then we are going downstairs to see the twins because I miss them and if they really did come here to see me then I want to spend some time with them."

Quinton looked past me, to his nephew, and grinned. "I love it when the real Ariel comes out to play," he said, sounding pleased as all get out.

I stood at the foot of the bed, in between them, awkwardly.

Enough was enough.

"Perhaps you should go downstairs and wait for us to join you," I rudely suggested.

Quinton aimed his grin at me. "It won't take you long to hang up your dreamcatcher," he told me knowingly. "Ty already put a hook in the ceiling for it two days ago."

"What?" I whispered. I whirled around and pointed my finger rudely at Tyson. "You," I screeched. "You tricked me into kissing you!"

Unrepentant, he shrugged and said, "Yeah. Can you really blame me, though? I had to try. And, to be fair, I'm still going to hang up your dreamcatcher for you. And, I did go out of my way to put that hook in the ceiling for it. That's got to count for something."

"He also put the protection spell into the thing," Quinton said softly, defending his nephew. "That took work, energy and blood to make for you."

I loved my dreamcatcher and knowing what Tyson did to it for me, to make it into some form of protection for me, made it all the more special.

I turned to Ty and found him watching me with a serious expression on his face. His brows were drawn, his eyes guarded, and his lips were pursed into a tight, thin line.

"Thank you, Tyson," I said softly with a small smile on my face. "I already told you I loved it and I meant it. Thank you for making it so it really will keep out the bad things while I'm sleeping."

I held my right hand out to him and waited. I needed his touch, the heat that came with the touch of his skin.

He walked over to me and grabbed ahold of my hand, pulling me into him. I collided with his side and he let my hand go. He wrapped an arm around my shoulders and pulled my front into his side. My boobs were smooshed into his ribs, but I didn't care. It was a little too up close and personal for me with Quint standing not five feet away, too close for comfort with an audience. I didn't think I was a big fan of PDA.

"Now," Quinton said blandly, making my eyes shoot to his face. "How about we talk about what I want to talk about now? I want to hear more about this kiss."

All air left my lungs and I almost hyperventilated. When I managed to draw in a shaky breath, my eyes were all for Quinton. Was he mad? He had kissed me first. Logically, I knew he had nothing to be mad about, he wanted this, he wanted me to be with all of them. That's why he encouraged me to come to Dash's house in the first place.

I got what he wanted from me. How could I not when it had been spelled out for me on several occasions?

I *got* it.

I did.

But standing here in the same room with Nephew and Uncle, both whom I had kissed. That didn't seem right to me because neither of them acted like they cared.

I cared.

I cared a whole lot more than I probably should.

"You aren't mad?" I asked Quinton cautiously.

Tyson pulled me in tighter to his side. If I got any closer, we would fuse together.

Quinton smiled at me and it was a new one, a smile I hadn't seen from him before. This smile was soft, sweet, and, scarily, very loving.

I didn't know what to do with that smile or the love I saw in it.

Frankly, it freaked me out. If I didn't have magic, then he wouldn't feel anything for me. I would simply be some unfortunate girl who moved in next door to them. The one who wasn't a witch and didn't have magic inside of her. They wouldn't have given me a second glance then, I was that girl. Was that it? Did they only like me because I was a girl and had magic? I knew that was the truth of it, which is why I wondered… why did I like them so much? Not all of them, of course. But, some of them I liked a great deal. Did I like them and feel drawn to them simply because they were male and had magic? Why would Quinton look at me with love shining in his eyes if it weren't for magic? He couldn't love me, he didn't even know me.

I wanted him to be mad. I didn't want him to be mad at Tyson and I didn't want him to be mad at me. I simply wanted him to be mad at the situation.

But that was stupid.

It so was.

None of them should be mad at this situation, or at me. This whole thing was so overwhelmingly confusing that I wasn't sure what to expect from anyone.

Quinton came over to where I stood in the safety of Tyson's arms. His hand came up and he cupped the side of my face.

His eyes were warm, intense. I liked this look a whole lot better than his cold, hostile one.

"No, baby," he said gently. "I am not mad. How can I be mad when I'm getting everything that I want? Besides, I got to kiss you first and that's all that matters to me."

Tyson grunted as Quint leaned in. He kissed me on the forehead and backed away.

Walking backwards, he said, "I will wait for you two downstairs. Don't take too long or I will come back and bring her downstairs myself."

He turned around and sauntered to the door.

Tyson's put pressure on his arm around my shoulders, pulling me in closer.

"You see what I mean?" He muttered. "He's a smug bastard."

My body shook with laughter and I wasn't entirely sure why I was laughing. Maybe it was a stress reliever. The last two hours of my life had been extreme and very bizarre. I had a feeling that extreme and very bizarre were about to become my version of normal.

I would take laughter over tears any day.

Tyson walked us over to the love seat and moved me so I was sitting. I immediately pulled my legs up to my chest and wrapped my arms around my knees.

I stopped laughing and watched him as he pulled my dreamcatcher out of the white box. He stood and toed his black boots off. I was glad he thought to take his boots off, I didn't want them on my new bed. Very considerate of him.

"Hold this for me," he said as he held out the dreamcatcher towards me. He shook the pretty thing in the air, telling me to take it from him.

I sat up and let my feet fall to the floor as I took the dreamcatcher from him. I held it up in front of me while he put a knee into the bed, then the other and he pulled himself to his feet until he stood on the the bed. He held his arms out at his sides, keeping balance as he walked to the head of the bed.

I spotted what I had missed in my earlier perusal of the room, a small, white hook had been screwed into the ceiling above where I would lay my head down on my pillow tonight.

Tyson held his hand out to me and I got to my feet. I walked to the bed and held the dreamcatcher up to him. He took it and hung it up on the little white hook.

With my hand, I smoothed out the comforter he had wrinkled by standing on it. As I did this he jumped down from the bed.

He backed up and squinted his eyes, studying his work.

"What do you think?" he asked me.

I backed up until the backs of my knees hit the love seat and I sat down, taking in the view.

What did I think?

I thought it was perfect, just perfect, like everything about the room. I loved it. The black looked good against the yellow color of the wall and I imagined the feathers floating around on a gentle breeze that would come in through the window if I opened it. Maybe after everybody left I could open up the window, lay down on that bed and watch the feathers move around above me.

"It's lovely," I murmured distractedly.

He laughed and said, "You're adorable."

I looked from the dreamcatcher to him and smiled. I liked receiving gifts. And I liked Tyson.

His eyes dropped to my mouth and filled with heat. I knew he wanted to kiss me again and I also knew I couldn't let that happen. Not at the moment. We needed to get downstairs and staying in here kissing would mean Quinton barging in and getting an eye full. I didn't want that.

I stood and practically ran to the door.

"Time to go downstairs now," I mumbled as I sprinted past him.

His laughter followed me all the way down the stairs, mocking me.

Chapter Twenty-Six

I SAT ON the floor with my back to the wall and stretched out in front of me. My feet were crossed at the ankles. They were sweating and felt like they were burning inside my socks. I shouldn't have picked a spot to sit that was so close to the fireplace because this was torture.

When I'd come down the stairs with Ty right behind me, everyone was in the dining room and they were all talking. Tyson and I stood back in order to watch the show.

"Don't look at me," Quinton said angrily. "I've never watched a movie with her before, there hasn't been time for stuff like that. I have no idea what she likes." He rubbed the back of his neck awkwardly. "You would have to ask Ty about what she likes."

Quinton had looked embarrassed by his lack of knowledge of me, and I'd felt so bad for him that I had actually taken a step towards him in order to help him in any way I could. Tyson had stopped me by placing a hand on my arm and I'd stepped back into him. He wrapped his arm around my waist and held me close to him. I got his silent message. He wanted to watch, and he wanted me to not interrupt and potentially ruin it for him.

"What about a horror movie?" Damien had asked.

The entire room had exploded in a chorus of very loud no's.

I had wanted to laugh.

"Scary is out," Julian had muttered. "She doesn't need any more scary shit in her life."

"That sucks," Damien had muttered sullenly. "I love scary movies. What, are we going to have to watch chick flicks or something from now on?"

I'd had to put my hand over my mouth to keep any noise I might have involuntarily made inside.

"We could watch the Titanic," Julian had suggested.

"What is it with you and that fucking movie?" Quinton had barked at him. "The second half of the movie is the best part and then it's ruined when that bitch lets him go, after promising she'd never do that. Who ends a movie like that? And, who the fuck watches that stupid thing like once a month? Titanic is out. I refuse to be forced to endure three hours of that bullshit."

"We are not watching the Titanic," Addison had growled. "My twin can't watch movies like that anymore. It will give him nightmares and he already had enough problems with sleeping, he doesn't need more. All those people in the water…" He'd taken a deep, shuddering breath and shook his head.

I had been holding my tongue every time something got said that I had no clue the meaning of because I hadn't wanted to be nosy and I felt like they would share things with me on their own time. That was the nice thing to do, the thing the old me would do. The me who would run away and hide at the first sign of trouble. I was trying to be stronger, bolder, less of a scaredy cat.

I'd slipped out of Tyson's arms and stepped further into the dining room.

Binx darted out from under the dining room table and curved his tiny, little body around my ankles. I bend down and scooped him up in my arms.

I'd cradled Binx in my arms and he immediately started purring. Goodness, I didn't even have to pet him to get him to purr for me. I'd cuddled him close to my chest and murmured, "Awe, what a sweet, sweet little boy you are."

I had looked up and caught them all watching me. I sighed. Oh well, it was likely something I would have to get used to until *they* got used to *me*.

"I'm with Quinton," I had told them in a shy, quiet voice. "I could only stand to watch Titanic the one time. I couldn't stomach watching the ending more than once. I more than positive there had been room for the both of them on that makeshift raft. Poor Jack died because he had the misfortune to fall for a rich, spoiled brat. And, then she just goes and marries another dude and has kids with him. What did it take her, like, two minutes? I mean, come on." I paused to shake my head.

I singled out Damien and gave him a small, half smile. He'd actually talked to me today and he hadn't been a dick. I could be nice to him, if he could try, then I would too. "And, I actually do like scary movies. I don't watch them much because I tend to do it late at night when I'm all alone. I freak myself out over every little noise, and I end up not sleeping. I tried to watch one in the middle of the day once and it just wasn't the same."

There.

That was nice, and I'd even shared a little about myself without having to be asked first.

I could do this.

"What's your favorite horror movie?" Damien asked me. I was glad to see his eyes weren't cold or bored but warm and interested in hearing what I had to say.

"*Strangeland*," I told him, and I didn't even have to think about it. That movie freaked me right out. It also made me never, ever want to meet someone off of the internet. There were a lot of freaky people out there and you never really knew who you were talking to. That movie, just, ugh.

Damien's eyes sharpened as he focused solely on me. "You've seen *Strangeland*?" He asked me in a surprised voice.

"Yeah."

Julian started laughing.

"He made me watch that movie with him," Julian told me. "He tried to watch it on his own and couldn't do it. He does that a lot. He might love horror movies and scary shit, but he always needs someone to hold his hand through it. And, you watch it all by yourself in the dark. Our brave girl."

Julian continued to laugh at Damien's need for hand holding. I didn't laugh. Everyone should have a hand holding buddy for when they wanted to watch scary movies. I was envious of Damien having Julian there for those things.

"Do you enjoy scary movies?" I asked Julian.

After a slight hesitation, he answered me, "No. I hate them. I like tragedies and love stories."

I liked those, too, but still…

"I'll do your horror movie hand holding with you from now on, if you want me to." I told Damien before I could think better of it.

Holy crap! This was Damien. Why would I do that, offer to hold his hand? He had a girlfriend… You didn't offer to hold the hand of someone who had a girlfriend.

"I-" I tried to cover for my error, but he got there before me.

"I would love that," Damien said in a husky voice while watching me with his warm, intense eyes. "You're saving Julian's ass here big time. Before I leave tonight, you're going to have to give me your number, so I can hit you up."

What?

Damien wanted me to give him my phone number? What was going on here? And, what about his girlfriend? Wouldn't that make her angry? I knew it would make me really, really angry.

"We aren't watching a horror movie," Quinton stated, cutting into the awkward silence that had followed Damien telling me he was going to get my phone number.

I had agreed with Quinton. My first night in a new place… I absolutely did not need to be watching a horror movie before going to bed.

None of this had anything to do with why I had stepped forward to begin with. I needed to forget about holding Damien's hand and get back to the important stuff.

I sought out Abel and found him sitting next to his brother. They were both staring at me intently.

"What's the deal with you and not wanting to watch people going into the water?" I blurted out. "Why would that give you nightmares?"

I didn't get it, and I wanted to know.

From here on out, if I thought about it, then I was going to ask about it. They never held off on asking me questions. Why should I hold off when they didn't? That wasn't how you got to know someone.

There were so many questions I never asked because I didn't want to be rude in doing so. That time was over.

The silent room had grown still. Everyone froze, becoming statues. They all looked brittle, ready to break at any second.

"Damn it," I had cursed myself silently. What had I said to turn them into brittle statues? What had I done?

It was like trying to waltz through a minefield with these people. If they could all come with an instruction manual, that would be extremely beneficial to me.

"I don't know if you're aware of this or not, but our parents died in a plane crash," Abel said in a small, subdued voice. "The plane went down into the ocean. There were very few survivors and our parents weren't among them. One of the survivors said there had been more of them but they lost a bunch of people to sharks. He said that our dad was one of the one's to be attacked by the sharks. Unless it's a pool, water freaks me out and I won't go in it anymore."

My heart had tried to break inside my chest, and I had wanted to cry.

Quinton had taken it upon himself to be in charge of what we watched after Abel's confession.

That was how I had come to find myself seated on the floor in Dash's living room in between my Salt and Pepper twins with each of them holding on tight to one of my hands.

Thankfully, Binx had climbed into my lap and he made everything seem so much better.

That cat seemed to love me. I fell in love with him right back.

Dash was on the floor with his legs drawn up to his chest and his back to the end of the couch furthest from me. Damien, Julian and Quinton were all seated together on the couch. Tyson didn't sit. He leaned against the wall beside the doorway with his arms crossed over his chest.

They had chosen a Tv show instead of a movie, and they picked Sons of Anarchy. Apparently, Addison was a huge fan.

After the first episode, my heart went out to Jax in a really big way. After three episodes, I was hooked. Gemma and her fierceness. Clay, who seemed like a serious A-hole. Tig, who was Clay's man servant. Opie, and his broken family. And, have I mentioned how hot Jax is?

The guys were into all the explosions and gunfire. I was into it because I fell in love with the characters.

After two and a half hours, Julian stood up and yawned.

"I'm headed home," Julian said. "Damien, are you coming, or, are you staying here?"

Damien put his hands into the couch cushions and pushed himself to his feet.

"I'm going with you," Damien replied to Julian. He then looked to me, and asked, "Where's your phone?"

"On my dresser," I answered.

"Right," he muttered, and walked out of the living room. I heard his feet as he thundered up the stairs. I assumed he was going to do something with my phone, probably put his phone number into my contacts. I was fine with him messing with my phone.

Addison and Abel stood up from the floor.

"We're going," the twins said at the same time.

I stood with them.

No way was I doing this movie night thing with just Dash. I wasn't ready for that closeness.

"I have to get something out of the Rover," I told them as I ran from the room. I sprinted up the stairs, passing Damien on his way down. When I got to my room, I grabbed my keys off of the top of the dresser and ran back down the stairs.

Headlights lit up the way as I walked to my Rover. I grabbed the box out of the way back and ran back to the house.

With everyone else besides Dash leaving, I was going to bed. With my tattered box. And, hopefully Binx.

My tattered box. A box full of shit I wasn't entirely sure I needed to look through. But, I was going to look through it because it held secrets my mother had kept hidden from me and I wanted to know everything. I'm sure I would change my mind tomorrow and not want to know any of it. But, this wasn't tomorrow, it was today, and today I wanted to know.

Chapter Twenty-Seven

I LEFT MY door cracked an inch in hopes of Binx maybe wandering in to sleep with me, and made my way towards the bed. I tossed the box on top of my new bed. It hit the bed and the contents spewed out all over my new black and yellow comforter.

I stepped closer, drawn to the pictures and pieces of paper that had spilled out of the box.

There were more pieces of paper than there were pictures.

Letters. There were lots of letters.

The pictures were great, but it was the letters that told the real story.

I grabbed one at random and unfolded it.

I started to read.

My dearest Vivian,

She's my daughter. Not yours. She belongs with me. I grow tired of hunting you down with my magic so I can send you these letters. Yet, you've done something to make it so I can't actually find where you are. Since you don't have magic, you must be working with an extremely powerful witch.

Did you tell them why? Did you tell them about her? You better not have.

You should really consider giving her to me now because I will eventually find you and I can promise you that when I do, you aren't going to like how it ends for you.

Goodness.

There was no signature at the end.

The letter confused me. How did you send a letter to someone when you had no idea where they physically were? Could magic be used for something like that? I didn't know, but the more I thought about it, the more I was sure you could use magic that way. I would ask one of the guys about it in the morning.

I was done with that letter, so I moved it to the side and picked up another one.

Vivian,

If you do not give her to me, I will kill you. She's mine and she needs me.

I'm tired of playing this little game with you, Vivian. Enough is enough. Give me my daughter or else.

Who was this crazy person who had been sending my mother letters? If what I was reading was true, then Vivian Kimber hadn't really been my mother at all.

I didn't even know how to feel about this. The writer of the letters had called my mother by the term 'sister'. But, were they male or female? I didn't know how to determine the sex of a person based on their handwriting. It wasn't in my skill set.

I picked up another letter.

Vivian,

I'm sure you're wondering how I found you. You can rest assured, sweet sister, I have not found you and my daughter. Though, I have been diligently looking. In searching for you, I've also been searching for a magical means to find you. I came across something interesting. A spell that would transport my letter to you without actually knowing your physical location. Actually, I think it allows me to send the letters to wherever Ariel is. Blood magic is a wonderful thing, don't you think, my darling sister? This way, you can hide from me all you want, but you'll never really be able to escape me.

Poetic justice, if you ask me.

Not that you've asked me for my opinion on many things. If you had, then you wouldn't have stolen my daughter from me.

I finished reading this letter and set it aside, on top of the other one I had read.

My hands were shaking.

This was crazy.

I snatched up another letter and almost tore the paper when I opened it.

My dearest Vivian,

Yesterday, our father died. He had a heart attack and it killed him.

Do you even care? I imagine you don't. You were always such a greedy, spoiled little child. Father doted on you, always giving you everything that you wanted. Do you remember, Vivian? He'd go on and on about how precious little girls with magic were. The joke was on him, though, right Viv? His precious little girl who didn't actually have magic at all. What started as his greatest achievement ended up being his biggest failure.

Is that why you took her? Because you were jealous that she had magic when you don't? Do you remember the day she was born? The entire coven came for it, to witness the birth of a baby girl, one with two parents having magic. She was a miracle baby. She was my baby.

You took more than my baby from me. My beautiful Maude, she never recovered. My brothers, they never recovered. I was kicked out of my coven when they found out the lengths I was willing to go to in order to find you and get back my daughter.

All I had left was father.

And, now he's gone, too.

I wish it were you who'd been put into the ground instead of him.

I put the letter down on top of the read pile and wiped away at the wetness leaking out of my eyes.

My chest hurt, and I struggled to breathe past the lump in my throat.

This was unbelievable. If what these letters said was true, I had had a family that loved me, wanted me, and my mother had stolen me from them. Then, she'd spent my entire life up until this point treating me like a lesser being because she was jealous of me because I was born with magic and she wasn't. I could have grown up with people who would have treated me like I was precious. I could have grown up around magic and had people to teach me my craft. I could have met my grandfather before he died and maybe I would have loved him, and he would have loved me back. I could have had a mother who loved me and a father who was willing to do whatever it took to get me back, even get kicked out of his coven for it. And, from the sound of things, he never gave up and years later was still looking for me.

My heart broke for this man, whether we were related or not, my heart broke for him. He sounded like he'd lived half of his life in misery because of my mother. Something we had in common.

I didn't think I could endure reading anymore of the letters. I didn't enjoy crying and knew without a doubt that the remaining stack of letters would make me cry more tears.

I picked up the picture closest to me and held it up for examination. It had been folded in half for a good long while and had a white line down the middle of the picture as a result.

A young, teenage Vivian Kimber stood next to a slightly older looking man. He had his arm around her shoulders and their heads were pressed together. Neither were smiling, but they didn't look upset, either. Just two people who were clearly close and comfortable with each other and not interested in smiling pretty for the camera.

The man was slightly taller than my mother and his frame was thinner. Their ash blonde hair looked to be identical in color and shade, marking them as siblings. Their eyes were the only major differences between the two of them. Where my mother's eyes were blue, this man had lovely green eyes. Eyes that matched mine perfectly in color.

My breath caught in my throat and my entire body stilled. The man in the photo had my eyes. Or, did I have that backwards? Did I have his eyes? I think I did.

I think I was staring at a photograph of my father, my biological father.

And, I didn't even know his name.

I looked at picture after picture of the two of them together. Christmas, Halloween, birthday parties, at the beach. They looked close, always with their arms around the other, posing for the camera and neither of them smiling.

I fell asleep with a heavy heart and a photograph of the man who was more than likely my father clutched to my chest.

I had never hated my mother more than I did in that moment and I desperately wanted to know his name.

Chapter Twenty-Eight
Marcus Cole

THE MAN I had been waiting for sat down in the empty seat beside me. The entire theater was empty except for two teenagers sitting in the way far back row whose only concern seemed to be learning how far down each other's throats they could manage to get their tongues. I wasn't very impressed with their effort, they should have been in school.

Then again, so should Ariel, and she hadn't been to school in well over a month. I felt like the absolute worst parental figure in the known universe at the moment because I hadn't even mentioned her going back to school yet. Her magic made her special and she didn't belong in a school with normal children. She'd be better off being home schooled when she could learn at her own pace and a lot of that learning would have to do with magic. It wouldn't hurt that she would be safe and protected better if she were home schooled.

I knew the James twins hadn't gone to school before they moved in with Quint. Why they were going now was a mystery to me. Tyson hadn't started going to school until a few years ago and I never understood that either.

"What happened to Vivian?" The man beside me spoke in a deep, guttural voice.

I had never been a man prone to violence, but I had a strong urge to turn in my seat and punch this piece of garbage in the throat.

Of course, I did no such thing.

"Vivian is gone," I murmured, answering his question.

"Where?" He demanded to know.

Here was the problem, I had no idea where Vivian's physical body had gone, but I thought she was no longer a member of the living. I had broken one of my own sacred rules and had used magic to scry for her. She was nowhere. Gone. Only the dead could not be found with scrying. And I had a feeling Vivian was good and dead.

"I do not know," I answered honestly.

Rain Kimber turned his head to the side, looking at me.

His cold, dead green eyes, eyes the same color as Ariel's, bored into me, making a chill slither down my spine. The man was empty on the inside and it showed in his eyes.

"Explain yourself, Marcus. And, I suggest you choose your words carefully."

The man was tall, rail thin and had hair the same ash blonde color as Ariel's and it hung down past his ears. He looked too young to have a daughter Ariel's age, he looked more like her older brother.

Hatred churned in my belly, like a filthy disease, eating away at me. I absolutely loathed this man and I cursed the day he had come into my life. If not for him, I would simply take Ariel and run. My father had had the right of it, women should not be forced into certain things.

Ariel would not be subjected to anything she did not want. Quint was the only reason I felt comfortable leaving her. The young man was capable, ruthless and would have no problem standing by and watching as your body lit on fire and burned down to ash if you so much as breathed wrong in Ariel's direction. I wouldn't leave her otherwise. Quint was as fierce as a person could get, he had to be with the way his father had raised him.

When I had told Ariel I planned on moving to be closer to my brothers family, I had expected her to say she would come with me. At the time, I hadn't known she'd grown close to the members of the coven. If I had known, I still would have offered to bring her with me. It was her choice to make, not theirs. When Quint had told me she would be staying with them I pulled a hundred grand out of my safe and given it to him on her behalf. I would have given it to her but after everything I had seen in the few short months I'd been blessed to have her in my life, I knew she would not accept money from me.

"Marcus," Rain growled in his gravelly voice.

Sighing, I cleared my thoughts and focused on the man. "When I got home after my brother passed, she was gone. Ariel claimed to have never seen her mother since she'd left with me in the middle of the night." I shrugged my shoulders. "What was I supposed to do, hunt her down? I had a dead brother to put in the ground and a seventeen-year-old girl to take care of. I didn't have the time to go looking for Vivian. I had assumed she'd met another man, probably a richer one, and had run off with him and left Ariel and I both behind. What more do you want from me?"

He leaned over the armrest that separated our seats in a threatening manner. The only reason I took it as a threat is because his body grew visibly tight, like he was ready to fight me at any given second if he had to. His cold, dead eyes never changed a bit. They also hadn't changed when he'd talked about his sister or his daughter.

"What more do I want from you?" He whispered in a dark voice. "What more do I fucking want from you? I want what that bitch denied me. I want my fucking daughter."

He stood abruptly and walked away on silent feet. His black trench coat billowed out behind him like a second shadow.

I turned my head back to the screen, not seeing the movie playing in front of me.

Instead, I was planning.

I needed to have a word with Quinton before moving. Quint had to know about Ariel's dad, I had to tell him everything.

I waited fifteen minutes after Rain left before climbing to my feet and exiting the deserted movie theater.

The urge to run out and find Ariel, kidnap her and go into hiding was strong. I had to shake it off because I knew if I kidnapped her, Quinton's coven would come after me and they wouldn't stop until they found us, after that, things would get ugly for me.

I left the movie theater with a ball of dread sitting heavy in my stomach.

If I got in my car now and started driving, I could get there by midafternoon.

I wouldn't rest until I spoke to Quinton. And, if he couldn't keep her safe, I would kill him.

Chapter Twenty-Nine

I SAT UP in bed and tried to rub the sleep out of my eyes. I had slept the entire night without waking up once, and, if I had dreamed, I didn't remember it.

I looked up at the dreamcatcher dangling from the ceiling and smiled.

The smile lived a short life because I noticed the letters and pictures spread out all over the bed. I must have fallen asleep while reading. There had to be years and years worth of letters, and I hadn't even made it through half of the box yet.

Purring came from the end of the bed and I grinned at Binx who was curled up into a little ball besides my feet.

Yes!

I wanted to jump up and down and cheer.

I had successfully stolen Dash's cat away from him. And, this had only been my first time staying here. I hoped I could continue to lure Dash's furry little beast away from him on the daily and maybe, eventually, Binx could turn into my furry little beast. If not, I might have to look into getting one of my own so I wouldn't have extreme pet jealousy.

Maybe I could see about getting one of those (so ugly, they were cute) hairless cats. They always looked ornery, and their wrinkles were adorable.

I wanted one.

"What do you think, Binx? A little hairless baby to play with? Or, do you think you'd get jealous and hate it for stealing away some of your lovin'? I bet you'd hate it."

And, I was talking to a cat like I was a freaking crazy person.

There was a light knock on the doo before it was slowly pushed open.

Dash walked into the room wearing only a pair of black and gray pajama pants.

Did he have a thing against wearing shirts when he was at home?

"Hey," he said. "I heard you talking. Who are you talking to?"

I smiled and pointed towards the foot of the bed towards his traitorous cat.

Dash sent a ferocious scowl Binx's way.

"I wondered where he'd gone off too. He usually sleeps with me every night."

I winced and apologized. "I'm really sorry for stealing your cat, Dash."

The entire sentence had been a flat out lie. I wasn't sorry in the least.

He opened his mouth but snapped it shut. His eyes roamed over my bed as he muttered, "What in the fuck is all this?"

My face heated. I had forgotten all about the letters and photographs scattered all over the bed. I would have pulled the blanket up to my chin to hide, but I couldn't even do that because I had fallen asleep on top of the comforter. And, I hadn't changed out of my clothes and into my pajamas. I probably looked like a rumpled mess.

I moved my pillow to my lap and scooted back until my back was pressed to the headboard with my legs stretched out in front of me.

I made kissy noises at Binx while I patted my lap and demanded, "Come here, pretty boy."

Immediately, the dainty cat got up and walked towards me. He climbed on to my lap and plopped down, curling into a little ball. His eyes closed, and he started to purr.

Goodness, he was adorable.

"Ariel?"

"Yeah, umm…" I cleared my throat, and explained, "It's all stuff I found hidden in my mother's closet."

I paused, thinking. My mother. Or, was it simply Vivian now? Aunt Vivian?

"It's all letters from someone who claims to be my father. That my mother was actually his sister and she stole me from him because she was jealous that I was born with magic and she wasn't, even though she was supposed to have been. There's a man with her in the photos. He, Dash, it's crazy, he looks just like us. Well, he looks more like me than her because of the eyes. I have his eyes. My mother's eyes were blue and this man," I leaned forward and tapped at a picture with my fingertip, "he and I have the same green eyes. It's insane. And, in the letters he accuses her of stealing me away from him and he's been looking for us for years. For years. It's like he's crazy. In one letter, he's nice and friendly. Then, in the next, he's telling her he's going to find her and kill her for taking me from him."

I stopped talking and slumped back against the headboard. Binx blinked big green eyes up at me, asking me to pet him.

"Jesus," Dash muttered angrily.

He didn't know the half of it. I didn't tell him about crying over my findings or desperately wanting to know the name of the man who'd written the letters. And wanting to know how to send a letter via magic without knowing the persons physical location.

What was I supposed to say to him? Hey, Dash. Good morning. Thanks for letting me move in with you! And, oh, hey, guess what? My mother might not really be my mother after all. She might be my Aunt. And, my dad might be her brother. He sends her letters using some magical juju that seems to work far better than an address and a postage stamp because he has not one single clue as to where we are. And, sometimes he tells her he's going to kill her. Other times he calls her "My dearest sister". My real mother's name might be Maude and my potential grandfather is dead. What are you making for breakfast?

Yeah, he didn't know the half of it and I wasn't about to share with him.

"Do you have coffee?" I asked hopefully and changed the subject. If he didn't drink coffee I might have to rethink these living arrangements. I liked my caffeine and if I had to be up in the morning I needed it to function. And I got whiney without my coffee.

He frowned at me and scratched at his beard. “There’s no coffee. I just got up and haven’t gone downstairs yet. I heard you in here talking and came in to see if someone else was here. I can make coffee for you, though, if you want me to.”

Boy, did I ever.

How sweet was he?

“I would love some coffee,” I gushed. “I don’t even care if it’s fresh. I would take yesterday’s coffee so long as it’s heated up in the microwave. That works for me.”

I would take day old coffee. Heck, I would take two-day old coffee. So long as I didn’t have to make it myself I would be happy with it.

I probably shouldn’t expect Dash to make my coffee for me and I certainly shouldn’t be asking him to do it. Forget this arrangement not working out for me, he was going to kick my butt to the curb before I even really moved in.

“I’ll make you coffee, sugar,” he told me in a soft sweet voice. “I’m going to warn you now, though. I’m going to call Quinton while I do it and let him know about these letters and photos. Knowing Quinton, he will probably rush on over before we are even off of the phone. I don’t want you to be surprised when he shows up here and badgers you with questions and demands to go through your shit.”

I wrinkled my nose.

“No, no,” I said. “Don’t you worry about Quinton. I know all about him. He probably won’t even knock on your front door before he just barges in. He does this to me all the time. And, I saw him to it to Tyson before when we were in his room. He didn't leave until after he had bossed us both around and made Julian feed me." I waved my hand at him, dismissively. "You go right ahead and call him. I know how to deal with Quinton. I've got him all figured out."

Dash smirked at me and my mouth dropped open in shock. I think that was number three now, and there were no demons to be seen.

"I love my room," I blurted. "It's lovely. All of it. Thank you. I even like my tiny closet."

"No girl likes a small closet," he shot back.

Boy, did he have a lot to learn when it came to me.

"Right now, at Mr. Cole's house," I told him, "my closet is pretty much an empty space with a few things hanging up and a couple laundry baskets. I couldn't fit more than one laundry basket in the closet in here if I tried. I love it. Wasted space is stupid. My coffin closet kicks ass."

He grinned, and asked, "Did you really throw a rock a Quinton's head?"

"Get out," I ordered as I pointed towards the door. We absolutely were not talking about Quinton and that fucking rock. Good grief. That stupid story was going to follow me to my grave

Dash held up his hands in defeat. "Alright, alright. No more laughing at your expense. You're going to let it go. You hijacked my cat, it's the least you could do. Get dressed and meet me down in the kitchen."

He walked out of the bedroom without bothering to look back.

I still had his cat in bed with me. I'd call that a win. Oh, and he was making me coffee.

This day was already off to a good start.

Chapter Thirty

DASH WASN'T UPSTAIRS, and he wasn't in the kitchen. I moved through the dining room, then the living room, not finding him. I was about to call out his name when I came to the mud room and stopped, snapping my mouth shut.

What was going on?

Dash stood in the open door with his back to me. He moved out of the open doorway and stepped further outside, completely leaving the safety of his house.

Who was he talking to?

"She's not here, buddy," I heard Dash say. "Maybe you should check at her house."

"She's here," I heard Chucky's angry rumble in response. "Her car is here, and I know she showed up here yesterday and hasn't left since."

What?

What the hell was Chucky doing here?

And, how had he found me here at Dash's house? First, he showed up at Mr. Cole's house. Now, he was here at Dash's house.

What in the actual fuck? He must have followed me. That wasn't creepy or anything.

I moved closer to the open door, unable to stop myself.

"Listen, buddy," Dash said, "you need to get off of my property. Otherwise, I am going to call the police on you."

That didn't sound like a bad idea to me. This stalker business was getting old and it had only just begun.

"What the fuck?" Dash growled angrily. "Did you follow her from her house and then sit out here all night at *my* house watching for her? That's sick. You're not right in the head, buddy, and you need to get your ass off of my property."

Slowly, I walked towards the front door. This was my mess and I didn't think Dash should have to deal with it on his own.

"I'm not leaving until I see Ariel for myself."

I pulled the door open wider and stood behind Dash. His scars were on display today and I hoped he didn't turn around because I didn't want Chucky to see them and say something nasty to Dash about them. That would be something he would do.

"I'm right here," I said, and Dash's body jerked in surprise. "Now that you've seen me, it's time for you to leave. Dash has asked you to go twice now that I've heard, and I think you should listen to him before he's forced to call the police on you."

"I haven't done anything wrong," Chucky snarled as he leaned around Dash to see me. Dash moved, trying to block his view of me. "But you sure as hell have. You and that other guy lied to me. You said you were coming back to school and you never did. I told you that I need to see you and that something happens to me when I go a long time without being around you. I can't help myself. How do you not care about that? How could you do this to me? All I want is to be around you. What's so wrong with that?"

Everything was wrong with that. Absolutely everything. I didn't care what Quinton said about there not being an antidote to his love potion. I would talk to all of them and they were going to come up with something because this was so out of control it wasn't even funny. I couldn't handle having Chucky show up where ever I was at. I couldn't handle having him stalk me like that. It wasn't just creepy, it was just a touch on the scary side. And I really didn't need anything creepy and scary in my life at the moment, or ever for that matter.

Dash took a step back, trying to shield me from Chucky's view. I wasn't sure why he didn't want the other man to see me, but he kept shifting around to hide me from him.

"Get it the house and close the door, Ariel," Dash ordered. "Lock it. Quinton should be here any minute now and we'll take care of this. I don't want you out here with this guy, though. Get inside. Now."

I hesitated, not wanting to leave Dash out here all alone with an angry Chucky.

"Who the fuck do you think you are?" Chucky screamed in Dash's face. "What, are you fucking her too now?"

"What are you talking about?" I asked in a shocked voice.

Chucky's head swiveled to the side and he glared at me with hostile eyes. I flinched at the rage I saw burning in his eyes. I didn't deserve this kind of treatment from him.

"You need to leave," I told him. I was proud of myself because my voice came out strong, confident.

"Ariel," Dash snapped. "Get your ass in the house. Right now."

"First you're hooking up with Tyson. Then, that other guy who said he was Tyson's Uncle. And now you're with this ginger fuck. People were right about you, you are dirty girl, like your gold digging whore of a mother."

Apparently, Dash had had more than enough of Chucky's mouth and he was over the whole situation because one second he was standing guard in front of me and the next second he put his hands on Chucky's chest and gave a mighty shove. Chucky stumbled back but didn't go down and Dash moved right back into him.

I let out a relieved sigh when I spotted Quinton's black car speeding down the dirt driveway.

"What?" Dash grunted.

I quickly looked away from Quinton's car and back to Dash. His voice scared me because he sounded both surprised and in pain.

My breath caught in my throat and my entire body froze for a second because I rushed forward.

Dash's hands were pressed to his stomach red covered his hands. He was bleeding. Why was he bleeding.

Silver flashed in the sunlight as Chucky moved closer to Dash, plunging a silver knife into Dash's stomach.

"No," I screamed as I ran towards them.

I made it to Dash's side as his legs gave out and his knees buckled.

I grabbed ahold of his arm as his knees hit the stone pathway.

"Dash," I cried.

His face was pinched in pain and his eyes were closed tight. I looked down and what I saw made my entire body start to shake and a sob leave my throat. Blood. There was so much blood seeping out of him.

"Ariel," Quinton screamed, and I heard the sound of running feet but I didn't look away from Dash.

Quinton was here. My light in the dark. Everything was going to be okay.

My head was jerked to the side as pain exploded in my face and my cheek felt like it had been ripped open.

My feet came out from underneath me and I crashed into Dash, taking us both down to the stone pathway. I landed hard on my side and Dash hit his back. My cheek burned, and I didn't care. I only had eyes for Dash and all the blood coming out of him. I hovered over him in shock as wetness ran down my face, blood and tears. I sat beside him in silence as Quinton pressed something into my face and I didn't even flinch. I didn't feel anything anymore, I was numb inside. I sat there in numb silence and watched his chest rise and fall until the paramedics showed up and they took him away from me. After that, I blacked out.

Chapter Thirty-One
Quinton Alexander

I STARED DOWN at my hands in my lap and willed them to stop shaking. It didn't work, and I hadn't really expected it to.

I should really get up and go back inside. I should have gone inside over an hour ago and the others were probably worried about me. It was shitty of me because they really didn't need anything else to worry about. Dash had made it through surgery and he would make a full recovery, he had to. Ariel was going to be physically fine. She had to have stiches and would have a scar for the rest of her life. I knew it was stupid, but that was the part I struggled with the most. They were both going to be wearing scars for the rest of their lives as a constant reminder of my major fuck up.

And, I had fucked up. I had caused this to happen to them.

If I had just left that fucking kid alone, if I had never put that goddamn potion together to make him fall in love with Ariel, none of this would have happened.

Instead, here we were, at the fucking hospital. And it was all my fault.

The wooden bench I was seated on shifted under the weight of someone as they sat down on it.

I didn't have to look to know who it was. He would always follow me and had been since we were little boys. I could walk into hell and he'd be right behind me, taking my back and ready to fight off anything that came at me.

I sighed and dropped my head into my hands.

"She's gonna have a scar," I muttered angrily. "Because of me, she's gonna have a scar. Every time she looks in the mirror, she's going to be reminded of what happened to her because of me. Fuck. I'm supposed to keep her safe, it's my job. And, Dash? Holy fuck. His entire back was already covered. Now, he's got some on his front, too. How the fuck am I supposed to even face him? I made him swear to me that he would take care of her while she stayed with him. I made him swear it to me. Do you think that's why he-"

"Stop it, Quinton," Julian whispered fiercely as he wrapped his arm around my shoulders. "You couldn't have known this was going to happen when you messed with that kid. If you hadn't done something to him, I probably would have. Hell, Abel and Addison were all for following him home from school and putting a beat down on him. He would have ended up in the hospital had they followed through with that plan. You don't think he would have come back for revenge afterwards, or used Ariel to try and get back at them? Tyson's been wallowing in his own guilt and misery since the first day of school. It was only a matter of time before he snapped and did something awful to him. Seriously, Quint, even Damien has this kid's address saved in his phone. He told me that he's been driving past his house every day. I do not know what that's about, or what he planned on doing. I just know that he planned on doing something, and whatever it was he planned, it was probably going to be huge. You and I both know he doesn't do things in halves. He goes big in everything he does. I can't even imagine… And this kid, from everything that I've heard of him, he would have come back with something. It might not have been this extreme, but something was bound to happen."

Julian trailed off, likely thinking about all the chaos Damien could have caused. If Damien was going to do something, he'd go out of his way to make sure it was big enough to place him in the spotlight. It was annoying as fuck.

"And, I've been thinking about what it's going to take to keep the scarring to a minimal. I don't think I'm going to be able to get rid of all of it, but I'm sure as hell going to try."

If anyone of us could do it, it was Julian. He spent a lot of his free time working with plants and creating new potions. He had to have hundreds of jars and vials full of things he'd created. Despite the fact that none of it was labeled, he seemed to know what was in every single jar. If he told me he'd find a way to get rid of as much of the scarring as he could, then I had to believe him.

"At least there's that," I muttered under my breath.

"Nobody blames you."

I closed my eyes in an attempt to hide from his words.

He was dead wrong.

Oh, I knew neither Dash or Ariel would blame me for what happened to them. None of the guys would blame me. But, I did. I blamed myself because I knew it was my fault. I would likely carry guilt over this until the day I died. Julian could talk all he wanted about what the others had wanted to do and how it might have eventually backfired on us all and maybe he was even right. Didn't really matter though because that's not how it happened.

All I had wanted was to keep our girl safe. It never occurred to me that a person would harm someone like that when they were in love with them. Stupid, stupid. I knew better. People in love do all kinds of fucked up things. Why hadn't I remembered that? I should have remembered.

"Quint," Julian said as he squeezed my shoulder.

I shrugged his arm off and stood. My fists were clenched into tight balls at my sides. I wanted to hit something. This burning in my gut was just waiting to explode.

I wondered if Julian would take offense if I punched him in the face. Maybe I would get lucky and he'd hit me back. I could go for some extreme violence in my life right about now. Just so long as I was the one causing it.

"Hey," Tyson called out from behind me.

I didn't acknowledge that I'd heard him. He needed to get away from me before I entertained the idea of punching him in the face as well. I couldn't hit my nephew, no matter how much I wanted to sometimes.

"You should go back inside," Julian advised Tyson wisely.

I couldn't agree more. The less people around me, the better. I didn't want witnesses for my potential explosion when it came on.

Tyson ignored Julian's advice and said two little words that made the fist around my chest loosen.

"He's awake."

I sighed in relief, the fight immediately going out of me.

I had known Dash was going to wake up, like I knew he was going to make a full recovery.

I knew it.

But hearing Tyson say that Dash had woken up, hearing it out loud, outside of my head, made me breathe a whole lot easier.

Dash was awake, and Ariel was going to be alright.

Everything would be okay.

Chapter Thirty-Two

I SLUMPED BACK in the chair, exhausted. My cheek felt tight, nothing hurt but it felt like my skin was stretched. There were twelve stitches in my cheek and I was going to have one wicked scar when all was said and done. I could live with a scar, just so long as Dash was okay. That was all I cared about.

I had been sitting in this chair in his hospital room for over an hour now, waiting for him to wake up. Quinton had tried to get me to go home but I had refused. Which home would I have gone too? The half empty one filled with moving boxes? Or, the one with blood all over the walkway? When I'd asked Quinton, he'd snapped his mouth shut and stormed off in an angry huff. I knew he hadn't been angry at me, it was the situation he was upset with, and I couldn't blame him for that, either. I imagined he was not feeling very good about himself at the moment. He'd been downright hostile to everyone since I'd woken up. And, when I insisted on sitting in here with Dash, he looked like he was going to explode and that's when he'd told me I needed to go home.

I could only imagine how guilty Quinton felt about everything. If he hadn't forced the love potion on Chucky, none of this would have happened. Then again, Quinton didn't freak out and stab Dash in the stomach multiple times and he hadn't been the one to slice open my cheek with a knife. I didn't blame

Quinton for anything. In fact, when I saw him next, I was going to give him a hug. He could use one.

Movement on the bed caught my attention and I looked up in time to see Dash's head on the pillow turn in my direction. His gray eyes were open, his demons shining bright for all to see. Now he had more because of me.

I leaned forward and placed my elbows on my knees.

"I should have gone inside when you told me to," I whispered in a hoarse voice.

"What the fuck happened to your face?" He croaked, and I flinched.

I got up from the chair and grabbed a cup of water off of a tray on a side table. I held the cup to his lips and held it there while he sipped at the water.

"We got into a knife fight," I told him as I moved the water back to the tray and sat back down in my chair. I knew I shouldn't be joking about it, but it was either joke or cry. "I'm pretty sure we both lost."

He blinked slowly at me and asked, "Where is everybody?"

I sighed heavily as I sat back in the chair and told him, "When they found out you were going to be alright, Damien and the twins went to the police station to find out what's going to happen to Chucky. Quinton needed to walk off some steam and Julian followed him to make sure he didn't hurt anyone. And, Tyson went to get us some coffee."

I think I covered everybody. There were so many if them it was hard to keep track.

"But you stayed," he said as he reached out with a hand, searching.

I immediately placed my hand in his and squeezed.

"I'm not going anywhere," I promised him.

He smiled softly and closed his eyes. It didn't take long for him to fall back asleep.

I sat back in the chair and watched over him. Which is exactly what I did for the entire four days he was in the hospital. It drove Quinton crazy, but I didn't care and, eventually, he stopped trying to get me to go home.

When Dash left the hospital, I went home with him.

Mr. Cole had showed up at the hospital to check on me and when I had told him I was moving in with Dash, he seemed relieved. I tried not to let his reaction hurt me, and failed miserably. I wasn't looking forward to saying goodbye to him, but I also wasn't dreading it anymore. I had Quinton, and Tyson, and my Salt and Pepper twins. Now, I had Dash, too. I had a family to call my own, and I wasn't alone anymore.

Everything would work out just fine. In time.

The End.

From the Author

Thank you for taking the time to read my book!
The next book in the Ariel Kimber series will be Blood Magic and does not have a release date at this time.
If you enjoyed the book, please consider leaving a review.

In my Facebook group (The Dollhouse), I asked about deleted scenes and people said they wanted to read them so here you go!

Deleted Scene

Mr. Cole's office was a room I'd never been in until now. I didn't know what it looked like before but I imagined it wasn't the mess of boxes that it was now. Moving boxes were spread out across the floor. Some of them were taped closed shut and others were open and filled with things.

The walls were painted the color of the sky on a rainy day. The carpet was thick and the color of pure, untouched snow. Black shelves ran along one wall from floor to ceiling. A massive, sleek black desk sat before a large picture window. There were no pictures on the walls and the shelves were lonely looking and empty.

Mr. Cole wouldn't be in this place for much longer and neither would I.

I stopped short in the doorway, not expecting to see Quinton sitting in a chair directly in front of the desk. Mr. Cole seated in the chair behind the desk, I expected. Quinton, not so much.

Ignoring Quinton, I looked at Mr. Cole expectantly and said, "You wanted to see me?"

He smiled at me kindly as he gestured to the empty chair seated beside Quinton.

I perched on the end of the chair and sat my hands in my lap. I twisted my fingers together nervously. I had no idea what this meeting was about. Mr. Cole had knocked on my door and asked me to meet him in his office so here I was. And I had no idea why. They had already agreed on where I'd live, now what?

"What's going on?" I rushed out before anyone could say anything.

Quinton chuckled from his chair beside me. I shot him a dirty look before focusing back on Mr. Cole. Quinton laughed harder.

"Alright, sweetheart," Mr. Cole said quietly. "We need to talk about a few things before we make this official. First, I want you checking in once a week. Of course, you are always welcome to call me or text me or video chat with me at any time that you want to. But I want you checking in every week. Quinton promised me he'd remind you and make sure you don't forget."

I looked at Quinton out of the corner of my eye and saw him smirking. I just bet he would do exactly what he promised Mr. Cole he would. I had watched him barge into the guys bedrooms and I watched him try to boss Tyson around like he was Ty's real parent. He was so totally going to try to parent me and boss me around.

"I can do that," I promised Mr. Cole. "I'll call at least once a week, but I'll probably text you more."

He nodded. "Good. That's settled. Now, you'll keep the Rover because I bought it for you and I meant what I said. It's yours, there were no strings attached. You'll keep your bank card and I'll be depositing an allowance at the beginning of each month for you. For whatever reason, if you run out of money or there's an emergency, simply let me know and I'll have more money put into your account. It will be more than enough to support yourself and I will continue this until your birthday where we will discuss what it is you'd like to do with your future. Now, this brings us to the next topic I wished to discuss with you."

He paused to give Quinton a look that I entirely missed due to the fact that my brain wasn't functioning properly. He was allowing me to keep my car and wanted to give me an allowance. Even after he knew I wasn't going with him, Mr. Cole still wanted to take care of me. I didn't understand it because I'd never had someone to care before. And he wanted me to check in with him so he'd know what was going on in my life and that I was doing well. This was all so very kind, *he* was so very kind, but I could not and would not accept his money. It felt too much like a handout.

"Marcus," I said, and the shocked look on his face made me realize how stupid I'd been before to not call him by his first name. I took a deep breath, let that go, and continued, "I will accept the Rover because my Bug is long gone and you gave it to me and I love it. It's also like my security blanket. As long as I have it I can go anywhere I need to, I don't have to stay if I don't want to because I will have a means to escape. I don't know why, I just…" I closed my eyes and whispered, "I need that."

I swallowed down my emotions with a shaky breath. I hadn't meant to get emotional and I hadn't meant to give anything away to Mr. Cole. He was still in the dark when it came to most of my mother's behavior towards me and I didn't want him to know more than he already did.

Shit.

Think fast, Ariel Kimber.

"About the money, though. I can't accept-" I attempted to protest.

"I don't want you to feel beholden to the Alexander's in any way. I also don't want Quinton to entirely support you even though he has offered to do just that. This is the only way I'm comfortable with you staying with them. I know you can do whatever you want and you do not have to accept these things from me as I am neither your parent nor your guardian. But, since I consider you my family, and I hope you do the same with me, it's important for me to take care of my family, which is why I'm moving. It means something to me to be able to be there for them right now when they need me. But I'm not going to be able to go if I don't feel you're going to be properly taken care of. So, do this old man a favor, sweetheart, and give this to me."

I wanted to argue with him and push the issue. I didn't want to take his money, it would make me feel like a freeloader. And I certainly did *not* want to live off of Quinton.

"I can get a job," I assured them. A job doing what, I had no clue.

"No." They both said together.

"Babe," Quinton groaned. "If you get a job, the guys will kick my ass. The other coven's find out you're working a job and they'll think we aren't treating you right and that they've got a shot at stealing you away from us. If you don't mind, I'd like to avoid that."

Mr. Cole picked up where Quinton left off. "I'd also rather you focus on school work instead of some job."

Oh boy.

I didn't think this was going to go over well for me. I licked my suddenly dry lips and clenched my hands together in my lap.

Out of the corner of my eye, I caught Quinton staring at my hands. His lips pursed and he frowned. I untangled my fingers and quickly shoved my hands under my thighs.

"Ariel?" Quinton murmured. "Something wrong?"

I hated it when people asked me that.

What's wrong?

Well, gee, let me think about it for a second. The person sitting beside me accidently killed my mother after she beat me and tried to drown me in the bathtub. The man sitting in front of me had been my mother's lover. He didn't know she was dead and thought she'd bailed on the both of us. His brother died in a horrible car wreck and now he was moving out of state. I was moving next door to live with the neighbors who happened to be all boys and, oh yeah, they were witches. And we weren't even going to get into the whole sharing thing yet. Yikes.

Now, ask me again, what's wrong?

I stared down at my bare feet and wished I had worn socks. I didn't like walking around barefoot unless I was in the privacy of my own bedroom, on a sandy beach, or standing on soft, green grass. I was weird that way.

"Babe."

I sighed. There was no avoiding him.

"I don't want to go back," I whispered.

"Shit," Quinton breathed out harshly as he sat back in his chair. "You're gonna kill me if you drop out of school. If you don't go, Ty and the twins won't want to go either. They'll give me so much shit. Ugh, Ariel, babe, this is no good for me."

This wasn't about him. It was about me and I didn't need him turning it around and making it about him.

"Why don't you want to go back to school?" Mr. Cole asked me calmly. Unlike Quinton, who hadn't even bothered to ask me why I didn't want to go back.

I thought about how to answer Mr. Cole's question honestly and finally went with, "The kids are mean. They said awful things to me because I was new and because of my mother. Now with her gone…" I trialed off and shrugged my shoulders. The words I'd left unspoken, spoke volumes.

It would be worse for me at school now. Much, much worse.

Mr. Cole placed his elbows on the top of his desk and dropped his head into his hands.

"Goddamn Vivian," He mumbled. "Goddamn her straight to hell and back. Worst mother I ever met."

I looked to Quinton with wide eyes. Goddamn her to hell was right.

Quinton bit his bottom lip and shook his head. I knew better than to say anything, he didn't need to remind me.

Secrets could be a dangerous thing when leaked to the wrong person. I didn't think we'd have anything to fear from Mr. Cole but it wasn't worth finding out if I was right or not.

Quinton eyeballed me and I knew he wanted to know if I was okay. I desperately wanted to reach across the short distance between us and grab his hand. This man I barely knew yet was one of the strongest people I'd probably ever meet. He had a moral compass that frightened me and was often times a scary man. And I wanted to hold his hand. I knew if I reached across the short distance between us and grabbed ahold of his hand he wouldn't hesitate to intertwine our fingers and he wouldn't give a crap about what Mr. Cole thought about it.

"There's an alternative school," Mr. Cole said, cutting into my thoughts.

I did not like the way this conversation was going at all.

Alternative school? I wasn't certain sure, but I thought that was supposed to be for the troubled kids and teen moms. Did I belong at a place like that? I didn't think I did. Admittedly, I *was* a troubled kid but I still didn't think I belonged in a special school and, if I had to go to school at all I would not be going to school where Ty and my salt and pepper twins weren't. We were supposed to stick together.

"I don't want her at the alternative school," Quinton told Mr. Cole. "That's a rough crowd and God only knows what kind of trouble she could get into there. It's not safe for her."

"I can take classes online," I said in a last-ditch effort to not be forced to go back to school. And there was no way in hell I'd be going to some alternative school. No, thank you.

Quinton lifted his left leg and rested his ankle on his right knee. "That could actually work for me," he told Mr. Cole.

I sat back in my chair and rolled my eyes. Quinton was taking his role as guardian a little too far, if you asked me. Not that either of them seemed interested in my opinion.

"She'd still be taking her classes just not in the actual school building and not around people who treat her poorly."

Alright, Quinton got points for that one.

Mr. Cole sighed and sat back in his desk chair. He crossed his arms over his chest and glared at Quinton. Ha! So it wasn't just me.

"Is this really what you want, Ariel?" Mr. Cole asked me without taking his hostile eyes off of Quinton.

Was this what I wanted?

Well, to be honest, no it wasn't what I wanted. I wanted to take the GED test and skip the rest. But, beggars couldn't be choosers and at this point I'd take what I could get. And, hey, if I didn't actually have to go to class it would still be a win for me.

"Yeah," I lied easily. "That's what I want." I scooted forward until I was sitting on the edge of my seat. I clasped my hands together and held them up to my chest. Time to go for broke. "It would really mean a lot to me if I could have your support on this, Marcus. I know you've already done so much for me, given me so much. I have no right to ask for your support in this and if you really think it would be best if I go back to school then that's what I will do. I won't like it, but I'll do it."

Mr. Cole waved his hand in the air, as if waving my words away.

From beside me Quinton grunted. He knew exactly what I was doing with my hands clasped together and pleading eyes. I'd learned that Mr. Cole was a bit of a sucker when it came to me, something I loved about him. There was a lot to love.

"You're a good kid, sweetheart, if that's what you want to do then I will support it."

I slumped back in my chair and let out a relieved sigh. I wanted to jump up and down and cheer. I didn't have to go back to high school. That was easier than I thought it was going to be. I finally caught the break I'd been waiting for.

As they talked about the necessary paperwork that would likely need to be filled out, I let my mind wander. There had been so many changes in my life recently that it made my head spin. This was the first time in a month where I felt like my feet were planted firmly on the ground and a hole wasn't about to suddenly open up beneath me and I wasn't going to be sucked into the dark abyss.

Quinton and I both left Mr. Cole's office at the same time. I thought I would walk him to the door and see him out but he had other plans. He took ahold of my hand and pulled me along behind him as he made his way up the stairs.

"Quinton-"

He squeezed my hand. "I want to see your bedroom." He told me. "I know I've been in it before, but that doesn't count because I wasn't in the right state of mind to take in the view. And, I'm jealous because I know Ty's spent time in there with you and both the twins and Julian have been in there. Hell, I know Ty's even spent the night with you. I don't have the patience to be last and I'm not nice enough to wait for you to invite me on your own."

I laughed softly as I followed him to my bedroom. He barged into my room, dragging me along behind him. He liked to barge into other people's space uninvited.

"You know," I said quietly, "the only one I actually invited into my bedroom was Tyson. The twins and Julian weren't invited and didn't stay long."

Having him in my bedroom made me suddenly nervous. He talked about his jealousy and not wanting to come last like it was normal. He was far from normal, they all were, and the arrangement they wanted to have with me was anything but. I wasn't sure if he even knew that I'd overheard him with some of the guys talking about me, or if he knew that the twins told me that they'd all want to have a relationship with me.

Being a girl and having magic was a very rare occurrence these days. So much so, the girls with magic were treated like royalty, like a Princess. Or, so I had been told. Magic was a new development for me, something I never knew I had until recently.

Before I'd moved in with Mr. Cole the guys had all had a dream about me. They knew I was coming and some of them thought I was meant for them.

You see, the twins told me about the other female witches and their covens. Apparently, they ended up in a relationship with every member of their coven. They were treated special, precious and raised to think that kind of relationship was normal. The twins said that each coven dreamed of having their own female to share. My guys had almost had one but it didn't work out because she was an evil bitch. Because of her, some of the guys weren't open to trying out another girl. Well, that and one of them had a girlfriend and another claimed I was too young. They had no idea I'd overheard this last bit of information, but I had. It had slightly colored my view of them, and not in a good way.

None of this I was okay with and I had been avoiding thinking about it as a whole. I had a feeling though that with me moving in with them I would be forced to actually think about the situation. And I wasn't looking forward to it.

Blood Magic, book 3 in the Ariel Kimber series will be coming out in March 2018.

Ariel Kimber

Brothers of the Flame
Love Potion
Blood Magic
Tyson

Made in the USA
Columbia, SC
20 February 2018